"Melissa Ferguson delivers yet another sparkling, laugh-out-loud romance! *The Perfect Rom-Com* is a heartwarming story about chasing your dreams, discovering your voice, and finding love where you least expect it. With unforgettable characters and delightful humor, this novel is perfect for anyone who believes in second chances—both in love and in life."

—RaeAnne Thayne, *New York Times* bestselling author

"I loved this book! If you're looking for a heroine you can root for, a mean girl to boo, and a unique hero to fall for, this is your book. Bryony Page will keep you reading as she writes her way to the perfect HEA."

—Sheila Roberts, *USA TODAY* bestselling author of *The Best Life Book Club*

"In *The Perfect Rom-Com*, a successful ghostwriter longs to see her beloved book published under her own name. But her agent, who holds the keys to publication also holds the keys to her heart. Don't miss this fun romantic romp into the intriguing world of publishing!"

—Denise Hunter, bestselling author of *The Summer of You and Me*

"This clever and adorable romantic comedy is brimming with warm humor and a lot of heart. It kept me giggling and turning the pages to see what came next. What a delight!"

—Rachel Linden, bestselling author of *The Magic of Lemon Drop Pie*

"*The Perfect Rom-Com* contains two of my favorite tropes: friends-to-lovers and a road-trip romance. Melissa Ferguson handles both *perfectly*! I couldn't put this book down! And when main character Bryony finally clues into the fact that Jack is not *just* her best friend, it's the sweetest, swooniest of moments."

—Suzanne Allain, author of *Mr. Malcom's List*

"I can always count on Melissa Ferguson for sweet romances bursting with both wit and wisdom. Hilarious and heartwarming, *The Perfect Rom-Com* is comfy and cozy from the first page to the last."

—Bethany Turner, author of
Cole and Laila Are Just Friends

HOW TO PLOT A PAYBACK

"The perfect escape for lovers of dogs, second chances, and swoonworthy romance. Don't miss this one."

—Annabel Monaghan, bestselling author
of *Same Time Next Summer*

"Super cute! Melissa Ferguson's rom-coms lean more on the com than the rom, and this book is no different, delivering chuckles and giggles with an effortless writing voice, witty dialogue, and a cast of lovable characters. I was totally on board as soon as I read the premise, especially since it's a storyline I haven't already read more than a dozen times (give me all the fresh plots please!). You could say this is a grumpy/sunshine (although he's really not all that grumpy), enemies-to-lovers (although the hard feelings are only one-sided and misguided at that) slow burn, but I just call it a cute little romp of a book."

—Sarah Monzon, author of *All's Fair in Love and Christmas*

"It was so fun to sit in on the writer's room of a successful sitcom in Melissa Ferguson's delightfully charming and wonderfully quirky romance. There are so many sweet moments and wonderful characters sprinkled throughout, and I'm certain rom-com fans are going to fall in love!"

—Courtney Walsh, *New York Times* bestselling author

FAMOUS FOR A LIVING

"Calling all fans of slow-burn, opposites-attract romance! Melissa Ferguson brings another fresh, delightful rom-com in *Famous for a Living*. Cat and Zaiah are an imperfectly perfect match with swoony chemistry and plenty of back-and-forth banter. The gorgeous national park setting provides a lush backdrop for this fish-out-of-water story as influencer Cat hopes to escape a media fallout and finds much, much more. Readers who loved *The Cul-de-Sac War* and *Meet Me in the Margins* won't be disappointed in Ferguson's latest read!"

—Emma St. Clair, *USA TODAY* bestselling author

"*Famous for a Living* is a heartwarming and funny read with quirky characters and the occasional moose. It takes the reader on a virtual escape to the mountains and hot springs of Montana and the lofts and busy streets of New York City. Melissa Ferguson has given us a sparkling, sweet rom-com with a lot of heart."

—Suzanne Allain, author of *Mr. Malcolm's List*

MEET ME IN THE MARGINS

"Ferguson (*The Cul-de-Sac War*) enchants with this whimsical tale set against the evergreen culture war between literary and commercial fiction . . . An idealistic, competent heroine, a swoon-worthy hero, and delightfully quirky supporting characters bolster this often hilarious send-up of the publishing industry, which doubles as a love letter to the power of stories. This is sure to win Ferguson some new fans."

—*Publishers Weekly*

"A marvelous book on the power of positive feedback, the various struggles of being an emerging writer, and how to find a balance between work and life, this book is a very entertaining read."

—Book Riot

"*Meet Me in the Margins* is a delightfully charming jewel of a book that fans of romantic comedy won't be able to put down—and will want to share with all their friends. Readers will lose themselves in Melissa Ferguson's witty, warm tale of Savannah Cade and the perfectly drawn cast of characters that inhabits her world. This literary treat full of missed opportunities, second chances, and maybe even true love should be at the top of your reading list!"

—Kristy Woodson Harvey, *New York Times* bestselling author of *Under the Southern Sky*

"Ferguson has penned a lively romance for every bookworm who once longed to step through the wardrobe or sleep under the stairs. *Meet Me in the Margins* brims with crisp prose and crinkling pages as Savannah Cade, lowly editor at a highbrow publisher, secretly reworks her commercial fiction manuscript with the help of a mystery reader—and revises her entire life. You'll want to find your own hideaway to get lost in in this delightful, whip-smart love story."

—Asher Fogle Paul, author of *Without a Hitch*

THE CUL-DE-SAC WAR

"Melissa delivered a book that is filled with both humor and heart!"

—Debbie Macomber, #1 *New York Times* bestselling author

"Melissa Ferguson delights with a grand sense of humor and a captivating story to boot! With vivid detail that brings the story roaring to life, *The Cul-de-Sac War* brings us closer to the truth of love, family, and home. Bree's and Chip's pranks and adventures turn into something they never expected, as Melissa Ferguson delivers another heartwarming, hilarious, and deeply felt story."

—Patti Callahan, *New York Times* bestselling author of *Becoming Mrs. Lewis*

"Melissa Ferguson's *The Cul-de-Sac War* is sweet, zany, and surprisingly tender. Bree and Chip will have you laughing and rooting for them until the very end."

—Denise Hunter, bestselling author of *Carolina Breeze*

"With her sophomore novel, Melissa Ferguson delivers hilarity and heart in equal measure. *The Cul-de-Sac War*'s Bree Leake and Chip McBride prove that sometimes it isn't the first impression you have to worry about—it's the second one that gets you. What follows is a delightful deluge of pranks, sabotage, and witty repartee tied together by heartstrings that connect to turn a house into a home worth fighting for. I was thoroughly charmed from beginning to end."

—Bethany Turner, award-winning author of *The Secret Life of Sarah Hollenbeck*

"Witty, wise, and with just the right amount of wacky, Melissa's second novel is as charming as her debut. Competition and chemistry battle to win the day in this hilarious rom-com about two people who can't stand to be near each other—or too far apart."

—Betsy St. Amant, author of *The Key to Love*

THE DATING CHARADE

"Ferguson's delightful debut follows a first date that turns quickly into a childcare quagmire.... Ferguson's humorous and chaotic tale will please rom-com fans."

—*Publishers Weekly*

"*The Dating Charade* will keep you smiling the entire read. Ferguson not only delights us with new love, with all its attendant mishaps and misunderstandings, but she takes us deeper in the hearts and minds of vulnerable children as Cassie and Jett work out their families—then their dating lives. An absolute treat!"

—Katherine Reay, bestselling author
of *The Printed Letter Bookshop*

"*The Dating Charade* is hilarious and heartwarming with characters you truly care about, super-fun plot twists and turns, snappy prose, and a sweet romance you're rooting for. Anyone who has children in their lives will particularly relate to Ferguson's laugh-out-loud take on the wild ride that is parenting. I thoroughly enjoyed this story!"

—Rachel Linden, bestselling author
of *The Enlightenment of Bees*

"A heartwarming charmer."

—Sheila Roberts, *USA TODAY* bestselling
author of the Moonlight Harbor series

"Melissa Ferguson is a sparkling new voice in contemporary rom-com. Though her novel tackles meaningful struggles—social work, child abandonment, adoption—it's also fresh, flirty, and laugh-out-loud funny. Ferguson is going to win fans with this one!"

—Lauren Denton, bestselling author of
The Hideaway and *Glory Road*

"A jolt of energy featuring one of the most unique romantic hooks I have ever read. Personality and zest shine through Ferguson's evident enjoyment at crafting high jinks and misadventures as two people slowly make way for love in the midst of major life upheaval. A marvelous treatise on unexpected grace and its life-changing

chaos, Cassie and Jett find beautiful vulnerability in redefining what it means to live happily ever after."

—Rachel McMillan, author of *The London Restoration*

"Ferguson delivers a stellar debut. *The Dating Charade* is a fun, romantic albeit challenging look at just what it takes to fall in love and be a family. You'll think of these characters long after the final page."

—Rachel Hauck, *New York Times* bestselling author of *The Wedding Dress*

The Perfect Rom-Com

ALSO BY MELISSA FERGUSON

NOVELS

How to Plot a Payback

Snowy Serendipity: Two Christmas Stories

Famous for a Living

Meet Me in the Margins

The Cul-de-Sac War

The Dating Charade

The Perfect Rom-Com

A Novel

MELISSA FERGUSON

THOMAS NELSON
Since 1798

The Perfect Rom-Com

Copyright © 2025 by Melissa Ferguson

Published in Nashville, Tennessee, by Thomas Nelson. Thomas Nelson is a registered trademark of HarperCollins Christian Publishing, Inc.

Thomas Nelson titles may be purchased in bulk for educational, business, fundraising, or sales promotional use. For information, please email SpecialMarkets@ThomasNelson.com.

Publisher's Note: This novel is a work of fiction. Names, characters, places, and incidents are either products of the author's imagination or used fictitiously. All characters are fictional, and any similarity to people living or dead is purely coincidental.

Any internet addresses (websites, blogs, etc.) in this book are offered as a resource. They are not intended in any way to be or imply an endorsement by Thomas Nelson, nor does Thomas Nelson vouch for the content of these sites for the life of this book.

Library of Congress Cataloging-in-Publication Data

Names: Ferguson, Melissa, 1985- author.
Title: The perfect rom-com: a novel / Melissa Ferguson.
Description: Nashville, Tennessee: Harper Muse/Thomas Nelson, 2025. | Summary: "She's written dozens of smash hit romance novels. Too bad no one knows it"—Provided by publisher.
Identifiers: LCCN 2024041374 (print) | LCCN 2024041375 (ebook) | ISBN 9780840716880 (paperback) | ISBN 9780840716897 (epub) | ISBN 9780840716903
Subjects: LCGFT: Romance fiction. | Christian fiction. | Novels.
Classification: LCC PS3606.E7263 P47 2025 (print) | LCC PS3606.E7263 (ebook) | DDC 813/.6—dc23/eng/20240909
LC record available at https://lccn.loc.gov/2024041374
LC ebook record available at https://lccn.loc.gov/2024041375

Printed in the United States of America

24 25 26 27 28 LBC 5 4 3 2 1

To my former ESL students and all our wonderful times

NOTE TO READERS

Dear Readers,

This book is particularly special to me for two reasons. First, because of my own experience early on as a struggling aspiring writer, and secondly, because of my own previous work as an ESL teacher to adult immigrants.

I'll never forget the tender, fascinating, heartbreaking, and sometimes truly hilarious moments of my ESL students gathered together while I taught Idioms of the Day and check writing and so much more. Hilarious moments—like the scene where Bryony's student informs her about what happened when he told a police officer to "hold his horses"—were truly inspired from real experiences. Indeed, there are so many cherished memories I wish I could have stuffed into this book.

I made sushi with Japanese students, shared Turkish tea with my Turkish students, visited the Nepalian home of a student who shared wedding pictures of her weeping the day she met the man she would marry, on their wedding day, and left her family that moment to live in another country with new people forever. I grieved with students who came in some mornings struck by news of tsunamis, or earthquakes, or attacks in home countries, and laughed with a funny young woman who also casually mentioned her father was married to fifty women. I was relieved with students who escaped personal terrorist experiences and was saddened to hear when their own family members were not so lucky. I smelled wonderful things, ate wonderful things, heard wonderful things, learned wonderful things, but one thing I loved the most was that together, we all shared laughter. We all loved our *families. We all loved each other. It was truly a joyous time seeing what the world could be together, in harmony.*

And of course, as an author who has dealt with many, many rejections over the years, I have been itching to write the stranger-than-fiction world of publishing. The opening scene at the pitch session of the writers' conference is more true to life than you'd think, and it was pure fun to finally get it on paper! The literary world is a fascinating one.

The Perfect Rom-Com is my book lovers' twist on Two Weeks Notice, *and I hope you love Bryony, Jack, and all their friends as much as I did writing them.*

Warmly,
Melissa

CHAPTER 1

It was a dark and stormy night.

I mean, not *technically*.

Technically it's actually remarkably warm for a January afternoon in Nashville, Tennessee. Men and women of all ages are practically skipping down the sidewalk on the street below, twinkles in their eyes, hope in their chests. Just a moment ago I watched from the three-story glass wall of the conference center as one stuffy-looking businessman actually dropped his phone call to commence sharing crackers with a squirrel. *Crackers.* With a *squirrel*. Having a little lunch together on a green bench while taxis and tour buses flash by, windows down, hair in the breeze.

Everybody in all of the city is basking in the unusual sunshine.

Learning life lessons.

Having existential breakthroughs.

Except for me.

No, I, twenty-nine-year-old Bryony Page, have the distinct pleasure of my mind crackling like a thunderstorm while I pace outside the conference pitch room on my final day of the American Society of Writers conference, awaiting my final pitch appointment that will determine whether the past two years of writing my heart and soul out was life-changing or, in actuality, a complete and utter waste of time.

And then, of course, there's my sister on the other end of my phone. With her own particular brand of "trying to help."

"It's your last day, Bryony," Gloria says in my ear, a nails-down-the-chalkboard kind of twang in her voice. "You just have to buck up. Pull yourself up by those bootstraps. Slap that book on the table—"

"Proposal," I interject, pivoting on the thin hotel carpet.

A manager in the distance is frowning mildly at my legs, looking like he's calculating exactly how many times I have to pace this exact path before I'll wear a hole in his carpet.

"—and get back on that horse because you are going to have a *rootin' tootin'* good day, ya hear? This is *it*."

I pinch the bridge of my nose, trying to ease the tension. On the bright side, I'm not hyperventilating. Hyperventilating is what the man to my left is doing as he exits the pitch room and collapses onto the first bench he finds.

Neither am I crying.

Crying is what the woman to my right is doing while another conference attendee is shaking her by the shoulders, telling her to pull herself together because she has, according to the clock above the door, thirty seconds before she's up.

No, what I am doing is getting my pre-pitch pep talk. The same pep talk I've received from my sister the past three pitches over the past three days I've been at this writers' conference nine hundred miles from home. Only, as each day has gotten progressively worse, the rejections have piled up higher and higher, and the stakes have risen to dangerous levels, the pep talks have grown . . . weirder. Longer. Just worse.

My sister, Gloria: dignified court reporter in the courtroom, whimsical adult-child every moment out.

I know what she's doing, though. The harder she sees me struggle, the more absurd she gets.

Some people's love language is baking casseroles and sending letters. Hers is providing distraction—even at the cost of throwing on a Big Bird costume and dancing down a congested hospital hallway waving streaming blue ribbons (i.e., during our friend's seven-year-old daughter's recovery from tumor removal). And right now, without question she has at least four tabs open on her phone on websites about "Southern slang" while she grasps at straws for any sort of distraction from these tortured few minutes before my last and final pitch.

(Not to mention she found it raucously funny that I called her from a line-dancing saloon my first night during a "meet and mingle." Needless to say, life at the conference here in Nashville, Tennessee, is a far cry from our little borough outside New York City. And to my misfortune, it turned out, I did *not* happen to have any life-changing chats with agents while doing the Boot Scootin' Boogie.)

I let Gloria continue as I turn on my heels and pace beside the doors, taking in words like "highfalutin" and "can't never could" and attempting small chuckles every few moments for her sake.

And to my surprise, it's actually helping in a small way. Just hearing her voice rattling off anything, anything at all, braces me. It's not *fixing* me, mind you. But it's stabilizing enough that I'm not getting any worse.

At least eight people are pacing in the massive room around me (all of whom are contributing to the manager's stress). Most with heads bent, mumbling to themselves as they stare at their papers. Some, like me, on their mobiles, getting their own personal pep talks—that no doubt *don't* include phrases like, "There's someone for you, B. After all, there's not a pot too crooked that a lid won't fit."

And as the long hand on the clock strikes twelve, I feel an urge to flip open my proposal folder and recheck everything. Just one more time.

It's unnecessary. I've checked to make sure my papers were all there and in order at least a dozen times.

But I have to see. I have to confirm it did not magically disappear in the past sixty seconds.

My one-sheet. Check.

My business card crafted on some site I'd never visited before, where I ordered two hundred for the sole purpose of this weekend (and 197 still linger at the bottom of my bag). Check.

My sixty-page proposal prepared to tell literary agent Jack Sterling every single bloated thing about my life, career, and book.

I don't work as an ESL teacher. I am a philanthropic academian with a bent for loyalty and integrity in my fifteen years of service.

I don't have a gerbil named Biscuit my old roommate abandoned when she left me halfway through a yearlong lease. I am in the animal rescue service and provide therapy—via allowing Biscuit to come to my classes so my students can find comfort in stroking his soft black fur during anxiety-ridden testing weeks.

I do not have a newsletter of forty-six people comprised of 25 percent family and 75 percent students. I have a global-spanning news outlet with a roster reaching people from twenty-seven countries and counting.

I have three sample chapters.

I have a pen I can gift him that has my name and email, just in case he loses my business card.

I have a paper clip with my name and email I can slip on my papers in case he loses my business card, and my pen, and my proposal and folder, and all electronic receipts regarding my name and information.

I have . . . everything. Down to the bandages on my blistered heels from walking miles inside these conference halls the past few days and attending classes about how unprepared I was to do something as idiotic as try to sell my book when "don't you guys *know* that two million new books come out each year?" and "let's not even begin to think about the destruction wrought by AI."

I've diminished beneath celebrity speakers sharing their glory stories of old, writing books on washers and dryers before receiving the big phone call with the six-figure advance.

I've sat in on marketing classes informing me how I need to run a successful website, newsletter, blog, Goodreads, BookBub, Instagram, Lemon8, Threads, TikTok, Pinterest, YouTube, X, and Clapper account before even considering reaching out to an agent, because of course publishers can't publish books without successful authors. Never mind that it's impossible to *be* a successful author with a thriving platform on social media without actually having, you know, a book.

I've done one-on-one sessions only for editors to circle every page of my first seven and tell me precisely thirty-two things I did flagrantly wrong.

I've been rejected by three agents during three pitches. The whole reason I came.

If dictionaries were made entirely of pictures, there'd be a large photo of me under the word *defeated*.

My eyes flicker up to the clock on the wall and I swipe at one particularly annoying lock of brown hair that keeps falling over one of my eyes. The energy in the room is lifting. Shifting as people gather up their supplies and begin to stand.

"Are you done, Gloria?" I say into the phone.

She stops midsentence. "You feeling energized yet? 'Cause I can do this till the cows come home."

"I'm up," I say in a hush. "They're about to open the doors."

"All right, all right, I know you're . . ."—she pauses, clearly hunting for a clichéd phrase—"busy as a cat on a hot tin roof, so I'm going to cut to the chase 'cause this is key. Here we go!" she says, and I pull the phone from my ear after a thunderous clap. "Repeat after me: I, Bryony Sophia Page, am a strong and intelligent woman—"

My mouth remains clamped shut.

"—and I don't care if I have had three agents tell me my stuff was crap—"

The doors burst open, lanyards swinging from the necks of two conference staff. People begin to stream out.

"—or that that woman said my proposal wasn't worth the paper it was printed on—"

My heart begins to beat frantically. I clear my throat. My jaw tightens.

"—and I will not waste my time on anyone who's slicker than pig snot on a radiator—"

You can do this, Bryony. You have gotten this far—you can do this.
Do it for The Bridge.
Do it for your students.
Do it for you.

"—or waste my time on anyone who's as useless as a screen door on a submarine—"

A young woman's face is as red as a tomato as she walks unsteadily on skinny stilettos, eyes unfocused ahead as she clings to her dignity and, apparently, aims for a trash can.

Two more walk behind her, already pulling out their phones to break down everything that happened in the past fifteen minutes. The fifteen minutes that feel like both a lifetime and a blink.

Fifteen minutes.

That's all the time I have, ever again most likely, to sit before a real professional and give my novel a real shot.

"—because I am Bryony Sophia Page, summa cum laude in literature studies at NYU, beautiful woman with the voice of an angel—"

I flush slightly. I do like my voice.

"—and the best English teacher hundreds of your students have ever sat under. A world changer. And a heck of a writer with a story to tell. My sister."

"You changed your POV," I murmur.

And sure enough she's done it. She's managed to put a hint of a smile on my face.

"I'm going back into court, but I'm calling for an update the second I get out."

I nod and drop my phone tab down to silence it. Pause just before hitting the airplane button. Check one last time for a text message from Parker. Nothing.

Still nothing.

Of course, he has his own life and his life is on the other side of the world currently, but still, I had hoped he would've remembered to message me sometime today. Anytime, really. Given this moment has been all I've been able to think about the past six months.

I shake my head, forcing myself to remember. It's *hard* being in a long-distance relationship. And it's particularly hard when it's the middle of the night his time.

Every victory I'm awake for, eager to share about, he's sleeping through. And vice versa. It's hard to be present for somebody else when you can't even see the sun and moon at the same time.

I push aside my pride, ignore the little internal wound of neglect, remind myself about that one conversation when he said, "Bryony, it's impossible to bother me when I'm asleep. I'm just over here dreaming of you. How much better is a conversation with the real thing?" and quickly type the words: I'm about to go in. Final pitch appointment! Wish me luck.

It sounds a bit forced. And I'm rethinking the command to wish me luck, wondering if I should add something else, something light-hearted and totally off topic, when the typing bubble on his end forms.

I stare as people start walking past me for the doors, my feet planted to the ground.

And then the text comes, and I exhale.

Good luck, B. They'd be crazy not to pick you.

A smile is plastered on my face as I turn off my phone. My lucky charm text came through.

I slip my phone into my bag.

Inhale deeply.

You know what? The failed pitch appointments simply don't exist. They didn't happen. They are all behind me and might as well have been bad dreams. *This* is the only moment that counts.

I check the arrangement of the folder tucked under my arm one last time. Raise my chin. Focus on a confident stride. And walk through the doors.

The pitch room is bright and emotionless and expansive. Twenty-five or so tables litter the room with two folding chairs on either side. Agents sit on the side facing the doors, nameplates on the tables, faces alert to the new charges coming through the doors. Scanning us with a flick of the eye first to our name badge and any accompanying glossy ribbons on our lanyard (i.e., multipublished author, TIFA award winner, contest finalist) and then continuing the scan for any other clues that they can scrape from our bodies. We're the new recruits to the publishing army. One of us just may be, despite our pale faces and shaky gaits, the needle in the haystack they are hoping to find.

I already know what they see in me:

Bryony Page. Five foot five.

No lanyard of rainbow-colored ribbons falling down to my knees showing I'm important in any way.

Brown, uninteresting shoulder-length hair that matches the brown, uninteresting eyes and ensemble.

Department store clothing that shows, if you look closely, the hole where I pulled off the tag with my teeth. (So. At least I'm classy.)

In other words, utterly unremarkable in any way.

Agent Kerry Cross's eyes zing with mine as soon as I enter. She's perched at her table directly ahead, fingers looped through one another.

Immediately I avert my gaze.

She's the one who told me not three hours ago that my writing was "like eating a burrito. Burritos are nice, but they aren't filet mignon. And the publishing industry is much too congested for a *burrito*."

My eyes then land on Agent Tim Graves and ricochet away immediately like a bouncy ball let loose in the room. He was the one I actually had a tremendously pleasant conversation with—fourteen of the fifteen minutes, that is. He nodded with what appeared to be genuine interest as I rattled off details about my grandmother's history and the inspiration for the novel. He read my sample chapter thoughtfully. Laughed at my jokes. I remember I had glanced over while he read and actually felt *sorry* for the girl at the table to my right, sweating bullets as she tried to convince the disinterested agent on the other end that her story was not a total rip-off of Orwell's *Animal Farm*, that it was "just about a farm full of animals who overthrow the leadership and create a peaceful economy of their own . . . but . . . in *space*."

And then the one-minute bell rang, and I slipped out my business card, feeling incredibly sure of myself. I slid it over to him. Gave it a little tap with my index finger. Said in a quietly thrilled way, "Here's my information. This was an absolute pleasure."

And then, to my utter shock, he slid it back. "It was a true pleasure, Bryony. You've got real potential here. I look forward to seeing it one day out in the world."

And then he slid back *everything* toward me. All of it. As though he'd rented my materials from the library and had enjoyed them, but now it was time they return.

I slid my business card back. "That is so kind of you," I said a little unsteadily. "I so respect your opinion in this business. It would be an honor to work with you. Here is my email."

At which point *he* slid it back, with a few more confusing and uplifting niceties. We slid it back and forth several more times, and long story short, it was the *timekeeper* who eventually stepped in with a waiting conference attendee behind her, picked up the business card, and pushed it into my hands. "He's saying *no*. He's saying he *doesn't want you*."

Apparently, as I found out later, Tim Graves has a reputation for being nice to the point that he is *incapable* of turning someone down to her face. He just spouts out compliments and avoids taking on folders until the attendees eventually get it and walk away. Which worked for everyone, apparently, except the most desperate ones. Like me.

Okay. New plan.

I just can't look at anyone in this room. Every time my eyes lock with someone else's here, it's a punch to my confidence.

I'll just have to . . . keep my gaze to the floor, then find where I'm supposed to go by clues.

My eyes skirt around tables, focusing on shoes and laptop bags lying on the floor, and I glance up only for the briefest squint at nameplates before ducking back down.

It's not until I'm at the very end of the room, isolated from all the other tables deep in conversation, and wondering if maybe I need to turn around, that I finally spot the name.

JACK STERLING.

His nameplate is askew.

He's wearing a T-shirt. A charcoal-gray T-shirt—the kind of T-shirt that exudes quiet luxury in its simplicity. The mere fact that you can't tell if it's part of a six-pack from aisle six of the grocery store or handspun in the Himalayas somehow makes it all the more boastful. A blazer is tossed on the chair beside him.

His shoes are athletic. The brand name something foreign. His feet are crossed one over the other *on the table* as he leans back in his chair and thumbs through his phone, not a care in the world.

Not one single care.

He may as well be at home right now, watching soccer on the television.

One glance up to his face and there's no question that this is the man I'm supposed to meet.

They are the same striking gulf water–green eyes as those on a dozen tabs on my laptop—every ounce of research I could find about the senior agent of the titanic agency, The Foundry Literary. His squeaky-clean, freshly shaven face and perfectly trimmed and oh-so-slightly swooped brown hair is plastered on everything from decade-old interviews about the state of the publishing industry to the recent breakup announced on his former girlfriend's Instagram page. (Yes, I, and every other crazy conference attendee here, am a stalker.) Every single thing about his life and interests I could possibly find to help me create the mask I would need to wear to impress him.

The same coffee order in his hand I'd learned through a podcast Q&A two months ago. Black but for one pack of sugar.

The same thin, unconcerned lips as he looks through his phone.

Honestly, it's startling. Other agents and editors and their hopefuls are engaging in earnest conversation, and here Jack is, appearing like he's absolutely *forgotten* about me. As if he couldn't care less if I'm here or not. I'm not sure what's better: the unsettling intensity of other agents . . . or this.

I slide into my seat.

He holds up a finger. *Without looking at me.*

And it's a full, agonizing *three minutes* before he peers up from his phone. *Three minutes* out of a possible fifteen total where every tick of the clock rings in my bones. The chatter in the room has grown to a roar. The conversations and missions around me rush forward while I'm sitting here, stuck in the mud as I watch this man spin through his phone. And there is *nothing* I can do about it. I am completely at his mercy.

Stagnant. It's a good thing I wore my bland brown dress today because I have sweated through it.

And just when I think I am going to *burst*, he casually sets the phone on the table face down.

"Sorry about that . . . ," he says, without any sense of sincerity, and gives a startling clap of his hands. He drops his feet to the ground. His eyes skim over my lanyard. "Bryony. Whatcha got."

It's less of a question than a statement, because before I know it, he takes the folder from my hands and swivels it around to face him.

Just. Takes it.

Agents, in my vast experience of the past three days, *do not do this.*

They open the conversation slowly, like cats eyeing their mice carefully because they think it'd be fun to play a little before swallowing them. They say things like, "What's your name?" despite the fact it's written across your lanyard and printed on the sheet of paper before them. They ask questions like, "Where are you from?" and "Ah. So you're a Knicks fan, then?" even though it has absolutely nothing to do with anything. All just filler conversation to break the ice and warm you up before they inevitably eat you for supper.

And they certainly *don't* just snatch your folder from your hands.

But here Jack is, cutting straight to the stage reserved for the nine-to-ten-minute mark of the pitch. He's actually jumped us *ahead* of everyone else now. Flipped past the one-sheet without looking. The pages of character descriptions. My author bio. Platform (or lack thereof). Straight to: the ominous silent read.

I clench my hands in my lap, back straight as a rail as I watch helplessly to see what will befall my fate. His eyes jump down the page before he flicks the page over and reads down the next. And the next.

There's barely enough time for me to gather up this new situation before suddenly he's ready for a verdict.

He snaps the folder shut.

Pushes it toward me, making a terrible scratching sound across the table. "Yeah, this isn't going to work."

I feel a thump in my chest.

It takes a second to catch up from all the whiplash happening here.

Nobody just *starts* with horrible rejection like this. People at least beat around the bush before they suddenly slice you through.

"I'm sorry? Um . . ." Do I *want* an explanation?

But of course.

I have to *fight* this.

"Is it . . . ?" I venture.

"It's the genre."

He looks at me. I look at him.

He sighs. Throws out a hand. "I mean, what really *is* this? Is it magical realism? Is it biography?"

Ah. A question I can answer. A question I've been asked. I grasp for the familiar ground. "It's literary fiction," I supply unsteadily, "with a touch of magical realism. And . . . a bit of suspense. And . . . somewhat biographical. After my grandmother's life."

"So . . . a commercial dead end." He's smiling at me as though he's talking about something as superficial as which way it is to the bathroom instead of saying my book is "a commercial dead end."

And there he is. His hand sliding, *unbelievably*, toward his phone. As though this was a nice chat but this conversation is over.

"Is there . . . anything I can do?" I throw out.

"Unless you're hiding some amazing connections, you won't get anyone to pick this up."

Well. The other agents had said magical realism biographical suspense literary fiction was *unique* at least. Tim Graves called it "incredibly imaginative" and "never before seen in the industry"—which at the time I took as a massive compliment. Best not to think of it, actually.

None of them, at the very least, had called it a *dead end*.

"There's only a tiny piece of magical realism, for the sake—"

"How many words was this again?" He cuts me off.

I bite my lip. I knew this one was going to come up.

"It's 149,800."

I do not round up, specifically because I'm delusionally hopeful those two hundred words make a difference.

He chuckles a little. Under his breath. Like an insider looking at the pitiful, pitiful little girl who knows approximately *nothing*.

"Do you think you're Stephen King?"

I cast my gaze around uneasily. "What?"

"Do you think you're Stephen King?"

I'm falling into a trick question, I know, but have no choice but to reply. "No."

"Then what makes you think you can bypass all the laws of commercial fiction and write a book easily twice the allowed number? It costs the publisher money for those pages."

I am beginning to dislike this man immensely. (Of course I'll work with him—I'll work with a shoe if it could sell my books—but I am absolutely *not* going to enjoy it.)

"Right," I say slowly. "I know it's an issue. I know about King's 'kill your darlings' and all that. It's just, this novel—"

"Manuscript."

"—is about the legacy my grandmother has created within the organization I work for. It's just—and I know people must say this all the time—but there's nowhere to cut."

"There are approximately seventy thousand places to cut—"

"Every part is special—"

"Then put those seventy thousand words in a family scrapbook where they belong."

"If you could just read it—"

"I don't make the rules, love."

My nose wrinkles in distaste at his choice of words there. Who *exactly* does he think he is? A sweet old Southern woman at the grocery register? A brawny Scottish herdsman bringing his sheep across a gorge? These are the only acceptable people for such a use as "love," and he, with his scrawny bookish arms, is neither.

But there it is.

Time slows to a crawl as his finger, with the power of a judge's hammer, taps my folder two painfully slow, painfully definitive times.

And Jack, his phone flipped over now, doesn't even give me the decency of looking me in the eye as he says, "Pleasure meeting you. Enjoy the rest of the conference."

Enjoy. The rest of the conference?

The *six hours* left of the conference?

As if I haven't spent thousands of dollars and spent six months in savings and taken off work and traveled across the country for only the smallest glimmer of *hope* of fifteen minutes with four agents—*four*—for the pleasure of being told to "enjoy the rest of the conference"?

And this guy was my last shot.

And now here I am, with—I check the clock—ten minutes and twelve seconds to go.

A lifetime.

Does he even *know* how much I've sacrificed for this experience?

I sit here stiff as a board while his attention fixes wholly upon his phone. His frown is growing as he swipes down an email. A moment later, he rubs his chin.

I stand.

What else is there to do?

My head is pounding, my legs are numb, as I take the walk of shame between tables toward the exit doors.

Faces glance up in midconversation as I pass, people curious to scan my eyes for the tears. *What happened with her? Why is she leaving so early? Ohhhh, she met with HIM? A year-one conferee having a go at Jack Sterling? I wouldn't be caught dead wasting an appointment on him. Rookie.*

I can hear their thoughts. My face is hot as I try to ignore them all. *I didn't have a choice!* I want to cry out. *He was the only one left!*

I spent *six* hours yesterday in the appointment wait line, ignoring classes just to hope to snag an extra appointment beyond the three that were given me at the start of the conference.

Three appointments in exchange for the thousands of dollars at this conference felt unreasonable.

I had spent all this money. I had spent every waking moment of the past two years writing this story, ever since it came to my attention that my workplace and home, The Bridge Refugee and Immigration Services, was at risk of losing its funding and going under. Ever since I hatched the crazy plan that *writing* was something I could do. Write the story. Tell the story. Support The Bridge with the profit. Keep not only my ESL job but the place that was my community, my family's community.

Really, just my family.

It was a wild dream, but it was our last hope.

I had tried getting newspaper outlets to take up interest in saving the town's beloved program.

I had tried organizing fundraising festivals full of bouncy houses and balloons.

I had applied for more grants than my aching hand could handle writing.

I'd tried everything. But this.

Maybe it was a pipe dream. Girl writes book loosely about her grandmother founding this beloved community center, and it raises the awareness of just the right people who secure it forever. Maybe it was ridiculous. But the fact is, those stories *do* exist. Books do become bestsellers and go on to raise awareness for great things. Encourage recycling. Save trees. Fund foundations rescuing people from human trafficking. Remind people that humanity *can* do wonderful, incredible things when we come together. Books *can* do that.

A few select books *do* break out big.

Everybody thinks the lottery is crazy except for the one person who wins it.

Maybe, just maybe, it is my time to win this.

So I sat down one particularly helpless-feeling night and did the only thing I felt I could do. I wrote.

And wrote.

And wrote.

And before long, nobody could stop me from writing.

It began from a mission and ran on the steam of passion. Turns out, the only thing I love more than reading is writing. I love writing. I love telling stories.

I love shaping words and worlds within my story that bend to the dreams and hopes I wish the world existed on. I love that in a world so uncontrollable, I write so that the guy gets the girl in the end. The dog finds his family. The mother never dies.

So forgive me if yesterday, after being rejected from the third and last agent on my list, I rejected the upbeat conference speaker's advice to just "wait until next year's conference to pitch and instead make the most of those marketing workshops!" and joined the group of conference vultures.

The conference vultures.

It's a thing.

We are a thing.

For whatever reason (illness, signed a contract with another agent, sudden panic attack . . . probably the sudden panic attack), there is a system in place for "spontaneous bonus appointment openings."

A conference attendee calls and cancels his or her upcoming appointment and in that moment, the conference vultures—the small group of conference dissidents who ignore classes and watch with beady eyes for spontaneous appointments—pounce as a staff member scribbles the newly available name and time on the board.

The name of the agent or editor would be revealed.

Hands would fly through phones, researching the new person.

The conference staff would call up the next vulture number. I was number seventeen.

And so, on the day went.

AGENT THERESA JONES, 12:15.

~~AGENT THERESA JONES, 12:15.~~

EDITOR PHILLIP PARKS, 2:45.

~~EDITOR PHILLIP PARKS, 2:45.~~

The board filled up and emptied of names while you waited, watching the board like a stockbroker, anxiously researching anything you could find out about the person in question until your number popped up—on the delusional hope that everyone else suddenly lapsed into stupidity and didn't realize the name in block letters was a good one.

Agent Theresa Jones was single. A cat lover. Her author gave a glowing review about her in the acknowledgments section of a recent release, *The Gentlemen of Shanghai*. She won two apparently incredibly important awards in the past three years, given the general glowyness of the trophies and fluff level of her dress. She hobnobbed with a celebrity once, via the backdrop of a 2018 movie release. She was into knitting cat hats.

Agent Jones was kind and successful.

Agent Jones was a winner.

Ergo you and every other anxious author surrounding the dry-erase board wrung your hands with delusions of hope as you waited and hoped and prayed for Jones.

But of course, Jones would last on the board twelve seconds.

Cue bitter disappointment.

Then surprise! Someone just called in to free up a new appointment.

Cue delusional hope.

It was *exhausting*, sitting hours in that chair riding an emotional roller coaster.

There was one name, however, that always stayed on the whiteboard.

AGENT JACK STERLING 12:30.

AGENT JACK STERLING 12:45.

AGENT JACK STERLING 1:30.

Sterling, as it turns out, was also single—although the number of different (and yet all the same?) women who jumped in and out of his frames on his socials was concerning. An ego man. A Peter Pan. Red flag. Jack kept a small clientele list, no more than fifteen, and all the kind of names you'd see splattered everywhere from the CVS checkout line to coming out of the mouth of the eight-year-old you babysit. *Household* names. This is another red flag.

He wasn't desperate for fresh meat, and whenever he wanted, he could easily pick up someone with far more experience and credentials than you.

He was *too* good. *Too* established.

In fact, it was a little concerning to even see him here. Why *was* he here? He was by far the most successful and well-known agent in the business, the caviar of agents in the caviar of agencies. Even the conference directors tried to schmooze up to him at mealtimes and casually/not-so-casually slip him comments about their own books every other second (to the great frustration of their own agents; it's actually been a bit of a drama).

Jack enjoyed skiing in places where the mountains in the backdrop were just, you know, the Alps. And the goggles over his face were shiny in an intimidating, look-how-expensive-these-are kind of way.

All of these little facts lead to the glaring, waving red flag that is Jack Sterling. And all of this is what I want to cry out to the people eyeing me and say, "I was number seventeen! He really was the only one left!"

The doors give a painfully loud creak and every face in the world seems to turn, looking for the person who is actually *leaving*—what time is it now? I cast my eyes to the clock above the door and feel a thud—with nine minutes and five seconds left.

Unbelievable. Someone has jumped up to ask conference staff if she can take my spot in the remaining minutes.

The conference vultures really need their own reality TV show.

The staff member gives an exasperated sigh, as though tired of dealing with a bunch of lunatics, which is entirely what this place makes you become. "No. That's her time. If she wants to leave during it, that's her decision."

I nibble on the bottom of my lip.

A thought bubble forms.

It is, though. Isn't it?

It's *my* decision to leave.

Agent Sterling didn't officially throw me out. He didn't say, "Nice to meet you, now leave." In *fact* . . . My wheels are turning, my breath coming more quickly as I begin to pump myself up. There is a real chance that the pitch regulations require that agents and editors allow the full fifteen minutes. Maybe he isn't *allowed* to force me out. I've paid all this money. Maybe he *has* to let me give my full pitch.

My insides are gnawing at me.

It's a painful, hopeful plan I'm drawing up.

Putting my foot down isn't my strong point.

Being an inconvenience to someone, or even thinking about the *possibility* of being an inconvenience to someone, is right up there with dropping into a tank of jellyfish. Unacceptable.

Standing here even *considering* being a five-minute inconvenience to Jack Sterling is enough to make me queasy.

I feel a buzz in my dress pocket and pull out my phone.

Gloria's text comes in. GO BRYONY. THIS IS IT! I'M SO PROUD OF YOU!!!!!!!!!!!!!!!!!!!!!!!!!!!!!!

Gloria tends to demonstrate how much energy she is giving toward something in the number of exclamation points. It's actually a bit of a problem in her line of work. The lawyers don't exactly love it in their transcripts.

But sure enough, her text is just enough of a kick to get me to put my hand on the door handle. And once that is done, enough people's eyes are on me that I feel myself propelled to open the door.

Step through.

Force my shoulders back a little more.

And march straight back to Jack Sterling's table, steadily ignoring everyone's gaze along the way.

I may not *like* him.

I may not actually want to *work* with him.

But with dozens of auto-response rejections in my inbox, three agent rejections down, and a thick manuscript I've spent years writing in the dead of night on my desk, Jack Sterling is quite literally my last shot for getting my little (fine, massive) book out in the world.

So, Jack Sterling, move over. Because here I (politely) come.

CHAPTER 2

"So you were saying?"

I've decided the least explosive way to restart this conversation is by pretending the break in between never happened.

Oh, ha-ha. No, silly. I never left. That was just a little bubble in your imagination. You were daydreaming. I've been here this whole time. In fact, you were saying very nice and encouraging things to me before you daydreamed off. And the casual smile on my face, as if we are having the most mutually lovely conversation of all time, is proof of it.

I slide into the seat opposite him, and to say he is startled—his feet again propped on the table—is an understatement. His sneakers kick back, jostling the coffee mug in his hand and throwing little drops over that pretty blazer of his on the chair beside him. All four legs of the folding chair land on the ground with a thud as he drops his phone and coffee mug on the table and begins rubbing the droplets off his hand.

There's an expression on his face as he looks at me during all this. Something I'm not accustomed to seeing in my life's goal of never inconveniencing anyone.

His mouth is open. His eyes are bulging at me like I am an alien. An alien who's come in the middle of the night to stand over him while he sleeps soundly in his bed. And instead of reaching over for a little glass of water for a 2:00 a.m. sip, he finds himself being handed an Oreo from me. Green alien with an Oreo, smiling and full of goodwill me.

A new friend.

"I think you were saying the book was a bit on the long side," I continue casually, pulse thrumming at the back of my throat. "I *could* cut it. If you would read just a few chapters first to see what I mean though, that'd be very helpful in making sure we're on the same page. I know that *some books* are allowed to break the rules of commercial fiction. If they prove to have enough to say in this respect. Think of *Middlemarch—*"

"You are not George Eliot. And this is not the nineteenth century. And you do not have her level of talent."

"How would you know if you haven't read it?"

His brow quirks. And if I'm not mistaken, a tiny pilot light ignites in his eyes.

I shrug casually, like this is an ordinary conversation between friends. Because to me, it seems as if what Jack Sterling likes, given the twelve Instagram photos I've seen and the way he's responded with general indifference to the conference directors following him into the elevators, is to be surrounded by successful people. He respects people who respect themselves.

Now, I don't respect myself, but I can pretend.

He blinks a few times, surveying me. Then he leans forward. Just a smidge.

"What're you doing?" he says, and his eyes flicker down for a half second to my badge. "Bryony?"

The announcement of my name feels like a little shower of trumpets, letting me know I passed the first level and may proceed to the next. My smile broadens. Casually, of course.

Then dims a little in case it's too much.

"I'm discussing my book proposal." I clutch the folder to my chest. The folder feels tarnished now. As though if he looked at it now, he'd reject it all over again. Better to just keep talking. Focus on the fact that I am a human. It is simple to reject a piece of paper. *Look in my eyes, Jack Sterling, and let's talk this out rationally.* "And your amenability in reading a few chapters as we take this conversation further. I think you will find I'm a very agreeable person to work with."

He laughs. Chortles, more like. A chortle of disbelief, but not altogether . . . unhappy sounding. One corner of his mouth lifts as he peers into my eyes. "Amenability, huh? Where are you from? A Jane Austen novel?"

"Florence, New York. Present day."

"Nobody lives there."

"*I* live there."

His phone buzzes, but to my surprise, he ignores it. A long moment of silence ensues before he speaks. "Well, here's the thing, Bryony of Florence: I don't need you. I don't need anybody, actually. I'm really only here because I was sent here by the agency. Metaphorically drew the shortest straw. So, unfortunately, despite how much I appreciate your . . . pluckiness, I'll have to apologize, again, and tell you, again, that this"—he motions between us—"isn't going to work. But go try your luck on Davis over there." He points over my shoulder. "He takes on a new client every week."

And then he gives an apologetic smile. As though he is sorry but this is a good alternative. As though suggesting that Davis, who collects authors like a kid collects marbles, is not only impossible to get in touch with, *given I have no appointment*, but also a terrible choice.

Even *I* as a rookie know it would be better to go without an agent altogether, what with his rows of client authors on his web page and giant advertisement of that one semi-successful political book he represented fifteen years ago.

If there's one thing other attendees have harped upon the past three days, it's that just because you could technically *get* an agent doesn't mean you should. I've heard enough horror stories to last a lifetime.

So.

I have a choice here.

And really, I've gone this far into a land so far outside myself, I might as well just go all the way. "Terrific." I smile in return. "I'll keep that in mind."

Keep your shoulders straight, Bryony. Staple that confident grin on. "So. Are you big into skiing?"

That I'm-politely-letting-you-go smile slips off his face. "What're you doing?"

"The way I see it, I have"—I glance down to the large clock on his phone—"eight minutes and twelve seconds until our meeting is over. I'd like to make the most of it."

"And proving you stalk me on Instagram is the way to do it?"

I shrug. Although I'll be honest here, I feel like I'm about two ticks away from throwing up. "You have to know everyone does. I'm sure it's tiring, pretending you don't see everyone gawking at you. Might as well have it out in the open. So. Skiing?"

His brows crumple a little. He leans forward. "Tell you what. I'll give you your five minutes—"

"Eight minutes and twelve seconds."

"—but we're going to spend it doing something advantageous for the both of us. You say you're a team player, yes?"

"Yes."

"And you want to break into publishing, yes?"

"Yes. My ambition," I say, chin lifting as I rattle off my prepared speech, "is to spread awareness about the immigration services center in my community and use the proceeds to keep The Bridge from going under—"

"Then take a look at this." And now it's my turn to have something swiveled around and pushed to my side of the table. The screen is open to a document. A book proposal. Simple and yet roughly a hundred times more professional looking than mine.

I bite my lip, immediately regretting the eight-by-eleven stock photo of a bridge plastered across the cover of my folder and the title in 48 Times New Roman font.

"What's it missing?" he says in a serious tone.

"And this is . . . mutually beneficial . . . for me how?" I let my eyes drift down the page.

He waves a hand at the phone. "Don't make me say the obvious out loud."

It only takes a handful of milliseconds to see what he means. Ah. It's an example of what is a *good* proposal.

A boulder lodges in the pit of my stomach, but I ignore it. My nerves are going into overdrive from the length of this manic, adrenaline-inducing conversation. This is, oddly, both a nightmare and a dream come true, and I'm not entirely sure how much longer I'm going to make it until I pass out.

I'm meeting with the prestigious Jack Sterling. But he's rejecting me while informing me how absolutely laughable it is that I tried to hand off my preschool-level proposal to a man who represents—

My eyes land on the name on the proposal just above his own name and agency seal. I bite my lip, and a painful zing zips through my body.

Amelia Benedict.

No.

Can't be.

I can't have . . . in my hands . . . a super-secret book proposal from *Amelia Benedict*. I've passed books with her name on them a hundred times at the bookstore. Her little romances are usually on some table beside the register, always with a new cover. Always with something bold and bright. Somehow this woman puts out a new book faster than my milk expires.

"So." He leans in till his head is hovering over the phone, his eyes inches away from mine, bouncing from me to the screen. "Take a stab at it. What's it missing?"

Text notifications are dinging alongside a banner at the top of the screen every few seconds, all of which he ignores, so likewise I try to do the same.

I take a breath.

Focus, Bryony. You can do *this.*

But now I'm not just looking at a super-secret book proposal from a terrifyingly aloof agent who represents one of the biggest in the biz; I'm also seeing snippets of his private text messages from his private life on his private phone and trying very much to ignore them.

A message from someone named Ty saying: Just told Walt. He says he's going to sue you under tort law for negligently causing him to break his tailbone falling off his chair. Laughing.

A message from someone named Richie saying: Hanor's gone upstairs. Trying to get you fired. Not going to work but heads-up.

And then a message from Hanor that sounds very official and terrifying: I want to see you in my office the second you get back. With a solution.

And one from someone with a contact name of 2nd Floor Jann with the 300 Flower Pens saying: Are you kidding me, Jack? Could you just, for once, please leave Benedict's writers alone?!?

I try to politely ignore the notifications, despite the fact they are coming in from clearly important people in his life talking about very important details of his life.

Though he obviously cares less than nothing about the fact I'm reading them.

I'm *that* insignificant to him.

I'm the fly buzzing around someone's tea at a mobster's lunch meeting while said mobster is revealing clandestine codes to clandestine locks safeguarding clandestine money. I'm so unimportant that it doesn't matter that I hear.

Which I suppose is fair.

Who, after all, can I tell?

I run my eyes down the first page. Then realize the sum of it is only one page. One page before digging into the actual sample chapters.

Crap.

How many pages was mine? Sixty. With twenty pages dedicated solely to character descriptions.

Terrific.

The embarrassment nips me right in the face, and I feel two flames of crimson burst on my cheeks.

I really *am* pathetic, aren't I?

These past few days, the agents had been trying to tell me, and I hadn't quite gotten it. I hadn't quite *clued in*. They weren't the enemy, as it turned out. If anything, they were the nice guys trying to let me down easy.

They aren't the villains. I'm just the village idiot.

I glance up toward Agent Tim Graves with fresh sympathy and even more personal horror. I will *never* live down the humiliation of these past three days.

Focus, Bryony. You've still got—

"Three minutes!" a young conference volunteer calls out, and I turn to see her three fingers in the air as she stands in the center of the room, grinning madly. Three minutes left.

"So . . . you want me to find—?"

"What's missing, yes. A fresh eye."

Because that's literally all I can possibly be, I see now. That's truly the *only* thing I have that he doesn't right now. A fresh eye.

Something every person on the entire planet can bring right now: a different brain than his.

Super.

It's clear through the way he's sighing right now and pulling back in his chair that he expects very little. Even his eyes are glazing over my shoulder, and I realize this very well may be a ploy to get me to stop talking and leave him alone. If not physically, at least mentally. He's thinking, brainstorming about something important. *This* something that's important. And of course little old me is expected to consider this special book viewing and enlightenment a gift for my silence.

I read the first page, trying to concentrate.

"*Two!*" a conference volunteer mouths merrily, circling around the room with pageantry as she drops one finger and leaves the remaining two. This is, very clearly, an exciting job for her.

"Well . . ." I stumble, eyes back on the proposal. I try to keep reading, to formulate an intelligent answer, but the words under this type of pressure have become alphabet soup. All the letters are just floating around, a name here, an adjective there. There's a block somewhere between my eye and my brain that is seeming to stop the flow from seeing to understanding.

I scroll to the next page.

You have to do something.

Thumb up the screen to the next.

There's gotta be something better to reading this first chapter. A hook. My eyes rage down the pages, and my thumb begins flying from one page to the next.

"One minute!" the volunteer cries, panning the room with her gigantic lanyard of a thousand fancy ribbons and sadistic glee.

Where were we?

Oh yes.

A woman is leading the fun activities on a cruise ship. Singing. Dancing. A man is the leader of the cruise ship. Keeping the whole thing afloat. He is ordered to fire her, I grasp pretty quickly. But secretly he is in love with her. All fairly fluffy stuff that goes great with eating Doritos in the checkout line.

Nothing new.

Nothing to blow people's minds.

Nothing to expand their horizons and give them a deeper appreciation for the goodness of mankind.

And *a lot* of the word *glorious*. A glorious sunrise. A glorious lounge chair. A glorious schedule. Gloriously clean hair that frames her gloriously beautiful face.

Beautiful: That's all we get for character description here.

No, wait—we've got another one. Hot.

A hot, beautiful character with gloriously clean hair and a gloriously glossy face.

It's screaming for a Pulitzer Prize, really.

I jump, my backside literally breaking contact with the chair, as the volunteer rings a cowbell directly behind me. "Time's up!" she cries, and proceeds to give gracious nods and winks at various agents as if to say, "*I know, right? You're* so *welcome.*"

Chairs begin sliding backward. Bags are being picked up off the floor. Weeping, or shrill laughter, commences.

"Well, it seems our time is up here." Jack pulls an apologetic face, although his tone is entirely otherwise. He pushes back his chair and reaches out a hand toward me as though he is about to offer up a consolation prize of a handshake to make sure I know *without question* this is the end of the line. Our interview is over.

This is it.

This is my five seconds to say *something*. And it will be dazzling or nothing.

Come on, Bryony. What can you say now—NOW—short, concise, and knocks him off his feet?

I look down at the chapter, *nothing* coming to mind.

Nothing.

I can't say *anything*.

Well . . . that's not true, is it?

I'm supposed to say it's wonderful. I'm supposed to gawk and confirm that this book, the book he represents, is absolutely *inspiring*. Except for this teeny tiny typo right here on page 12 that could change the whole thing.

Before he is standing all the way, I blurt out the one thing that is true.

And, unfortunately, the one thing I'm not allowed to say.

"The one thing wrong with this is . . . everything."

CHAPTER 3

"Everything," Jack says. "Just . . . everything."

Jack Sterling's startlingly green eyes narrow to slits, and for quite some time he just stares at me.

I shrug. "I am trying to find something that is good about this book and coming up short."

"Nothing. You, very literally, can think of *nothing* good about this book. Amelia Benedict's book."

I shrug again.

Then, just as the cowbell-ringing conference girl leans over us to whisper it's time to "move along" (a person whom he ignores entirely), he smiles.

Jack really smiles, for the first time. I've *finally* given him something to smile about.

Then he shakes his head like I pulled a good one over on him. Reaches out his hand fully now and, this time, pretty much grabs my hand and shakes it. "And let me guess. You could do better."

He doesn't give me a chance to answer.

"Very . . . *unique* to meet you, Bryony of Florence. Nice even. You're plucky. I like that. I hope you and your very large manuscript spend some quality time together deciding which limbs to cut off. Perhaps I'll see you next year—if, heaven forbid, I am forced to return to this place."

I give up.

If "spend a year chopping up your beloved manuscript and then on the horrible off chance I'm here you can possibly see me at another pitch session" is the best I'm going to get, it's time to call it. I'm not cut out for Jack Sterling. Or this conference, for that matter. Or clearly writing.

A gust of wind blows through me. This must be the feeling people have when they finally accept their own inevitable death. The small, very small consolation prize here is the knowledge that I did my best. I fought to the end. And at the very, very least, I was honest. I will go out with my dignity.

I smile back at him as I take up my folder and rise. "I like all my words, Jack. I don't think there will be any cutting. And as for your client's romance—"

"Amelia Benedict's?" he adds with the tiniest flicker of "*You know, the Amelia Benedict?*"

"The one," I continue with a nod. "Objectively speaking here and polite niceties aside, I *could* do better. For starters, drop the third point of view of the event director's dog—it's not cute; it just comes off as weird. Give the captain a second-in-command position so he has someone actually in charge who has the authority to tell him to cut the girl. Cut out 70 percent of the 'supers' and replace them with meaningful descriptors, and delete all references to Extellilango. It's not a real place. It doesn't sound like a real place. And if you are going to create a fictional place, you should at least make it sound *remotely* plausible instead of a location you'd find in *Star Wars*. But really, if she's going for somewhere on *earth* that's warm with volcanoes, she should just go with Punalu'u Beach or Mosteiros Beach in the Azores, or Reynisfjara, Iceland. Personally, I'd go with Reynisfjara."

He's looking at me with incredulity again, and I add, "I teach ESL to adult immigrants and refugees—as I tried to explain with the Why I Wrote My Book page. I've learned something about their homes in the past fifteen years."

Oh dear. The adrenaline that has fueled me the last fifteen minutes is fizzling out to a jittery end, and I find myself anxious to get out of here in the next ten seconds. Because in about ten seconds, I have no doubt that wherever I am, I will be slumping down under the full weight of defeat. Probably crying. Like a wind-up toy crumpled over in the corner.

And I'd really rather not be a slumped-over, weeping toy crumpled on the floor *here*.

His smile wilts a little as I let go of our shaking hands and pull back. "Anyway, take my card. Better yet, take a handful." And like a claw machine game, I reach blindly in my bag and grab a handful of stragglers. Two or three business cards flutter to the table.

And with impending tears pounding at the doorsteps of my eyes, I give a tight smile and stride away as quickly as my heels can take me.

Just like all the other recruits here.

Who didn't make it.

• • •

"And then what'd you do? Say that last part again. *Slowly.* You know what? Just start over. I wanna hear the whole thing. Move over, Jerry. I have critical news on the line!"

Never mind that Gloria is elbowing a bunch of lawyers in a hallway during an adjourned court session to hear my story. I'm sure the lawyers believe it's genuinely important, too, by the way she's acting. And in a small way, the unique mix of incredulity and pride in Gloria's voice as I run through the details of my defeat four hours prior is at least a little soothing. A little balm for the soul after spending the past four hours wallowing in self-pity and humiliation as I packed up all the discarded pencil skirts and rumpled blouses littered around my suitcase and checked in online for my return flight to New York.

I dumped the rest of the business cards in the bin.

Over a hundred of my little faces smiling up at me from the trash can, beside the words in romantic italics: *Fiction That Inspires.*

What does that even mean?

Apparently, according to Gloria, this is all very, very sad but *on the bright side*, look at how brave I was! Who cares, according to Gloria, about this manuscript (I corrected her pretty quickly on that one), when just *observe* this wonderful life lesson! Bryony the Brave!

Bryony, the girl who could go back in time and tell that old group of childhood frenemies that no, she didn't deserve to be treated like the punching bag of the group whenever they wanted someone to pick on and, ergo, she would rather play with no one at all.

Bryony, the girl who couldn't put her foot down with her roommate at uni and say, "Look, *Tiffany*, I know you like having Brian over, but *I'm right here. On the bottom bunk.* And no, I do not want to go elsewhere at three in the morning."

Even now Bryony, the girl who never quite had the gumption to tell the neighbor at the apartment gym, "Right, well, the thing is, I don't *want* to move over from the treadmill to the elliptical just because you came in. I don't *care* that you are training for a 5k. I don't care that you have '5k' tattooed on your bicep. I'm walking at a snail's pace on my thirty-minute jaunt while on chapter 13 of my audiobook, and I *like* my treadmill."

A *ding* rings out from my phone at the same time the elevator announces its arrival, and I look down before the doors open, seeing the Uber notification that my car's waiting downstairs.

"Start when you sat down at Jack's table. No! Start when we got off the phone."

"Fine." The doors open and I step into the elevator, staring at my own frowning, impatient, exhausted face in the elevator mirror along the way. Grimace. I look worse than I thought.

Eyeliner has rubbed off one eye fully and not the other. (Tears always come more fervently on the left side. Is that just a me thing?) Flyaways in my tangled ponytail abound, thanks in large part to the post-episode brisk ten-block walk from the pitch session straight to the hotel. I didn't finish the conference. I didn't say goodbye to anyone. I just left as insignificant and alone as I came. I'm wearing sweatpants, the comfy kind with threads at the knees from the thousand times of going through the washer in the past decade. A

thick brown cardigan is wrapped around my T-shirt at the waist—
bulky. Ready to beat the chill of the airline air.

Bryony Page. What agent would be crazy *not* to want this?

"The sad, sad story of Bryony's life began," I say, yanking the
ponytail elastic out with one hand so I can at least *try* for a better
ponytail in public, "when she sat for six hours with the other conference vultures while other more successful conference attendees
shook their heads with jeering eyes and odious expressions—"

"*Ooooh*, she's going for the rage words," Gloria says gleefully,
knowing how my vocabulary expands when I'm heated up.

"—only to secure, after said six hours, the most eremitic, vainglorious, and least desirable agent of all time—"

"*Vainglorious*, I love it," Gloria interjects.

"—and when time came for the doors to open, she directed herself toward Jack Sterling's table—"

"Via staring at people's shoes because she was too embarrassed to
look up—"

"Thank you. I'd forgotten that," I say. "And then eventually at the
back of the room she bumped into Jack's—"

And then something in the mirror catches my eye, and I stop.

Stop dead.

Right there.

As I grip the handle of my suitcase and forget to breathe.

You hear these things about Tennessee. Of bedazzled belt buck-
les. Of barefoot children carrying around chickens under their arms
like cats.

These are the rumors. Inflated stereotypes.

Except for this moment. At 6:12 p.m. on Saturday evening, January 23, in Nashville in a bedazzled pink elevator in a bedazzled pink
hotel with "Friends in Low Places" playing over the speakers.

Where Jack Sterling's reflection in the multiple mirrors around
us penetrates me with his startlingly green eyes that look at me from
all directions.

It's a nightmare. A honky-tonk nightmare.

After a small eternity of staring at each other, a tiny smile lifts one side of his face.

"Vainglorious," he says, breaking the ice. "Well. That's a new one."

I think . . . I'm going to . . . die now.

Yes. I believe that's the only possible response in this moment.

"You know, it's about time, Bryony of Florence. I was two more elevator rides up and down away from banging on your door. Honestly. I didn't take you for a person who tends to be late. But"—he waves a hand at my appearance—"then again, I didn't take you for being so . . . *athletic* either. It's a good plan, by the way. Much preferable to those stilettos you kept trying to face-plant in."

"Wh-what?" I stammer. Then look down to the rolling suitcase in his hand and back up again. "What?"

My cell phone is dangling in my palm now, my hand going limp from my ear. Vaguely I can hear Gloria through the line asking about what's going on.

The elevator door dings as the doors open on the next floor down.

A mother and her young son stand on the other side. She takes one look at me (and probably my tortured expression), grabs the shoulder of her son to stop him from stepping on, and the doors shut.

Jack resumes. "Anyway, I like that. 'The most eremitic, vainglorious, and least desirable agent of all time.' Snappy. Maybe I'll add that to my byline."

I raise a finger. "How did you—" I pause. Restart. "How did you know—" Pause again. "And you were about to bang on *my* door?"

It's no use.

I'm in a dream missing a bunch of crucial bits of information, and there's just no way to start this conversation.

Jack, for his part, looks like he's ten pounds lighter than he was four hours ago.

He actually looks like the only thing keeping his feet on the ground are weights in his shoes.

In fact, it's suspicious.

He's staring at me right now like this is *exactly* where he wants to be and I'm *exactly* the one he wants to be with.

Here. In an elevator.

He nods at me. "Funny. For the chatterbox you were four hours ago, I thought you'd have at least two pages worth of words to throw at me now. Well, I'll just take the lead then. I'm talking about the flight we're about to go on."

He's said the word *flight* as though this should make perfect sense.

"You're in my elevator," I say. "At my hotel." I press my lips together when he doesn't respond to this. "Are you . . . staying at this hotel?"

"Oh no," he says with a half chuckle as though *of course* he wouldn't be caught dead in a place that uses cowboy and cowgirl hats for labeling the restrooms. "No, but you had a lot of handy information in that folder you gifted me today—"

Accidentally left behind on the table in the whirlwind of adrenaline and extreme disappointment and would *rather die* than walk back in that room one more time to get it, more like.

"—which made it incredibly easy to spot you now."

My brows crease. "Track me, you mean."

"Spot," he corrects with a raised finger. "I prefer the word *spot* when you're finding someone who wants to be found. And you did—at least you did four hours ago—want to be found. If I recall correctly, you actually tried to staple yourself to my side."

My nose wrinkles. "It wasn't that bad—"

"Were it not for the annoying bell girl, I think you would've trotted along after me home—"

"That is absolutely *false*—"

"Probably would've moved next door to me if you could—"

"Hang *on*—"

"Anyway, according to your very organized folder system"—he pulls out the folder and taps the color-coded tags—"I like this tab system here. It's handy, even if it smells of desperation. We have a flight to Newark leaving in an hour and forty five—"

"*We*? You're on the same flight?"

"It took a while to get the flights rearranged, but I am now. Because *obviously*"—his hand makes a rolling motion as he elongates this word—"I have a very busy schedule, and I can think of no better way to start off this relationship than by spending six hours squeezed together on a plane, through two plane rides, a handful of layovers, at least two airport Starbucks, and one Cinnabon—do you like Cinnabon? You seem like the type of girl who likes Cinnabon—going over everything. We're going to hit the ground running, so I hope you don't mind me assuming—particularly given your eager, some would say fanatic, display today—that I won't be holding you up."

Relationship.

As in, Jack and me.

Tied together in a *working* relationship that lasts, presumably, far more than fifteen minutes. Because . . . and then it hits me with a thud . . . he liked my book.

I left the folder.

He took the folder.

My chapters were in the story. (Along with pages and pages of character descriptions.)

He read my story.

The image of Jack in his hotel room, leaning back in the hotel chair with his fancy shoes propped up on the executive desk, sunshine pouring through the window beside him, folder gripped in his hand. Lips moving as he reads. Eyes wide, zeroed in on each word. The TV is on, but he no longer hears it. Somebody is knocking at the door—food service—but he doesn't notice.

He is moved.

Moved enough he drops his feet down with a thud and slams the folder on the table with a declaration I had dreamed about happening over and over (never with him, but it still works): *I want this book!*

He must want my book. It's the only logical conclusion.

"I'll call you back," I murmur into the phone and hang up amid Gloria's protests.

I turn fully to Jack now. Face him head-on. "You liked my book?"

And to my surprise, he looks like this question is of little significance. He's actually waving with one hand like my question is a fly he's trying to swipe away.

"Your book. Yes. I read through the forest of trees you chopped down for pages you left me, and yes, once you're past the initial thirty pages, you have something. It's not *ready* by any stretch of the imagination, but it has potential. And no, I don't throw that word around like confetti to every wannabe writer I meet. I don't tell everyone they have 'potential.' But that's not my proposition here. I have an offer for something that's . . . well . . . quite frankly, unturndownable. Much, much bigger than your book."

My stomach drops at his words about my novel—only the passion project that has gripped my heart and soul the past two years—and the way he so casually tosses it aside.

But however I look he doesn't seem to notice, because he continues. "I want to see if you'd like"—he pauses momentously, steepling his hands to his lips for a long moment and then letting go with a flutter of his fingers as if they are needed to accompany his next grand words—"to be the ghostwriter for Amelia Benedict's next book."

My entire body freezes but for the tiny sliver between my brows that creases into a tiny line above my nose.

I stay this way so long that Jack drops his hands. Points vaguely at my head. "See, now, what's this mean? I'm sorry. I don't know you enough yet, so you'll have to clarify. Are we in shock now? Because, unfortunately, we will have to quite literally run to the airport in a matter of seconds—"

The elevator dings and flings the doors open. A man steps inside. A couple follows suit. The doors slide shut and down we go to the final floor.

"I know this is a . . . unique offer," Jack continues, his voice lowering.

"I'm thinking," I say, and this time it's me waving away his words like a fly.

"Then I'll help you process," he continues, not missing a beat. He's closed the gap between us now. I can actually smell the this-is-my-special-first-class-seat aftershave on his skin. "Amelia Benedict releases three books a year. Seventeen are out to date. Six more under contract to release through this year and the end of next."

"How many ghostwriters are there?"

"Three."

"Has she written any herself?"

"Just the one. Her first."

"Was it any good?"

"As a doorstop it's excellent."

"Then why did she become a hit?"

He gives an incredulous little screw of his brows. Inches back from me just enough to gaze at me properly. Gives a little *don't you know?* smile as he surveys me. Like I'm some adorable little Girl Scout who just stumbled upon his front door and asked about stock trading. "Because we're in publishing, Bryony. We stack the deck."

But of course. Little Amelia Benedict. Daughter of multimillionaire father in the hotel industry. Celebrity mother in entertainment. Heiress with money and time to spend how she pleases. I suppose it should come as no surprise that her publisher would pick her books to soar.

"Anyway," he continues even more quietly, "one of our writers is midway through a novel set to release next October. One just took maternity leave. And the last one, the one for the book you previewed yesterday, left recently due to"—he pauses, then settles on the words—"an incompatible work environment."

"You dated her."

"I went on *a* date," he counters briskly. "I was just unaware that the conditions of *a* date with Greta meant I was supposed to become immediately blind to all women henceforth and forevermore."

"And evidently this situation wasn't your first time," I say.

"And evidently you're very good at lying and pretending not to read other people's texts."

The elevator doors slide open to an overwhelmingly pink hotel lobby. We grab our suitcases and stride forward.

"So, as you see, this puts me in a sticky situation," Jack continues, in step with me. "But lucky for me, your overpowering presence came along just when I needed it—"

"I prefer to consider myself prepared—"

"—and the really leech-like vibe you gave off—"

"My sister called it a self-respecting use of boldness."

He throws his hand in the air. "The point is, you're suited for the job. You have good instincts, and you *clearly* have no problem using words. So how about it? I'll have my assistant email you the current manuscript, and you can hack away at all those *supers* all you like." He pauses. "Not to mention, the pay is great."

He speeds up as we approach and then move through the revolving doors, pulling his trendy suitcase and leather laptop bag resting on top along. A man is waiting on the other side, exhaust rolling around his gray suit as his hands rest on one another. Like he's at a wedding. Or a funeral.

When he sees us, he strides forward, reaching for the suitcases. *Both* of our suitcases.

I hesitate on the sidewalk.

A *ding* sounds on my phone, and I glance over to the beat-up dark blue Corolla with the word *Uber* slapped across the dented passenger door. The man inside is tapping the wheel impatiently. He's staring at the revolving door. Waiting for his rider to come out.

It's time for my decision.

I can go with the dented Corolla or with the man in the suit, waiting beside a plume of exhaust that actually smells sweet. Like cinnamon.

Well. It isn't exactly Sophie's choice now, is it?

And before I know it, I'm cruising along the interstate beside Jack Sterling in a completely foreign world of crisp black leather and the lingering scent of cinnamon and even a glass bowl of peppermints on top of a variety of fresh beverages in the mini fridge across from us.

Me, without any forewarning, having gone from the lowest of lows to this situation in a blink.

Jack is rummaging through his bag and pulling out an official-looking set of papers. "The contract's a boat, but it's all very simple. You get paid for writing this and any forthcoming books, and you don't tell anybody about it."

He pulls a pen out of his shirt pocket.

"Or what?"

"Oh," he says, waving a hand over the insignificant question, "you go to jail for the rest of your life, I don't know."

"I go to *jail for life*," I say incredulously, eyeing the pen and papers like they are handcuffs ready to snap on my wrists.

"Are you *planning* on telling people?" He laughs. "Are you and your Facebook following of twelve people planning to seize the Benedict fortress by night with pitchforks raised?"

He's grinning at himself.

He's actually enjoying his little jokes.

I sniff. "It's 242 people, thank you very much."

"Oh. Well, in that case . . ." He clicks on the pen and hands it over.

I stare at it for a moment. Spin the sleek metallic silver between my fingers.

A plan is forming. A decision.

"I'll do it on a condition."

And there it is again. That little spark that lights in Jack's green eyes as I butt up against him, surprising him with a challenge. "I can give you fifty thousand on the advance and 15 percent royalties, but that's the highest they'll go—"

The numbers quake in my ears. If I were completely honest with myself, I would've taken a *five-hundred-dollar* offer for my manuscript, and Gloria would've thrown me a party like I belonged right up there with Stephen King. But this isn't *my* manuscript, is it?

This isn't even *about* my book.

"Allow me to be clear."

My chest is banging so hard, my white T-shirt is making little hiccups. Painfully obvious hiccups. To the point his eyes flicker down.

"I don't want your money."

He raises his eyes back to mine, a dubious expression etched on his face. "Is that so?"

"I'll take no royalties. And I will write this one book for Amelia, *and one book only*, while you take the time to find a proper replacement moving forward. One you apparently don't want to date. Maybe just play it safe and find a man. But what you will give me in exchange for my work is representation. You will take *me* on as your client, and you will represent me and my manuscript until *Water Under the Bridge* finds a good publishing home. That's my deal."

Jack purses his lips.

His hands steeple together again and he leans back, surveying me for so long I see the sign for the airport out the window.

It's terrifying, actually.

He's not breaking eye contact.

And now he's gone quite immovable. Even at a turn that swings us hard left enough that I grab for the handle, he sits unmoved.

A sense of dread comes over me.

I've gone in too strong. In this game of poker I've played too hard and said the wrong thing and bargained too high, and now I'm going to lose it all.

My thoughts are reeling as I think through all the should-haves and could-haves.

Then he throws his head back and laughs. "You know what? I'll take you and your little book on, Bryony Page, but you're getting your fifty thousand and your 15 percent. Actually, what the heck. Just for this book let's make it twenty."

"What about fifteen being the highest you could go?"

And then he pats me on the shoulder. "Congratulations, Bryony Page. You are now in the inner world of publishing. Don't trust anybody or anything they say. I have a feeling we're going to have a great time."

CHAPTER 4

TWO YEARS LATER

"Oh, the inspiration for *The Seven-Year Holiday* was a fun one. Every winter my family has this sweet little tradition of heading to a tiny town in the mountains of Vermont, also called Stowe—"

"It's Woodstock, Maine," I murmur under my breath.

"And"—Amelia throws out a hand—"of course you know where this is going." She has a lilt in her voice, as though she's sharing a cute little secret with the crowd. "There's the most charming little café in this community—"

"It's a bookshop," I growl-whisper.

"Where everyone gathers around, just like every day after a long day of skiing, and it's surrounded by these people who become like *family* after so many years of wintering together. The Barnhartts. The fabulous Donohues. And . . . and everybody else. That's when you realize what it's all about. That *this*—" Amelia's shiny blonde hair and shiny blue eyes and shiny white teeth practically shimmer as she draws herself up even farther off her chair and gives a commanding pause. Those in the room collectively hold their breath.

Eighty people in the eighty folding chairs of the crammed bookstore grip *The Seven-Year Holiday* hardback in their hands as they lean forward, waiting for her never-before-heard wisdom and never-before-heard words.

I clench my teeth from my perch in the back.

I also clench my book. Clenching so tightly that the shiny, slippery cover is tugging off and crumpling in my hands.

She lets the silence sit for an eternity. Like she's waiting until she actually *can*, in fact, hear a pin drop. Her eyes peer through the bookstore windows behind us, as if she is actually expecting every taxi in New York to come screeching to a halt so we can all hear her very important point.

Finally Amelia's animated face opens even further as she spreads out her hands. "That this," she repeats with a high and attention-demanding tremor, "is . . . what it's *all* about."

A hum of awe goes around the room.

"*What is she even saying?*" I hiss. "*This* is what *this* is all about?!"

Her hands rise slightly toward the heavens, and she bows her head with a humble smile, and it's at this exact moment the room goes mad. People are clicking their cameras madly, fingers tapping on the little red circle on their phones twice as fast as they were before. People drop down to their notebooks, hastily scribbling her words in their journals with heavy-handed exclamation points. Somebody to my left circles the words "*This* is what *this* is all about" in red pen at least five times.

Oh my *gosh*.

Could there be any fewer brain cells in these people's heads? They're mindlessly following along! Mindless, I tell you!

The cover of the book twists in my hands like it's made of tissue paper. A low squeak escapes through my clenched lips. I'm a teakettle about to explode.

I see Amelia's publicist's eyes shoot to me from her station at the front, then watch her discreetly send a text on her phone.

Jack's phone dings.

And suddenly, I'm enveloped as he wraps his arm around me. Gently taking hold of the book with his free hand, Jack whispers in my ear, "Ooookay, Bryony. Let's remember why we are here, shall we?"

"I don't know why we are here," I snap. I look like a little turtle underneath Jack's wing. An angry little turtle that some kid keeps as a pet and shows other kids, saying, "Look at Gus! Isn't he adorable?"

I am not adorable.

"In the spirit of *comradery*," Jack supplies, completely unfazed by my temper tantrum. "We're here to prove how well we can *work together* after the *incident*."

(So I threw Amelia's cup of lemonade in the trash can a little "aggressively." And in the aggression, the lemonade flew on her face. And I laughed. But to be fair, she *told* me to put her lemonade in the trash can because there, and I quote, "weren't enough fresh lemons in it.")

"Let's go over this again," Jack whispers. "What is Amelia's job?"

He moves to pull the book out of my hands, but I cling to it like a stubborn child.

"Being the stupid face," I whisper.

"And what are you?" He ignores my jab.

"The big brain inside the stupid face," I sputter.

Mona, Amelia's publicist, is blinking furiously at the both of us now, and despite the warning code from his coworkers and how "serious" he's supposed to be at this "serious" event, the side of Jack's mouth has slipped up into a sideways smile.

"Fascinating." The interviewer beside Amelia nods like a trained seagull with her poised head bouncing in time with her poised bouncing heel. "That's a point that's right on target with what I said in my own novel *Make Way Through Havana's Scarlet Wind in the Quick of Night*." She flashes a hopeful look at the audience. A look that screams, *"Are you going to buy? Are any of you going to buy my book now?"*

"So tell me," the interviewer continues, "in case there is *anyone* here who is possibly the last person on earth to read your latest"—she pauses to laugh at her own joke, and a couple of good souls chime in around the room—"how would you sum up your book? What would you say is the *heart* of this story?"

"Oh, goodness." Amelia laughs as if this is the first time this question—the question that has been asked approximately three hundred times at the last three hundred stops on this tour—is completely out of left field.

She pulls back several strands of her shiny hair. "I don't think I could sum up this book even if I tried. There's just *so much*. You know? But you know what? Why don't *I* hear from *you*? I hear myself all the time, but I would *love* to hear firsthand from my fans."

"*The Seven-Year Holiday* is a heartwarming rom-com," I whisper furiously, "about two people who run into each other in a café bookshop on summer holiday, exchange life-changing advice, and agree to meet every year—without ever talking in between—to give and receive life-changing advice all over again. It's about *laughter* and *love* and *healing* wrapped in the powerful bond of trust between two people who come to rely on each other more than anyone else in the world. Not about 'holidaying with my rich besties' and that 'THIS' INEFFABLE 'THIS' IS WHAT IT'S ABOUT."

Mona's making wild Morse code at Jack with her blinks now, her brows shooting up and down in a mechanical motion.

"Okey dokey," Jack whispers. "Time to go."

I can feel Jack's chest shuddering with silent chuckles while he grips me tighter and pulls me to standing. It's not a choice here. He's got me in a vise grip and I'm moving. Not that I would *choose* to stay.

I'm still clenching my book to my chest as I whisper, "And another thing!" when his hand covers my mouth as he wheels me around. He waves over his shoulder to Mona—who looks like she's about to keel over that moment—and pulls me through the doors into the sweltering heat of an evening in June in the middle of Somewhere, Manhattan.

The air is thick and sticky, with both the smell of macarons from the pastry shop next door and the scent of gasoline from a city slick with sweat in the midst of an unusually hot summer. It's crowded and loud, painfully loud, as it always is on a Wednesday night when half the city is on their way to dinner and the other half of the city is serving it. And my ears, the ears of a Florence citizen unaccustomed to being in the center of the City That Never Sleeps, pound with the sudden onslaught of honks and sirens and conversations in passing.

Jack, meanwhile, is oblivious to it all as he swivels me around outside the door. "Are we done? Are you proud of yourself?"

"Mildly."

"Now you're going to be all over the news."

"Right." I cross the book over my chest protectively. "The group that said she was 'a generational role model' after she went over her morning makeup routine is really going to put two and two together. They'd blindly follow her off a cliff."

"Hence why you two are the perfect team." Jack grins down at me while I stand there frowning at him, clutching the half-torn international bestseller that's actually *quite* meaningful and has been on the bestseller list for twenty-three weeks and running. "She's got the magnetic personality—a certain . . ." He pauses, thinking of words. "Merry cultlike air, if you will, and you are very"—he halts—"smart."

My frown deepens.

"And spritely."

My frown deepens even more.

"But mostly very, very smart. A woman of wits. The trendsetter of our literary time."

It's targeted flattery. A shallow pass for forgiveness. But still, this mollifies me. As he knew it would. As it always does. Not entirely. Not even 50 percent of the way. But enough that my shoulders defrost enough for him to take a step forward.

"There we go," he says, patting me on the head. "That's a girl. So. We'll just cross the signing off our to-do list. Terrific job collaborating; you really gave it a C-minus, D-plus effort. And now it's off to dinner."

He slips his arm behind my back and redirects us toward the car waiting at the curb. "Now, what'll it be? Cibo e Vino or that little shack of yours with all the box televisions and questionably sourced meat?"

"Gok-Oguz," I reply promptly.

"Of course it is," he says, not missing a beat. He holds the door open for me. "Hop in. Bob, take us to Florence, please."

"I want to talk about my email." I slip into my seat.

"And I want to talk about mine." He waits at the open door.

"I mean it," I say with a serious expression.

"Back at you. Now move." He unceremoniously nudges me over.

I glance at the glowing little bookshop as the car begins to move.

The deep green one-story brick building with greenery bordering its doors is nestled between towering complexes, even more festive given the great multitude visible through the glowing windows for the sold-out event. People are milling around the sidewalk, craning their necks to look around the rows of window stickers announcing Amelia's new book. Phones out. Cameras snapping.

One person keeps pacing around a life-size foam board of Amelia Benedict, looking like she's going to make a break for it.

This is what Amelia's events do to perfectly normal citizens. Turn them into fanatics who stand outside sold-out bookshop events, trying to steal foam posters.

This, for the record, is what my life has become saturated with the past two years. My whole life. One massive conversation around one single name: Amelia Benedict.

Day and night. Amelia. Benedict.

It started with leaving that writer's conference and taking a mostly euphoric six-hour flight with Jack as the reality of representation for my book sank in. I was indeed going to be a writer. I was indeed going to have the book that took my heart and soul and give it the wings to fly. Jack Sterling of The Foundry Literary Agency was going to represent me and my book and take it places so that I could use the profits and awareness via publication to save my struggling workplace and my grandmother's greatest legacy—on that one condition, of course.

That I rewrite that sham of a book for Amelia.

So I settled in and hunkered down for six months of a rewrite of somebody else's novel. Which surprised everyone by blowing up beyond anything they'd ever seen.

Which turned into my writing a quick book called *Smuggler's Paradise* after the other ghostwriters couldn't keep up the hype.

And by the time of that release, I was already three chapters into *A Room for Rose*.

I was a workhorse, and somewhere in there, the conversation shifted away from *Water Under the Bridge* to whatever Amelia's book should be next.

Soon enough, I—or rather Amelia—was landing on bestseller lists for unprecedented months that stretched into an eternity. The first three books were optioned to movies six months before they even released, and before I knew it, the other ghostwriters were long out of the picture. It was just me and Amelia. Amelia and me.

Stuck together by Gorilla-glued dollar bills.

I was able to move apartments. Get a place of my own with a view of rosebushes instead of the back side of buildings out the kitchen window. Walk barefoot around my own freshly restored hardwood living room.

I became an anonymous monthly donor to The Bridge—although, admittedly, I had deeply underestimated the depths of their financial straits. Turns out the operating budget of a twelve-thousand-square-foot rented building with twenty-two employees that serves 340 immigrants per year was much, much higher than my donations. And with government budget cuts cutting The Bridge's services at the knees two weeks ago, the reality is that my donations were enough to bide a little time on a boat that was already sinking, but now time is up.

Now is the moment of reckoning.

"Ah! Teacher Bryony! *Buna ziua!*" the owner of Gok-Oguz says when we pull up twenty minutes later, clasping my hands warmly. "I thought you would be coming! You are in for a good game. Three minutes to halftime. Come in." The longest pause in history occurs, and then he turns to Jack and says, "Jack."

"Serghei." Jack nods.

Serghei gives the briefest nod to Jack through such deeply slit eyes, you'd think he had closed them entirely. But then I cough and they open up, big, brown, friendly eyes around his tanned, deeply lined, highly spirited face. He walks us to a little table crammed into one corner of the small Moldovan restaurant, surrounded on all sides by eager Spanish soccer fans.

"What's going on this week?" Jack's eyes slide over the row of TV screens.

"UEFA Conference League Final," I say without missing a beat, eyes running down the menu.

These are not facts I wish to know.

These are not facts I seek out.

But Gok-Oguz is a staple in town, not because the food knocks it out of the park (although it is good), not because the sticky, bleach water–smelling laminated tables are particularly nice, but because Serghei is a gem in the community. Larger-than-life personality. The kind of guy you meet once and he sees you. Really *sees* you. And remembers you. Makes you feel like you are important to him and, ergo, the world. Like your presence is something that makes his day brighter. Like you matter.

And that trumps sticky tables.

He was one of my earlier students (thirteen years ago?), which is funny because at the time I was nineteen and he was fifty, and while I helped him get through English classes specifically directed toward helping him get his GED, he always called me Teacher Bryony. For the first few rounds of students who went through my class, I tried to get them to call me Bryony. I was so young. I was so ignorant, really. They were the ones who had much, much more life experience. All I was doing was teaching them how to write a check for a test and on fun occasions throw in an idiom of the day.

But everybody called me Teacher Bryony.

Everybody around the world who differed in every way possible seemed to be in agreement on one thing: I was a teacher and a teacher gets respect. Permanently.

So here I am. Hundreds of students later and still known all around town as Teacher Bryony.

Or here, Teacher Bryony with, cue tiny growl, *Jack*.

"Half-and-half sweet tea for Teacher Bryony with extra lemon," Serghei says, beaming down at me as he slides the tea my way. It's stuffed to the brim with lemon slices, which I note with an appreciative grin.

"Thank you, Serghei." I take a sip to show my gratitude.

"And *Jack*," he says.

A cup of water drops on the table in front of Jack. Water droplets sprinkle onto the laminate of Jack's menu.

Jack looks at it dubiously. "I believe I asked for bottled."

"Bottled water." Serghei waves a hand at the cup. "Opened for you."

"Ah. Wonderful." Jack eyes the cup of water that looks pretty much like lukewarm lake water. "Do you think you could add some ice cubes?"

"Fresh out," he says, and turns toward the kitchen.

"I'll take a Coke too!" Jack calls out as the kitchen doors swing in Serghei's wake. He looks at me. "Do you think he got that?"

"I think you're getting toilet water until you die," I answer, halfway into spooning ice cubes and lemon slices into his cup from my own.

"You think he'd forgive me eventually." He takes a paper napkin from the dispenser and wipes up the water from his menu.

"You think you'd have remembered not to stand me up." I set the spoon back on my napkin.

"I forgot to come out here to Timbuktu—"

"—thirty-two minutes by train—"

"—for dinner two *years* ago—"

"You didn't forget." I smile as I snap open the menu and scroll over the options. "You knew perfectly well you were supposed to meet me here to go over Amelia's notes and conveniently *forgot* when that new acquisitions editor said, 'Oh golly gee, Mr. Sterling, I'm new to the city and have absolutely no idea how to walk into a restaurant and order food in this great big place all alone. It's just *soooo* different from Orlando.'"

"I liked you better when you were in awe of me. Where's the simpering, leechy Bryony who loved me? Can we bring her back?"

"Ship's long sailed."

A ref blows a whistle across one of the many screens, and a unanimous moan runs through the room.

Silence hovers between us.

"So." I flick up the menu and let my eyes drift over it. "How's Claire?"

"Fine," he says promptly, scanning his own menu. "How's Parker?"

"Fine."

There. We got that little bit of courtesy out of the way.

Every time we end up at dinner together, I approach the subject, just to clarify our terms. We are agent and client. Friend and friend. And look here! We've established that openly, again, just to make it absolutely, perfectly clear should it come up in conversation with our significant others.

I finish spinning the little gold band on the ring finger of my right hand. The ring Parker gave me just before he left for Auckland, Russia. The one he told me belonged to his mother at one time. It didn't signify that we were engaged *obviously* (I mean, we had only been dating four blissful months before he left to teach ESL across the globe), but in his words, "I'm leaving something priceless behind, and I promise I will return for it."

I exhale, recalling distantly the moment precisely twenty-seven months ago.

At the time it was supposed to be twelve, and that twelve turned into sixteen, which turned into eighteen, and now here we are, twenty-seven months later.

I'm not actually sure how *significant* things are with Claire. In fact, I'm not even totally sure that's her name. But I don't care, really. The point is, in case Parker brings it up, it's been written down and recorded. At precisely 7:12 p.m., I brought Parker up at a work date with my agent and friend. See? You can pull it up on the (very likely broken) camera perched in the upper corner of this restaurant if you like.

Not that Parker has ever brought it up.

No, for the last few months in particular, our troubles seem to lie elsewhere. For us it's more of a challenge of figuring out how to simply *connect* when our time zones are quite literally polar opposite.

"Is that her name?" I say, glancing up.

"Who?" Jack says.

"Claire."

"Oh." Jack pauses. His brows screw up like he's thinking hard. "No," he says finally. "I think it's Chloe."

"Huh," I say mildly.

"Mmm," he returns, and gazes at the menu.

A few minutes later Serghei returns, arms loaded down with dinner plates alongside a platter of his famous round braided bread.

"And for the Teacher?" Serghei pauses at our table.

"I think I'll go with *chiftele cu piure* again."

"Good choice," he says. "Fresh delivery of pork today."

"I'll take that too," Jack says.

Serghei drops the plates on the table beside us and walks again through the swinging doors.

Jack turns to me. "I think he's starting to warm up to me."

"I think it's wise you've finally given up and just started ordering whatever I get. It's what he always gets you anyway."

"Does it make me look less pathetic here?"

"A millimeter less so, yes."

"Terrific."

Cheers go round the room over a goal, and for a moment we watch the screens.

"I wanna talk about the email."

"What was her name?" Jack says suddenly.

"Who?"

"The editor."

"Let's not sidetrack. The email."

Jack sighs. Sits back in his chair. Crosses his arms over his chest in a way that says, *I knew we'd end up here, but I still don't like it.* "Can we at least get some cabbage rolls first? They'll go well with my tap water."

"It's been six months." I hate the frustration in my voice, the way I've taken to stirring the straw around my lemon tea at a rate that's created a little whirlpool. But it's been *six months* since Jack had a conversation with Florence Peters and she got back with a request for the manuscript. *Six months* in the hands of a real editor at a real publishing house who has all the power in just her tiny index finger to type the word *yes*. All the power in her one finger to change my life, Gran's life, and hopefully The Bridge's life, forever.

I'm allowed to be anxious here. I'm allowed to be frustrated, especially considering that once Florence Peters was someone from Pennington Publishing. Hathaway & Root. Laury & Co.

It's been one painfully long revolving door spinning possibilities in over and over. Two years ago I thought the conference weekend was an unbearable emotional roller coaster that fried the nerves. Little did I realize that no, this is just publishing. In general.

Jack sighs. He hates when we have these conversations. But I can't help it. It used to be that I directed our conversation toward *Water Under the Bridge* at the tail end of every phone conversation. Then slowly, over time, the conversation tapered off as Amelia's books became more in demand and everyone around me invested in this ghostwriting secret became more successful.

The conversation shifted to making more books. To praises for the rom-coms I wrote. To praises for how well they were selling. How I resonate with people in the rom-com market in a way that's special, that's powerful. And would I be a dear and squeak in another book, real quick, to make the most of a charged moment? And how would I like another 2 percent royalty? And a nice big fruit basket to boot?

"Bryony." Jack rubs a hand down his face. "Do you think I enjoy making money?"

"Yes." I purse my lips. "But—"

"Do you think I send out manuscripts to people who have the power to send me back six- and seven-figure offers just so I can deny them?"

I inhale a tense breath. "No. Of course not."

"Do you think I have a filing cabinet somewhere just for very special books that *would be* international bestsellers that I keep hidden, just so I can feel the thrill of knowing no one will see them except for me?" Jack waves his hand in the air. "That perhaps I go down to my secret filing cabinet, on lonely nights under a milky moon, to read and laugh sadistically?"

My nostrils flare. I hate when he does this. "No."

"Then don't you think the *second* I got word from Florence, I'd be telling you? Just like I have every other time I've gotten *any* news about *anything*?"

I exhale through my nose much like a bull steaming down after a fight. "Yes. I know. It's just, it's been *six months*—"

"A drop in the water of time in publishing, particularly for someone trying to get her foot in the door. Give it another seventy years. Maybe eighty—"

"We should have heard by now," I press, ignoring him. "If it's this 'potential international bestseller,' then it should've been picked up by now. Shouldn't it? Seriously, Jack. *Really*?" The chip in my voice gives away the depth of my insecurity, and for a moment Jack regards me.

He reaches over. Puts his hand over mine. Pointedly ignores Serghei in the distance crossing his beefy arms over one another, tapping the butcher knife against one bicep. "The market is oversaturated, Bryony."

"I know," I say more quietly, because Jack's given me this talk before.

"You are competing with quite literally millions of other books."

I nod. Just as I nod every other time.

"And part of my job, part of you trusting me to do my job, is to know when to pounce for the sake of your career. Right now isn't it."

My chest tightens. "But you just said you sent it to Baker. Are you saying they won't get back with us?"

"I'm not saying that. I'm saying I've sent it around because you keep pestering me to do so. But the fact is, and you know this, I think the book could use some slashing. And you're still an unknown author, with zero platform of your own—" He puts up a finger to stop me from interjecting. "Despite how incredibly frustrating it is to in reality be writing under Amelia's name—"

"And we can't—" I interject all the same.

"No."

"And there's no way to just, you know, *let* people wink-wink know—"

"No. I'm not going up against the Benedicts. No. Not unless we wanted matching orange jumpsuits, no."

I grind my teeth and let him continue. *This* is maddening. The secret is maddening.

"The reality is, you've written an obscure—albeit talented—tale that's approximately 30 percent too long for the traditional market with approximately four too many genres Vitamixed together. To add a cherry on top, we're in an election year and the two politicians everybody's eyes are on right now have decided to hire a little ghostwriter of their own and throw some ink on the page for a boost."

Jack squeezes my hand. "Let me be clear, Bryony. I think you are a brilliant writer—*everyone in the world*, whether they know it or not, thinks you're a brilliant writer—but your time just hasn't come. Yet." His eyes hold mine and he sighs. "Don't look at me like that. I hate it when you look at me like that."

"Like what?" I draw back and plunk into the back of my chair, my hopes deflating.

"Like I've crushed your dreams. And can you do something about this?" Jack gestures at Serghei, who is eyeing him now, elbows on the cash register, still with knife in hand. "Can you please . . . you know . . . laugh or something before this takes a tragic turn?"

I purse my lips defiantly.

Wait.

Throw out an exaggerated "Ha-ha-ha."

And I know what Jack's doing, how he's using himself as a distraction to ease my unyielding disappointment and continued anxiety over waiting on my manuscript. It's a funny thing, writing books that turn the world's head but at the same time being unable to tell the world, "But look, look at *this* one!"

It's an impossible-to-explain feeling, enjoying with quiet pride that you have done a good job at your work, but at the same time enduring incredible frustration in being unable to prove to publishers that you *really do have* what it takes. I may not have a million followers on a glowing platform. I may not have six books under my name with glowing sales and a strong readership to give them a sense of security. But I *am* Amelia Benedict. *I* wrote *Smuggler's Paradise*, the novel set on the beach that sat on the *New York Times* bestseller list for a whopping fifty-six weeks. *I* made people laugh and cry at the end of *A Leap of Faith* and flock to the internet begging for more.

If only *anyone* could know the truth.

"Honestly, Bryony, what I don't grasp is how you can't just *be happy*," Jack continues. "You have achieved the goal of every writer who has ever existed. You are successful *and* you get to claim anonymity. *You* aren't receiving death threats. *You* don't have to squeeze into all those dresses you say you hate in your closet for all those interviews. *You* don't have to worry about smiling all the time. You just get to hole up in that apartment of yours and write to your heart's content. *And*," he says, raising a finger, "let's not forget the little point that *you* are making *sixty*—not *six*—times the amount with this little 'side hobby' you don't appreciate than you are going to get for your literary–magical realism–historical fiction–nonfiction memoir with a dash of mystery. *You* are *the* writer for Amelia now. *The* one. With a higher salary than any ghostwriter on the planet now. Thanks to me. So how about we just drink to that and not worry about anything else? I'll let you know the second someone jumps on board with your book. But in the meantime, let's just enjoy what we're building up for you here. Now. My turn. On to my email. I know you saw it."

This isn't the answer I want.

It's never the answer I want.

But we've talked about it enough that it's enough to live on. Crumbs to keep me going another day.

Enough hope to subsist for a little while longer.

Serghei sets our dinners on the table, and after the typical back-and-forth between Jack and him, we dig in. Honestly, I think they both kind of like it.

"Do you think you can get it in by August?" Jack says, fork punching into a meatball.

I frown as I dip a meatball into my mashed potatoes. There's that exhausting pressure again. "I don't know, Jack . . ."

"Two weeks earlier. Just two weeks." Jack makes an inch motion with his fingers, as if what he's saying is the easiest thing to do in the world. Just like the time I turned in *A Room for Rose* and he read it over and suggested casually that I should write it again from a different point of view.

No biggie.

Just casually make the story come from the perspective of an entirely different person in time.

Better yet, turn it back in in ten days. Why not?

"The thirtieth?"

"The twenty-fourth." He throws his hands out. "So. On the *other* end of the two-week spectrum—"

"As in three weeks. Three. Weeks."

"Which, if you think about it, is great. You won't be wanting to work over your family beach trip again. In a way, I'm *saving* you. From yourself."

"*You* were the one blasting my phone with messages last time," I retort.

"And *you* were the one keeping your phone on replying to them. We're both addicted to work. I'm the only one who can admit it. So, obviously, that means I'm a step ahead of you in the program."

I roll my eyes at him but do recall the horror of spending my last vacation holed up in the little rental house's bathroom, sitting on a pink frilled toilet seat with my laptop, trying to ignore the clammer of thirty extended family members crammed into a two-thousand-square-foot seaside cottage having dinner, all while I finished up the last of a revision that was, according to Jack's endless messages, "absolutely urgent."

I consider through a few bites, then shake my head.

This has become the cycle since The Foundry Literary dropped the other ghostwriters. After the other ghostwriter's book came out, five months after my own *Sunset over Santorini*'s explosive entrance, there was disappointment on the publisher's end. On the critics' end. On the world's end. Sales weren't thriving, even though this was the "same" author. Critical reviews started to come in, slamming Amelia for being too rushed and tempted by quick money and throwing together a sloppy book. Reviews came in calling the much-anticipated novel a flop. Saying the plot was one-dimensional and riddled with holes. The characters lacked depth. The language lacked depth. The takeaway message was nothing beyond "Life's short, so by golly, buy an extra pair of shoes!"

(A message that critics noted was in direct contradiction to my own message just one book prior.)

And when the third ghostwriter's book released shortly after that, the whole publishing team exploded when it was met with the same results.

One flop and fine. That's life.

Two books and that's a pattern that needs to be nipped in the bud *immediately*.

So it wasn't much of a surprise to me when they gave the ghost-writers the boot. It was, however, a surprise that after a few further failed ghostwriters' attempts, they came to me with the offer: 22 percent royalties. Two books a year. And the "honor" (secret honor) of being the exclusive ghostwriter for Amelia Benedict.

I countered with one every ten months because the thing is, I didn't even *want* the job. Not exactly. Not *this* job. But the reality, as I kept reminding Gloria, was Jack was my agent. He was the only one who could get my book, *mine*, through the door. Get my *name* through the door.

And call it people pleasing or using standard logic, but I couldn't risk losing his, or the agency's, favor.

After all, I literally had nothing to convince another agency to pick me up.

I had no other options here.

They countered with one every seven.

I countered with one every nine.

They countered with every eight *and* a really nice espresso machine. I'm talking nice. The kind that could keep me awake for weeks.

(They really are my dealer, aren't they?)

And eventually we landed exactly where they wanted, with one book every six months. Two books a year. And an espresso machine.

I said yes, *despite* not wanting to go beyond the first book. *Despite* the fact I still worked at The Bridge full time with absolutely no desire to retire from teaching—even if it did pay peanuts (and yes, I guess technically I was volunteering given the fact I was the Anonymous Donor). *Despite* the fact my life could barely sustain squeezing in the time to write one book in a year for somebody else, much less two.

So here I go, carrying a surrogate pregnancy and delivery of a book for somebody else every six months. Nursing the pains of creating life on the page through many sleepless nights only to deliver my work into the hands of somebody else.

Which is fine.

I'm a tiny bit bitter, but it's *fine*.

And it might truly *be* fine, except that *this* is what I get every few weeks. Emails asking if I can push up the deadline just a smidge, because "we really need to get it in before the holidays." Calls saying, "You know, if you could make it by April so we can get the line editor we want locked in, then that would be just so, *so* great."

I get told frequently that I, Bryony Page, am just so, *so* great.

The last book they managed to weasel out of me in five months and thirteen days.

I cave every time.

Despite myself.

"Fine. But *no earlier*." I stab a meatball. "Not a millisecond earlier than August twenty-fourth. You tell them that."

"Absolutely," Jack says, flashing a grin.

I fully anticipate him to flip his phone over and type it in, informing somebody or other on the publishing side the good news, and wait expectantly.

He continues eating, and when it's clear I haven't budged, he looks up. Eyes the meatball held in midair on my fork. "What?"

"Are you going to tell them?"

His grin widens. "I did this afternoon."

My brows crease, and I pause while a round of cheering goes around the room. "You told them . . . what exactly? You *told* them I agreed to turn in the manuscript in August?"

"No, I told them that last week. I told Susanna five minutes ago that August *24* was your final word and that you wouldn't want another demand for the deadline being pushed up a millisecond earlier."

"You didn't say that."

"I did."

"You didn't write *millisecond*," I counter.

And to this he slides his phone over to my side of the table. Sure enough, his email reads:

> Hey all,
>
> Note that Bryony is prepared to give you the ms August 24, and to use her words: "not a millisecond earlier."
>
> Also to note: stop sending her plaques. She doesn't like plaques. She's not a plaque person. The last plaque I saw with the vague "To Bryony Page, for a job well done" was not only a bit taunting (given my client Amelia just publicly posted your gift to *her* of the Cartier 18-karat rose gold watch with exuberant praise), but it was being used as a doorstop to her backyard. Gifts of flower bulbs are a better choice. I am told she likes them from random human beings' backyards on Etsy. There's also a home goods shop in Brooklyn called The Six Bells with a particular mug dotted with sheep she has been eyeing. They direct ship.

I laugh with incredulity. "How did you— I mean, Jack. Down to the millisecond—"

His smile screams he is incredibly proud of himself. "It's my job to know my clients. Just like it's my job to eat flat meatballs in the middle of this jungle—"

"Florence has thirty thousand residents. It's hardly a *jungle*—"

"—while Serghei threatens me with knives. I'll take that." He lifts his hand for the bill a waiter drops beside us. Flourishes the company credit card. Slides it into the black folder on the edge of the table.

"I do want that sheep mug."

"And the sheep plates. And the whole happy sheep set. As I've heard. Approximately one hundred times."

"All right, do it. If you're so good, tell me what Cadwell is thinking right now." I throw out another one of his clients.

"Simple. He's thinking, *Oh, how grateful I am to have Jack in my corner, and which character's life can I possibly traumatize enough to make into an eighteenth book in this dying series?*"

I grin. "Fine. He's a dead giveaway. I could've said that. Ann?"

"'Oh, how grateful I am to have Jack in my corner, and I can't wait to retire next July.'"

My brows collapse into a straight line. "She's in her sixties. She won't retire."

"She will. July thirteenth, the day after she finishes her contract. She'll book a cruise to the Bahamas, and I'll never hear from her again. Wait and see."

The thing is, the moment he says it, I can actually see it. See Ann dropping off the side of the earth and never returning. And I'm amazed at Jack's intuitiveness. Just a begrudging bit.

"Now." He weaves his fingers together on the table and looks at me seriously. "Back to business. I have something deathly important to say."

Nobody else could see it, probably, but there's a mirth in Jack's eyes, and I can see a little game is afoot. He's quietly asking me to ease up, to shift topics, to take the foot off the gas pedal of our serious conversation and let him move from Agent Jack to Friend Jack, to let me shift from Pestering Client Bryony Page to the girl who ignores him as she hauls a giant tub of animal crackers into his perfectly detailed vehicle and force-feeds him elephants dipped in chocolate on the interstate despite his protests.

To shape-shift away from the man I've been having the power struggle with to the man who lets me sleep on his couch after late nights in the city, just so I can pound on his bedroom door and hear his growly "unearthly-hour-of-the-day-Bryony" and we can skip downtown in the morning light with pastries in hand, watching all the stores open up one by one.

I twine my fingers together as he does, press my elbows on the table, and lean forward, chin on my hands. "Okay. Shoot."

"I've been giving it a lot of thought."

"I'm ready."

"And I need your full support on this."

I wait. My phone between us rings, Parker's name lighting up the screen.

Jack's eyes dart to mine.

A wordless pause lingers in the moment, a choice, and I make it. I tap the silent button on my phone and flip it over.

A whisper of approval flickers in his eyes.

"We need to rename our bowling team. I'm going to walk in there and pitch, and I need you to back me up."

My brow tweaks. "You don't like Pin Pals?"

"I hate Pin Pals."

"You don't think Pin Pals has enough swagger?"

"The swagger is significantly lacking."

"Counterproposal?"

"Rolling Thunder."

"Willing to compromise with Gutterly Ridiculous?"

He gives a sharp head shake. "No."

"Spare Me the Details?"

"Afraid not."

"How about Bearly Trying? How cute would that be? Little bears in hats for T-shirts has some real potential."

"I'll quit on the spot."

I sit back in my chair. Rub my nose. Sniff. "Buy a round of onion rings and drinks for the team tonight. Wait precisely five minutes and twelve seconds before pitching. I'll see what I can do."

Jack flashes a full grin and we move to stand. "That's my girl," he says, and I feel a trill, light hummingbird wings against my chest, as he pushes my chair behind me and nudges me forward by the small of my back.

"Good night, Serghei," Jack calls loudly—and totally unnecessarily—over his shoulder.

Serghei grunts gruffly from the kitchen door, looking not totally displeased by the attention.

"Oop. Mustn't forget this." Jack snatches up the phone I'd left on the table. Sets it in my hand.

Oh right.

I'd forgotten.

CHAPTER 5

Interstate Bowl is, in a word, busy.

In a series of words, it's full to the gunwales of polyester shorts and replete with the scent of nacho cheese dip and tobacco. James, one of the many high school employees tasked with keeping up with obsessed middle-aged league members who have decidedly made rolling heavy balls down a glossy surface a major part of their identity, is covered in a cloud of bowling shoe disinfectant beside the jukebox, which is beside the cheap food bar flanked by splitting red-cushioned stools.

I plop my shoes on the floor next to Gloria and sit down.

"He loves you." Gloria casts her gaze over at Jack, who's leaning against the bar.

I shake my head. "He dates more women than are in this building."

"What women? Look around." Gloria takes in the swaths of males around us. Fair. "And *dated*. Past tense being the key tense here. I think he's waiting for you."

"For what?" I throw out, giving a disbelieving laugh. "I'm right here."

"Have you forgotten Parker so easily?"

My face warms slightly, internally slapped by surprise at the remark. Of course. Parker. Only the guy I've been dating across the world. For two-plus years.

"Jack loves you."

"He's *paid* to love me, nothing more." I lace up my bowling shoes. They are a smidge too big, given they were a graduating gift to me last year from a teammate and, you guessed it, former student. Actually three whole lanes are made up almost entirely of former and current students.

My idea for the Wednesday Night Hangout came three years ago on a whim. Partly because I knew it'd be good to help them practice their English outside of the classroom and partly because they became friends.

I missed the students when they graduated the class, and they missed me.

Hence, a hangout.

And what started as a social outlet for students in the middle of a cold, dark winter turned quickly into a weekly gathering, which turned quickly into a league. Or rather, a set of leagues. Enough students, both past and present, came to fill up six teams. And before we knew it, we were the Pin Pals.

Which, naturally, Jack resents.

"You actually think that your agent would haul that stupid bowling ball you got him last Christmas on a train forty-five minutes out of the city, put on that T-shirt jersey he complains about to us *every* week, and throw such pathetic balls that you had to appeal to the team to keep him—which of course everyone did because it's *you*—because he's paid to? He's not your bodyguard, Bryony. He's not *paid* to stick around."

"Of course he's not. He sticks around because my brain and hands are now precious cargo to Amelia and the agency, and as such, part of his job is to secretly make sure I don't go off and ruin everything by becoming an alcoholic or falling in love with a billionaire on a remote island or losing one of my typing hands in a freak bowling accident. Or who knows?" I stand up. "Maybe he's afraid that if I'm left alone too long, I'll leak everything to the press."

Gloria inhales furiously through her nostrils. As she does every time we have this conversation and I refuse to give in.

"But really," I say, smiling, "we all know it's because bowling night with my students is reality television on steroids, and he comes for the drama."

I wiggle between people up to the screen and, before tapping in our names, check the opposing team. Their name is the Striking Pencils. (It was Spitting Vipers, but Lakshmi has a fairly terrifying backstory and now understandable phobia of all things snake, so the team generously switched it to what they called truly intimidating in light of their current lives: English academia.) They're out Lakshmi and Phuong tonight, but I see already on their two screens Galina, Chen, Miho, Saliha, Abiola, and Abiola's first wife, Tiwa, as well as Abiola's second wife he pretends is his sister (don't get me started), Ayo. Plus Jose.

The next two lanes over are covered up as well.

It's a full house tonight.

I type in Abdallah. Socorro. Gloria. Fatima (a sweet fifty-five-year-old woman who has lived in America for over twenty-five years and is only now brave enough to seek English classes). Otieno. Eman. Then I move to the next lane and type in Mr. and Mrs. Azarenka (our elderly and slightly terrifying Moldovan couple who refuse for propriety's sake to be called by their first names). Jack. Me. And the ever-quirky but not-totally-unhandsome newest member to our group, the twenty-five-year-old German student, Albrecht.

He sits next to Gloria, frowning deeply as he watches her reaching for a nacho from the center of the booth. Not going to lie, this happens a lot. He's the resident Gloria starer.

Abruptly, she turns to him, nacho in hand. "*What*, Albrecht? What is it now?"

"You are bad with logic," he says, staring at her. "You eat nachos, then complain every week your stomach hurts. You should keep me near to remind you."

I bite at a smile tugging my lips. Gloria does, in fact, eat nachos every week, and every week complains about a stomachache afterward.

"I like stomachaches." Gloria thrusts the entire nacho in her mouth. "In fact," she says through a mouthful, "I *vove* them."

"You were also late today. You make people worry."

"Three minutes does not count as being late in America, Albrecht."

"Perhaps you should let me call and remind you because you are so forgetful."

And cue the next hour of backhanded compliments and Gloria-Albrecht bickering.

"Abdallah, you're up anytime," I call over my shoulder, pretending not to see him flirting with the girl in the pinstriped top and skirt holding a platter of cheeseburgers and fries. Which I have to hand it to him is bold—flirting in a second language when you're only four months in is not for the weak of heart.

I wait thirty seconds and, when he hasn't moved, call louder, "*Ab-dall-ah*."

"Hold your horses," Abdallah calls, then flashes me an unsteady grin.

I flash a tight smile right back. "Correct usage. Wrong time. Get over here."

As Abdallah shuffles over, he says, "You know, Teacher, I use that to the police today at the airport."

"*What?*"

"They want me to move out of the line, the, uh—" He hesitates, motioning with his hands something undiscernible.

I wait patiently. I'm used to waiting.

Giving my students time to fight the battle to find the word is essential in helping them win the war of language learning. It's a simple process: giving them confidence in the classroom to raise their hands and use words gives them confidence to step out of the classroom and order a meal, which gives them confidence to step out into the world and get their license, and a job, and make friendships with coworkers and neighbors. And have big, beautiful lives.

This is the goal.

Patience is key.

"Parking zone," he says at last, with a little glint in his eyes. He's proud of himself for calling up the words, and I smile, proud of him for remembering them—at four months in no less.

"And?" I say.

"And I say what you teach us. I say"—he enunciates the following words with a broad smile—"hold . . . your . . . horses."

Oof. All proud feelings gone.

I squeeze the bridge of my nose. "Oh, *Abdallah*. And how did they respond?"

He laughs. Replies with a jilted, "They did not like it."

Abdallah is one of my newest students, a nineteen-year-old Middle Eastern refugee who, despite the kidnapping of his uncle that led to a threat upon his family's life, carries a zest for life that makes him able to pretty much charm his way out of most things. Oh, and a fondness for using my idioms of the day in inappropriate situations and later bragging about it in class. Always, I'm pretty sure, to rile me up.

"That's not—" I shake my head. "No, we'll talk about it tomorrow. C'mon. It's your turn."

As I look back, my eyes catch a glimpse of Jack over by the jukebox, his brows furrowed. He stands in the middle of the crowd, staring at his phone.

A work frown, of the more significantly displeased type. Last time I saw him so engrossed and unhappy, I asked what it was with a laugh, thinking it was nothing more than a bad manuscript, and he told me his client had died.

I can't help wondering over what it is this time.

At my turn, I knock down eight pins.

Socorro, who is always using the aisle of my classroom during breaks to practice with a baseball (much to the chagrin of my desk lamp and Saliha, who always ends up getting a baseball tangled around her skirt), rejoices flamboyantly over a strike.

Gloria, who just got her nails done and decided she didn't "need" to put her fingers in the holes in the ball, gets zero.

I look over at Jack.

"Order up," Pinstripe Girl says, sliding paper bowls and cups to the woman beside him.

I frown as I watch her flash a smile at Jack, who doesn't look up.

My frown becomes a little disgusted as she leans over the counter toward him, her bubblegum lip gloss grin in his downcast face, and asks him if he wants anything.

"Jack," I call, and he veers off from staring at the phone and our eyes meet. I nod toward the lanes. He jump-starts our way.

"I mean," Gloria says, "I see women in *court* lying their heads off for their deadbeat, money-smuggling husbands who are less in tune than the two of you."

"Impossible. I'd never go to jail for Jack. They don't have a bowling league."

"Bryony." She's eyeing my hands. I've transferred some of Jack's Oreo ice cream sandwich sundae (the man's weekly kryptonite) into my bowl and begun spooning off my peanut bits onto his.

"So," I say, as Jack slides into the seat beside me. "Who was it?"

There's a pause from him, and I add, "On the phone?"

"Oh, just Pat, having his weekly mental crisis." Jack scratches the back of his head, then reaches for the bowl. It's a curious pause, the kind that he tends to give when he's bluffing about something and about to lie to me. One of those, "No, no, of course I didn't erase that side character from your manuscript I told you was disturbing. I'm merely an agent, Bryony. Why would I go messing about with your slash Amelia's work? And yes, I *do* understand and respect that what you are doing is art, even if you don't get to put your name on it."

He did.

He entirely erased my favorite, possibly creepy, side character from *Smuggler's Paradise.*

"Pat . . . *Henderson*?" Gloria says with a little hiss wavering on awe. I cast her a look that says, *"Stop it. Or I'm going to give you the talk— again—about how we don't dump out the contents of our purses and then thrust them in Jack's hand whilst begging him to do us a teeny tiny favor and get his client's autograph on them."*

I decide I don't care enough to press for reasons behind Jack's dodginess and move to the more interesting matter. "Did you tell him

I saw his books at Costco the other day? Tell him it was ten. I saw a full *ten*."

For being a man with four million sold copies and ten years of dedication to the literary field, you'd think he'd have more self-esteem than he does.

Jack shakes his head, unwilling as always to stoop to this level of affirming obviously successful authors.

"I'm going to meet him for lunch next week. Want to come and tell him the *revolutionary* news that he is in Costco yourself?"

"Fine." I hand him a spoon. "He'll love it."

"Great." He digs in. "I'll bet." He waves a spoon at those around us. "Have you discussed with everyone yet the change to our appalling team name?"

"I've been thinking on it, and we already have the T-shirts. The team name is going nowhere."

"I'll buy new T-shirts."

"They don't want new T-shirts."

"I'll make them less pink."

"Maybe we all *like* pink."

"Striking Pencils changed their name. Tell you what. Let's just take *their* name. I'd much rather have a cobra on my back than this"—he motions to my shirt—"this . . . pink angelic turtle."

"Striking Pencils had a team member with a terrifying python backstory. Do *you* have any terrifying flying turtle memories you'd like to discuss?"

"I once was at the beach and a hundred hatchlings sprouted and began finning toward me. That count?"

"On account of that being a miraculous highlight of your life and the thing people dream would happen to them, no. Keep thinking. I'm up."

And I can't help seeing Gloria's face watching our interaction as I lick the whipped cream off my spoon one more time before I set it down and move to stand.

And I can't help feeling the tiniest little glow in my cheeks as I pick up my ball to bowl.

Which I squash, of course, with the pound of the bowling ball as it lands on the lane and races fiercely toward the pins. It's 1 percent because Jack is my agent, and all of my hopes and dreams rest in him (and is it even legal?). And another 1 percent because I'm pretty sure he's dating two or three women simultaneously at the moment.

And the other 98 percent because I'm dating Parker, and I am, above all, a woman of integrity.

We lose our first game. Win our second. And after a couple hours, the swirling disco ball that at one point in the evening was fun is becoming sad as it slowly circles on and on, and the music from the jukebox that once was energizing now just pounds in the ears. The scene around me is starting to sag, as it does every night when it gets past nine thirty and the bed begins to call.

Overall, it's a perfectly lovely and typical Wednesday night.

Jose, of course, invites people to hop on over to his apartment for part two of the evening, and the same youthful souls who always say yes to hanging out till 2:00 a.m. (and don't mind surviving on a handful of hours' sleep and copious amounts of caffeine the next day) say yes.

Meanwhile I shrug on my coat, my body already leaning toward the exit doors.

"I'm slammed. I have a depo at nine and two tomorrow in the city," Gloria says as she gathers up her things. "What time are you teaching? Want to meet me for lunch in between?"

"Can't. I teach to noon and then I'm heading into the city myself."

Gloria's eyes narrow. "I thought you were on a tight deadline."

"I thought you just asked me to lunch regardless of your tight deadline," I respond with an equally *ho-ho-ho now* air.

"What do you have going?"

I shrug. "Just work things. You know how it is with my contract."

"On for helping me find a wedding present tomorrow, yes?" Jack says, suddenly at my side, his T-shirt already stripped off and crumpled in his hand, crisp oxford in its place.

Gloria's smile grows as she turns from me to him. "Funny. I didn't know that shopping for wedding presents was part of Bryony's contract."

"Of course it is," Jack says, readier than I could ever be with a snappy reply. "Under section 13b: Client will make every effort to support the emotional well-being of agent in question and vice versa as needs fit. Subject to include," and then he rattles off very quickly, "weddings, funerals, birthdays, social gatherings, and serving as a plus-one within twenty-four hours' notice."

I cast him a look, prompting the reminder of that one time I ended up breaking dinner plans to be his plus-one for a wedding in Staten Island on a random Tuesday.

"Four hours' notice," he amends. "Pending exceptional food." He gives me back a look that says, *I told you there would be a cotton candy station. And there was.*

Gloria throws up her hands. "All right," she says, walking between us, "good night, you totally-platonic-not-even-technically-friends agent and client. Have fun—or not—tomorrow buying registered plates together. I'm going home to break up with Benson and rethink my life choices."

She gives us a little wave and is at her car door when I hear her scream.

Albrecht has popped out beside her and is leaning on the hood of the car, hands in pockets. "See?" he says in his thick German accent. "See how you would feel if someone tried to get you? Good thing I am here to keep you safe."

Jack follows me to the passenger side door and pops it open. I laugh off Gloria's previous words, my cheeks still a little bit hot from her comments directed at us. "It's unfortunate, you know."

"What?"

"She spends forty hours a week steeped in courtroom drama. Her whole worldview is unbalanced. I honestly don't think she can imagine a drama-free relationship." I drop into the passenger seat.

"Which we definitely have." He takes my bowling ball bag from my hands.

"Absolutely." As I'm clicking the seat belt into place, I feel him bend and lean over me, a whiff of his freshly laundered shirt tickling my nose as he brushes past me. I freeze, hands holding to the seat buckle. He reaches up to the overhead row of buttons, presses the trunk open feature.

Slowly.

It must be the conversation prompting it, but I feel all the air zip out of my lungs and discover I'm holding my breath.

On the way back out he pauses, just as his face is inches from mine.

He turns by degrees toward me.

There's a slight, almost roguish twinkle in his eyes. "Sorry. Opening the trunk."

"Sure," I say, a little more breathlessly than I meant.

This is nothing.

This means nothing.

It's mere chemistry. When two people get this close in proximity and have this much of a natural, *practical* life connection, this is the result. Mere. Chemistry.

My eyes drift to his lips, then quickly rise back to his eyes. I force an easy grin. "How's Claire?"

"Fine," he says promptly, scanning my eyes. "How's Parker?"

"Fine."

We are all. Just. *Fine.*

Jack drops me off at my apartment thirty minutes later, and then I do as I do most nights: slip into bed and open my laptop.

Stare at the blinking line on the white screen, waiting for my "masterfully woven" written words. Words that are supposed to be written by "one of the wittiest and most brilliant minds of the twenty-first century," and precisely not one who still feels a little sick from too much *chiftele cu piure* and ice cream.

I'm in a tricky spot in my new draft. Twenty thousand words in and currently having a hard time seeing where the characters are going to go. Currently they lack depth, and a thousand questions hover around me over the computer, begging to be answered so I can move on—what exactly *is* Beau's backstory, and why exactly does she *care* so much about holding on to the house in Beaufort? What makes her feel *alive* about it? What *essential* value does it add to her life? How does it make her who she is today? Basically, why exactly does it matter to her *so much* that the guy—what's his name again?—is trying to swoop in and take it out from under her? The son, isn't it?

And more important, how can I make the manuscript funnier? *Funnier.*

Lighter.

Brighter.

In the words of Jack, "Fewer ashes of death and more sparkles." Because as Jack again said, "Nobody wants to put doom and gloom in their beach bag."

It's my unique challenge, keeping my books light as a feather while still conveying a meaningful message and not, now to quote Amelia, "all the super-boring stuff" that weighs people down.

Rom-com, unlike my *Water Under the Bridge*, is unique in that sense.

Laugh and fall in love and resolve some of your existential crisis while you go.

Spend a few hours with your eyes skating over pages of happiness, all while the more serious bits of your life get to rest their legs. Take a break.

Laugh your heart to healing, I like to say. Now there's a tagline.

Because laughter is a part of life too, isn't it? Something not to be dismissed as it stands side by side with more serious matters of growth and grief. I'll never forget the first time I laughed after Mother passed, the brief inhale of air before being plunged underwater again. Laughter is life. To laugh is to live.

And when done right—and isn't this the challenge, to do it right?—I do find a specific joy in melting together both magic and message.

Not that Amelia appreciates it.

Or the publisher even, at least those above Susanna's head.

Push. Push. Push.

The goal is to get it out there *faster* instead of *better*, and that, despite myself, I cannot give in to.

Which is *just great* because you know what that means? It means that here I go again, stressing myself to the max to meet a deadline to keep others happy while refusing to lessen the quality I demand of myself. For an end product *nobody* will really care about quality-wise but me. I'm punishing myself here, and not even for my own name. Just . . . *super.*

A little ding goes off on the bedside table from my phone and I look over at it, catching my eyes on the little frame of me with all my students from a surprise birthday party last summer. My hair was shorter then, and in my hands is a massive bouquet of yellow flowers—a generous gift from my students. The snapshot was taken just before Chen and Takeshi ended up heading back to Taiwan—a sweet moment before our little gang of students broke up and people moved on. Some on to the next level of courses. Some to jump that and go straight to their GED test and beyond. A few started community college courses. A few are still in my class, taking a slower, gentler route. But the beauty of them all is how we still keep in touch—even despite sometimes being a whole world away.

This. *This* is what I want.

My simple, sweet life of teaching.

But also writing books I love.

Oh, and also just casually falling into millions of dollars somehow and saving The Bridge from complete destruction.

No problem.

CHAPTER 6

"Now that's the thing, Bryony. I did not trick you. Stop yelling that and get your head inside before I get pulled over. I did not kidnap you. I am just very casually, on this abysmally humid Friday in July, taking you out for dinner. You said you wanted to eat out of the city."

"Referring to, oh, *I don't know*," I cry out as Jack cruises us over the bridge, spitting hair from my mouth as the wind beats my face, "maybe somewhere like *Florence*."

"You said you were tired of eating at the regular spots. You said you were bored. So voilà"—he gestures at the fan vents—"air-conditioning enough to host an aurora of polar bears."

He's trying to distract me by using the interesting fact I learned during a research rabbit trail about a group of polar bears being called an aurora. It's not going to work. I will not be deterred.

"You asked me if I was 'in the mood for tomato pie,'" I spit out. "You did *not* say the tomato pie would be in *Philly*." I watch as the sign for Philadelphia whips by.

"We both know you know the best tomato pie is at Gaeta's on Singapore Avenue, which happens to be in Philly." He frowns at something and adjusts the mirror. "Is that ketchup all down my shirt? Exactly how long have I had ketchup running down my *shirt*?"

"But I didn't know it was for *this*!" I exclaim, ignoring his question, to which the answer is roughly four hours, since we stopped at the hot dog stand this afternoon—the stand I love that he hates.

"A mere two hours. It'll fly by." He grabs a wipe from his meticulously laid out console between us and begins wiping. I stare at the stretch of interstate ahead of us.

Something is suspicious in all this.

Something I'm missing.

We always end up taking each other places we'd rather not be. That's kind of a staple of our agent-writer-colleague-friend-but-not-too-close-friend-support-system relationship. We are oil and water. City mouse and country mouse. A little too delicate and a little too cynical about life. I made him join a bowling league he hates, and he takes me to the trendiest, stupidest, appetizer-for-birds restaurants he wants to try out. It works.

But this?

This is something different.

There's something here.

I frown.

"Amelia's going to be there, isn't she?"

And to this, to my incredulity, he gives a little shrug.

I'm already groaning before he can reply.

I'm a toddler, I know.

I'm throwing a temper tantrum, I *know*.

But really, my situation is much more legitimate when comparing it to a hostage situation.

I could swear I hear a *click* beneath my window as he surreptitiously relocks the door on the off chance I try to open, tuck, and roll.

I snap my fingers, remembering vaguely one of the millions of emails I end up CC'd on against my will. "She has some event tonight. At the *Pennsylvania Convention Center.*"

"Is that tonight? Ah, you're right. So it is. Oh." He raises his finger, as though this is a novel idea. "Well, it might be nice to get together a group chat. Perhaps you two can even discuss the book you're working on together—"

"Not together—"

"—right now. Maybe you could even brainstorm over that scene you're stuck on."

"*What?*" I screech, gritting my teeth together.

"What?" He shrugs. "You call me at all hours of the night to make me listen silently while you talk about whether the house needs to be 'representative of Beau's childhood' or whether Pete's actions were so villainous readers will find him unredeemable or whether the pomegranate juice should be *on* the table or *beside* it. Amelia has plenty of opinions—"

"Too many."

I'm on the back end of a dozen ridiculous emails she sends per day. Ideas she just likes to throw out at random.

> Just got back from Morocco. It's stunning. We must make it there.
>
> Look at this fantastic green juice mix I've been making. Put it in. In fact, she just has to be a fitness guru—it's important to encourage my fans to live better. To *be* better.

All when I'm thirty thousand words into a piece of work that has *nothing* to do with green juice and is three thousand miles away from Morocco.

Does anybody even *know* how hard it is to randomly throw *Morocco* into a book about a low-wage baker's attempt to scrape together finances and move beyond a rough past to get back his daughter lost to the foster care system, all enveloped in a hearty rom-com?

Very hard.

"Never. Ever. In my life would I *ever ever ever* seek to brainstorm with that woman. She already casually adds plagues into my life *every* time I have a conversation with her. Not to mention, the woman *literally* replied when asked if she uses a dog-ear or bookmark, 'Oh, bookmark absolutely. I'm a vegetarian.'"

I give him a grim face.

Jack chuckles quietly at that one.

I will not be dissuaded.

I level my gaze. "If you recall, that was the same interview where she was asked, 'You are so active in your tours! How on earth do you have time to handle both writing and all of these visits around the country?' And she said a breezy, 'Writing is just *so* natural, if you really think of it. I just jot down a little problem and follow the trail to its natural conclusion. Honestly, I think the real challenge is figuring out how to make it from Atlanta to Nashville in rush-hour traffic with your lipstick in place. I mean, believe me. To get to all these *beautiful* events with you *wonderful people* is the real challenge. But'—cue high-pitched giggle—'that's the business of entertainment!'"

Jack chews his lower lip as he desperately tries not to smile at the idiocy of Amelia's words and prove my point. And, I imagine, he's also trying pretty desperately to dig up some redeeming thing to say.

"Stop." I hold up a hand. "Don't even try to free her from that horrific interview. No. No no no no no. I don't care how great the pie is, I don't want to meet her." I slice my arms in the air. "I can't take it. *No* more meetings."

And then something occurs to me. I give him a suspicious squint. "What happened? What dumb thing did she do?"

What exactly has caused this disruption in my life?

It's maddening. Maddening to live a life joined at the hip with someone who can manage to screw up so much. We're conjoined twins. Dependent on each other and yet I'm consistently feeling that I carry 90 percent of the weight.

Jack tilts his head, as though trying to pick his words carefully. At last he says, "Well. She didn't have the best interview this week."

"And?"

I essentially gave her CliffsNotes for the talk on the book. Note cards detailing what *precisely* she should say in little snippets about the book. This is *not* my problem. She should *read* the books she continuously claims are *her own*.

"And . . . the team has come up with an idea."

My voice lowers further. "And?"

"And . . . the reality is, we need to have a group conference and make some decisions. For better or worse, you two are stuck together."

"It's worse. It's definitely worse."

"And it's a good job—"

"That I do *away* from her in the safety of my cat pajamas—"

"And you *like* your job—"

"I like that *my* book is getting closer to contract with *you* as my agent—"

"And you have a contract saying you will show up on occasion when requested to be there."

That's it. I pop open his glove box, take hold of his obsessively organized pairs of sunglasses, and start dispensing them in various spots around the car. "You should've told me."

He commences picking up the sunglasses from the dash and gearshift. "And you would have found some excuse to hide in your apartment and renege your contractual duties if I'd have told you about this meeting ahead of time. And then that would lead to a broken contractual relationship. And that would lead you to lose your job. And your primary source of income—because we both know you teach for next to nothing. And your precious opportunity to squirrel away money *for* the job from which you get paid next to nothing. The place where you actually pay them to teach. As in, indentured servitude. So," Jack says, turning up the air coolers on my seat. "Amazing *tomato pie*."

I give him the death stare. Partly because it's very cruel what he's doing, and partly because I know he's right. I would have found an excuse, *any* excuse, not to be within yelling distance of Amelia. Not because I yell, exactly, but because she does.

"And don't worry. I'm going to do my best to make this a pleasant conversation for everyone. I am *on your side*." He gives me what is supposed to be a meaningful look.

I frown. "Don't give me that look. You also give her that look."

"I do not."

"Yes, you do." I throw my hands over my eyes. "Don't give me any look right now that you give all your other clients to woo them into trusting you with all their heart and soul."

"Believe me, Bryony. You're the only one getting this look."

I wait for several seconds, my feet on the dash, eyes squeezed shut. Then I venture a peek at him.

He's there, looking at me with that same expression. The kind of look in his eyes that says, "*Let's just jump off this cliff together. It'll be okay.*"

And then you do. Jump off an entire stupid cliff like an idiot and smack flat onto the ground three hundred feet down.

We stare off, minus the flicks back to watch the interstate, for some time.

He with his "*Trust me, I'm harmless*" gaze, me with my "*I hate everything about this moment and possibly you too*" glare.

At last, he caves.

"You know what I think?" He shifts gears rapidly. "I think we need to get you that standing desk you were moaning about the other day for your neck pain. Let's throw in the ergonomic keyboard too. A business expense covered by the agency. We need to keep your health a top priority."

"*Jack.*"

But he's already calling up Siri to call up his PA on the phone. She's answered and he's telling her to run down the internet and find the best standing desk company cards can buy. She says they have one in black and one in mahogany.

I jump in asking CJ about a whitewash option, and ta-da.

He manages to successfully distract me until we are, in fact, in Philly. Once inside the small restaurant, we are directed to a giant booth in the corner. The one tiny sliver of light in this is that Jack was honest about one thing, and we actually ended up at Gaeta's after all.

Just to throw more stale basil onto the evening, four pinched smiles greet us as I sit down and slide the Gaeta's menu out of the way. Bright side: The tomato pie is truly the best and only thing worth getting here—as Jack and I discovered last year around the Fourth of July. The rest of the menu is just made up of filler words. I wouldn't be surprised if they didn't even know how to make—my eyes flicker down to the menu and read a random line—sautéed shrimp.

Jack motions for me to scooch over, closer to the four figures, as he scoots in beside me.

I'm stranded here now.

Locked in.

Mona from publicity sits directly opposite me. Midthirties. Die-hard publishing type. Always up with the latest trends. Always trying to get her authors to partake in unorthodox methods to keep them on the leading edge, like setting that one eighty-year-old up in a desk and chair on a floating sheet of ice to do a "fascinating" news video interview detailing his new fiction book—written in tandem with a real, live PhD—of which the main character is a scientist studying the effects of climate change on the Antarctic glaciers. And oh, by the way, please be careful not to slip, Richard. That kind of thing. She's got a new hairstyle today. Actually, she always has new hair. This time it's razor cut at the jaw, no doubt symbolizing her cutting-edge approach to life.

Susanna, Amelia's/my editor, gives me a sheepish, apologetic smile. Early forties. Two young kids who scribble adorably on her papers sometimes and leave her perennially, nervously on edge. Her hair is done up in what looks like yesterday's bun. Her big round glasses are adorable on her rounded chipmunk cheeks per usual. She looks at me wearily, but friendly lines bracket her smile as though she, too, was dragged here somewhat against her will.

Amelia's young lapdog, Penny, sits beside her in head-to-toe yellow, poised already with pen in hand. Amelia takes Penny every-where, because apparently Amelia doesn't understand how to use her phone for note-taking and consequently treats Penny like a living Siri. She seems nice enough, not that I know her very well, considering

Amelia trades out the Pennys like she trades out her cars—which, for the record, is roughly every three months.

And then directly beside me is Amelia, looking faintly confused as to why we have ended up in a place with entrée items below forty dollars. Her spine juts straighter than a fishing rod toward the ceiling. She looks like she is trying very hard to touch the faded red vinyl booth she's sitting on as little as possible. A vibrant pink stretch of pearls matching a vibrant pink silk blouse rests on Amelia's perfectly sculpted neck, all framed by perfectly bouncy bottle-blonde curls. Even her vibrantly pink and impossibly thin stiletto heels look like they are hovering just above the sticky floor. And really, would it surprise me? To discover Amelia is a witch?

"Ah, the dream team all together," Jack says with a grin as exaggeratedly big as his voice. He raises a finger for the waiter beside him. "This calls for celebration. Two bottles of your finest champagne for the table, please."

I clear my throat. Jack adds begrudgingly, "And a sweet tea."

Amelia's glossy lips do a little pucker my way, and I'm already beginning to ball my hands into fists in my lap, readying for whatever nonsense she brings. But a little *ding* rings out from her phone. And then she's gone. Gone into the little words on her screen, scrolling and tapping like her life depends on it.

She does this, for the record, a lot.

I take a deep, already-exhausted-by-this-experience breath.

The rest of the restaurant is crowded, as all the restaurants lining Singapore Avenue are at this hour. The walls are covered in yellowing vintage posters of bottles of olive oil for twenty-five cents and bunches of tomatoes on the vine for five pennies. Little fingerprints smudge the glass, and I wouldn't be surprised if they haven't had a spray bottle on them in years. But whatever the atmosphere lacks, it makes up for in the air.

The room is one big perfume bottle of basil and garlic and freshly baked bread and, of course, roasted tomatoes. And given the number of tomato pies I see around the room, all propped up on pizza racks on tables, I imagine they go through hundreds of tomatoes a week. Acres worth.

Music plays loudly over the speakers, something indiscernibly old-fashioned and Italian and cheery—the kind of music that puts people in the kind of mood to spend money and eat tomato pie. And the loudness and the smudges and the general stickiness of the floor and ceiling and menus are forgivable. It's always forgivable because the food is *that good.* The environment of it all mixed together is *that good.* Everyone understands and accepts this, even cherishes it, because this is Gaeta's way.

Much like a sun-dried tomato taken straight out of the jar is inedible but becomes indefinably delicious when used within the secret sauce, so the smudges and stickiness and loudness all combine to create an extremely memorable kind of place.

Magical, if you will.

When you go to Gaeta's, you are guaranteed to leave like everyone else, arm in arm with your friends and a to-go bag in your hand as you sing "Que Será Será!" with a smile on your face.

"Can you turn it down?"

My head snaps to Amelia.

The waiter, standing beside me with the wine cork in his hand, snaps his head to Amelia.

Everyone in the room, it seems, has snapped their head to Amelia.

She looks at me, then Mona, the waiter, and finally Jack, who, to his credit, looks just as personally assaulted as everyone else within earshot.

"It's just . . . a little loud." Amelia shrugs as if to say, *"This is absolutely no big deal."* As if walking into a perfectly imperfect place and immediately demanding change is *no big deal.*

After a few seconds with no response, she adds, "It's just"—her eyes bounce around to each of us—"I have to *speak* in two hours for an *event.* And I am just trying to be careful not to lose my voice."

"Then simply stop talking, Amelia."

A pause ensues as everyone's eyes swivel to the last person on earth to say this to Amelia. Jack.

If there's one thing about Jack, it's that Jack does not offend his clients. I believe, in fact, one of Jack's main career responsibilities is to keep his clients puffed up at all times. This, he takes as his personal responsibility. Your books don't sell (not that I've personally experienced this part, but I've heard him plenty of times on phone calls), Jack is there to tell you it's simply the market's fault. Shame on the market. Shame on the whole economy. Never fear, your next book will pick up and race along like a two-year-old stallion.

You're struggling to write and voice that you are a failure? Jack is there to tell you that it's the weather. It's unseasonably cold, and with the cold front, *nobody on earth* has been able to get *any* work done and haven't you even read the latest news? (Cue him conjuring up some obscure article with whatever he wants to prove.) Work ethic is down 18 percent with these rains, and the best thing you can do right now is book a cruise. Yes. A cruise. A cruise will solve all your writing problems.

Half of Jack's job seems to be swiveling you, the author, around enough times that you're dizzy and then halting and pointing the blame on anything and everything aside from yourself or him. It's the economy. The weather. The ridiculous publisher and their ridiculous demands (though this one typically comes right before he decides to push you off the cliff toward another publisher).

Jack does not ever, now that I think of it, encourage personal responsibility. I believe he thinks of us authors more as show dogs. Lavish us with bubble baths and put bows on our ears so we can prance around performing our best.

It's why I hardly ever take his words to heart.

And why precisely at this moment, his words are incredibly jolting.

"The team has a lot to say in the next hour regarding ideas and plans," Jack continues, "and you have your voice to protect, so just relax and let everyone else do the speaking as much as possible, mmm?"

Amelia, ever the victim of flattery, releases the tension in her eyes and sits back.

Her pupils are actually undilating before our very eyes. Like Dracula. It's downright creepy.

She seems to recall exactly where she is and sits up again.

Jack slides her a drink and motions for one of the women to begin.

"Soooo," Susanna begins in a singsong voice, the least offensive one among them. Her smile is frozen on her heart-shaped face and her cheeks hold a rosy glow. She swipes at her phone. "Shall I start us off?"

Amelia's phone dings and then rings. "I'm listening. I have to do some work while you talk, but I'm here." Amelia does not even so much as look Susanna in the eye as she swipes her phone. "Yeah." She pulls the phone to her ear, all while pointing at Penny.

Penny snaps her pen on her paper and begins scribbling.

"Of course," Susanna says sheepishly. "Terrrrific."

I drag my sweet tea toward me and plunge my straw in.

"Everything," Susanna says, "I should say to begin, is great. It's *great*. We have been thrilled overall with this system over the past two years and how your partnership has turned out. Your books—"

"*My* books," Amelia interjects, cocking her head with her phone glued to her ear.

"Yes," Susanna says with a smile at the reminder Amelia has given, yet again, that I have no ownership. "The second person, single *you*," she continues, and I stifle a smile at this oh-so-tiny bookish comment and Susanna's oh-so-tiny pinched eyes. "And the Brooks Publishing team in general cannot be more excited to see what's in store for us over the course of this next year. We have no doubt *Babies over Bayou* and the next two releases will be even bigger blockbuster events."

"Two?" I cast a look (i.e., glare) at Jack.

He grabs my balled-up fist beneath the table. Gives a little shake of his head as if to say, "*No, they've definitely got that wrong, but it's of such little significance let's not bring it up now.*"

I dig my nails into his palm, just enough to see him wince.

"But?" I say. Might as well get to the massively bad news before the pie comes. Don't want the taste of massively bad news to ruin the one highlight of tonight.

"But." Susanna pulls a little *oh dear* face. "At the event last night—and that really was a wonderful event. Nice job as always, Amelia"—she flashes a huge smile at the top of Amelia's head just in case she decides to look up—"but there was that one teeny tiny, uh . . . episode . . . during the Q&A that set us all thinking about our upcoming book launch."

Susanna pauses. Takes a breath.

So this swing's going to come Amelia's way then. This is a free show for me.

I lean forward, taking a suck of my tea.

"Episode?" Amelia's head snaps up.

"Not *episode*." Mona jumps in with her low, efficient tone. "More like a moment of truth. We just realized something after the Q&A that let us know we need to redirect the ship here. All to keep it running smoothly."

Amelia's eyes squint so much that those extremely long false lashes she wears for events overlap each other, looking ready to get tangled and blindfold her. It must be a big event tonight at the conference center, because the bigger the event, the longer the lashes are. And tonight they're long enough to block her from reaching her wineglass with her lips. She blinks a few times until they let go of one another.

"Which is?" Amelia prompts suspiciously, dropping the phone from her ear and giving Susanna and Mona her direct attention. Just daring them to criticize her "rigorous art of entertainment."

"Bottles over Books went off with a bang. We had such a line out the door the police got involved. They thought it was a *rage party*."

"The event was *extremely productive*," Mona reaffirms.

Susanna clutches her wine and commences to take tiny, sheepish sips.

"*You* were great," Mona continues, when Amelia doesn't show any sign of calming down. "You have a very specific"—she pauses, finding the word—"*warmth* that draws people to you at these gatherings. We're always using footage of you at your events to show our other authors, demonstrating how to perfectly capture your audience."

Amelia sniffs. Looks to Jack.

"You do have a gift," Jack says.

Amelia bypasses me and looks to Susanna, who is nodding on repeat silently.

"But," Mona continues, when several seconds have passed and it has been made sufficiently clear that everyone (minus me) at the table has properly stroked her ego, "when you referred to a character as 'my sweet spot, Sam'—"

"That? *That* is your concern?" Amelia interjects with a laugh. "So his name is Nate," she says, flapping a hand. "I have *so many* books. Authors forget their characters' names all the time."

"But he is also a serial killer." Mona cuts to the point. "And you said he was inspired by your real-life childhood crush."

Amelia pauses and looks up. Blinks several times. "Nate is a *murderer*? The dog-loving love interest?" She shoots me an accusing glare.

"He isn't a love interest." I feel the rising need to defend myself. "He's the neighbor."

"How can he *not* be a love interest?" Amelia says. "I have *pages* of emails from fans telling me they *love* Nate."

"Sounds like there's something wrong with *your* fans," I reply, and Jack's knee jabs mine beneath the table.

"I think what everyone's trying to get at here," Mona jumps in, "is that you are right."

She lets that sink in for a moment, because we all know Amelia likes to hear that phrase.

"You do have *a lot* of books coming out each year, and because of that it's just becoming easier and easier to make a misstep. We need to change something about our setup because, unfortunately, some of your answers to the questions about the book just didn't line up with the content inside it. And if you weren't able to go over the Power-Point that was sent over—"

"I was traveling last week," Amelia snaps defensively, as though this is a logical excuse to dismiss the fact that I created and sent the PowerPoint over *four* weeks ago and it was a sum total of ten slides. Ten. She's not even asked to read my *books* anymore. They asked me at the last minute to whittle down my eighty-thousand-word novel into a mere ten slides that would take a total of ten minutes to go over, and she couldn't even manage that.

"Traveling makes it tough," Amelia says.

Susanna is nodding like a bobblehead in the face of this comment, despite the fact she herself has told me she sometimes reads over three hundred pages a day for work. Three hundred. A day.

Mona looks to Jack, and Jack takes the lead. "And what that tells us is that you are just far too busy and need some help. Your work is extremely demanding, Amelia."

Flagrant lie.

"You are busy."

Another flagrant lie.

"And frankly, we just can't afford any more near misses. The world is watching you"—Amelia smiles at this little reminder—"and recording every second of it. And right now, the worst thing that can happen is if people start puzzling bits and pieces from every second of your life and drawing conclusions we'd rather them not draw. If we don't take this more seriously, this whole thing could slam to a stop. It's hard enough to get every question right at these interviews even when you *are* the writer of the book. And we're starting to deal with obsessed-level fans, the kind who annotate every other line with color-coded pens and Post-its and form diagrams on their walls to discuss on fan accounts. These people are getting their PhD in

Amelia Benedict books. And soon enough, we'll have one misstep too many, and no offer of free signed bookplates can cover it up."

He finishes, and a tingle goes down my spine.

This is the closest he's ever come to giving any of his clients a true critique, which can mean only one thing: He means it. Whatever happened at that event last night was truly *so* close a call that he was willing to put his neck on the line for this.

Amelia, with a firm exhale of breath, flips her phone over and puts it on the table face down. There's a finality to the movement. A symbolic seriousness to her motions. "Fine. What do I do?"

"You can cancel the tour—" Mona begins.

"Absolutely *not*," Amelia snaps.

But of course she won't.

We are all entirely convinced the motivation for Amelia isn't so much the money (given her being a Benedict heiress, she'll never lack for anything) as the fame. It's the need to talk to people. To be seen by people doing important things at important places. Sitting in prominent seats at said important places with her lovely, bouncing, shining hair.

Amelia Benedict, in her very own shiny spotlight, just like her mother.

To take that away is to take away her reason for life.

"Or," Mona says pointedly, "we have another, potentially better, plan in mind. And it's Bryony we have a couple requests for."

Oh no.

"Bryony." She shifts her attention to me. "We're going to try to reel in as much interview time as possible from now on. Take out the spontaneity factor. Of course there are always going to be those spontaneous questions that come in during the signing portion or Q&A, but at least for the first portion, we can try to control the situation.

"I'll email the venues a list of ten preplanned questions we can all agree upon *here*, *tonight*, so we can all feel confident knowing we are reaching the public in a more contained atmosphere. Sometimes venues are particular about their events, sometimes the panels and the structure of the event just won't allow it, but overall, we think this is a good plan. We have a second step to the plan we want to initiate to try to cover any problems that arise from those open Q&A sessions, but right now, can you help us by answering these specific questions?"

I'm sucking in tea from my straw and nodding at the same time. So I was kidnapped for the purpose of providing answers for the discussion questions tonight. Easy peasy.

In fact, aside from inhaling Amelia's overly pungent beachy perfume (she also tends to follow the rule of "the bigger the event, the more dousing in perfume"), this is even a bit of a treat.

Tomato pie. Sweet tea. Gaeta's glorious atmosphere. If I'm painfully honest with myself, I even like talking books with Susanna and Mona—so long as Amelia falls into doomscrolling the internet for paparazzi photos of herself under the veil of "work" and doesn't interfere. Actually, being personally asked about the books I wrote makes me feel in the tiniest way special.

A little interview of my own. About the book I hugged so closely for hours and weeks and months.

"Terrific." Susanna claps her hands as she snaps open her laptop. "Does this sound good to you, Amelia? Shall we start this new plan tonight?"

"Yeah. Fine," Amelia says with a little shrug, her eyes starting to droop toward her phone.

"And so you can *listen* here to what Bryony says so you're ready, okay?" Susanna says, with the softest little nudge that screams, *"For the love, please listen so you don't try to crash all of our careers, okay?!"*

Which is the tricky thing about Amelia, as a matter of fact. Her math skills aren't the brightest, and so despite the fact that the one book she wrote a handful of years ago garnered ten thousand sales, only roughly fifty times less than what her books sell now in the first year, she was and forever claims she is the original author. The real writer. Hence why Susanna and Mona can't convince her to worry much about her little ghostwriter secret. Because to her, she *is* the writer. Sometimes she throws out a little line suggesting a setting or occupation to me and somehow thinks that equals her *actually* playing a major role in the writing portion. I'm just a Penny to her—the person jotting down those eighty-thousand-word little details surrounding her brilliant concept of "make her a yoga instructor."

"Okay," she says, but she's already sucked into her phone.

I exchange glances with Susanna and Mona and, for a moment, do feel for them. It's like trying to convince a toddler to eat her peas. The best you can do is put the plate in front of her and sit there, desperately hoping she picks one up and ingests it.

The tomato pie comes to the table and we dig in—while Amelia picks here and there at the iceberg in her salad. Penny scribbles furiously through the questions. Should I buy her a stenograph machine like Gloria has for court reporting as a Christmas-in-July present? Help with the inevitable carpal tunnel she is getting as we eat?

The questions are typical.

"What was your inspiration for *The Seven-Year Holiday*?"

"In chapter 5, we see Nate returning to his elementary school as they open up a time capsule from thirty years prior. Why does he find the compass? What's the meaning behind the compass?"

"What was it like writing the scene where Nate is given the contents of his former best friend's capsule addition? Why is the baseball card poignant?"

At one point Amelia lifts her head to interrupt my lengthy answer to "What is the most difficult part of writing a book?" with "Picking the cover," followed with a syrupy laugh that forces laughs from everyone else, after which she points to Susanna and says, "Write that down."

The cadence of the rest of the hour goes pretty smoothly, though. Mona asks a question, I answer, Susanna types and coughs every once in a while to grab Amelia's attention. Mona asks a question, I answer,

Susanna types and coughs with a poignant, hopeful stare in Amelia's direction.

It's all pretty cut-and-dried until the last question, when Amelia pulls away from her social media stupor and fixes her attention on us. "What was that last question?"

"What are you working on next?" Susanna says. "And Bryony said"—Susanna looks at her computer screen—"'I don't want to give too much away, but I'm thirty thousand words into this heartwarming story set in one of my favorite places on earth: deep in the heart of the marshlands of Beaufort, South Carolina. A single parent of nine-year-old James moves in next door to a third-generation farmer and her own nine-year-old, and when the children become fast friends, they spark something and ultimately teach their parents about how life is miraculous when people, against all odds, sacrifice for the well-being of one another.'"

Amelia frowns. "Where's the romance?"

"It's with the parents," I say.

"Where's the comedy?"

"There's humor. It's woven throughout."

"I don't know how it can when it sounds like you're so busy dealing with 'sacrificing' and 'miraculous living.'"

"Amazingly enough," I say with a snap in my tone, "books can be romantic comedies *and* use more descriptors than saying the guy was 'a billionaire and, like, super hot.'"

"Bryony has managed to make room for it all. That's what makes all these books so special," Susanna adds quickly, nodding fervently between us.

Amelia squints. Opens her mouth.

We wait for her to speak for ten seconds.

Then wait again as she tilts her head, screwing up her forehead in thought. She presses her lips together with a faraway look, as if this is all *really* important and it is vital that she be the one to figure it all out.

At last, she comes to "Change it to the Keys."

"What? No—"

"Nobody goes to Beaufort. Key West is *the* place to go. Key West is the destination where people want to plop down in their beach chairs and read something fun. Beach reads are for *beachy* places with white sand and dolphins and sunshine, not slimy seaweed and alligators. It's a marketing thing," Amelia says with a wave of her hand, as if I would *never* get it.

I bite my bottom lip. *This* is why I try not to tell her anything about the book for as long as humanly possible. Preferably until it has already gone to print.

I can't just "change" it to Key West. Key West is pretty, but *Beaufort* has the vibrant Gullah culture sitting side by side with modernized *Simple Living*–style farmhouses. *Beaufort* has the low country. *Beaufort* has the culture of a little Charleston in its downtown bayside living without giving up the history of generations of people who still live there. *Beaufort* has Spanish moss draped over live oak trees. *Beaufort*, more specifically St. Helena Island, has the kind of quiet the boys need from my story.

Uh-oh. I've done it again.

I can feel the rising mother bear inside me longing to throw myself over my story, protect it feverishly from anyone who dares to take my cub from me.

I *love* my story.

I *love* the vibrant green of the black gum trees outside James's window and the symbolism of their color drifting to wildfire orange in fall.

I *love* the sound of the gravel as Theo's mom's truck crunches down the long residential driveway leading to their pristine white, newly constructed Plan A103 farmhouse from page 39 of *Simple Living* magazine, directly beside the russet-colored single-wide resting on cinder blocks with the loose hinge on the swinging front door.

I *love* the spit of gravel and kick of the boys' legs as they race side by side for the school bus, their parents watching from the front porches with coffee clutched in hand.

I *love* the message I plan to bring to the story.

And I know I'm not supposed to, I know it only causes heartache for me, but I can't help it. I'm a surrogate mother and eventually I have to give this baby away and it drives me *insane*.

"And drop the kids," Amelia says.

I feel it. It feels like she just slashed the two little boys in half.

Their history, gone. The world never to see what beautiful things they did together.

Their whole lives, gone.

My face must be draining of color because Jack steps in. "Amelia, I've heard all about this story. It's going to be great—"

"Kids *out*," she says more firmly. "I *hate* books with kids in them. People hate kids enough in *real life*. Nobody wants to hear more about *other* people's children when they're trying to read and escape their *own*."

How? How is this the same woman who wins over millions of people through her television interviews? There really could be twins here: one evil, the other the angel the evil one lets out temporarily to do interviews.

Susanna, who just five minutes prior had showed everyone a picture of her daughter getting third place at a gymnastics competition, stares down painfully at her laptop with inflamed cheeks.

Meanwhile, I'm a teakettle. My head is suddenly aching. Spinning. There are so many consequences to just changing the setting to Key West and dropping the main characters (whom, again, I *love*). A sick and unsettling feeling persists in the dizziness. A growing shock. A mourning. A weight of a hundred bricks dropped on my head. Thoughts whizzing in and out.

The deadline is in three months. I'm struggling as it is.

A thought forms: Maybe I could just write them into a different story. Tuck the boys away safe and sound and write them out on my own later.

But when?

When would I ever have the time?

I'd have to completely change everything to do that. The parents need to be different. The message, different. Their jobs different. Houses. Lifestyles. Names. Hobbies. Motivations. Longings. Backstories.

To keep this book as my own and give it any hope of meeting the world one day, I'll have to shelve the whole story now. Drop it into the proverbial file cabinet and write fresh.

Can I do that?

Could I ever have *time* to bring my own story to life?

And who would even publish it?

And why is it so congested in this tiny booth? I can't breathe!

My breathing is shallow and small.

The feeling of Jack to one side and Amelia's silky, smelly blouse on the other is making me painfully claustrophobic. My knees knock against the bottom of the table. I have no space to work.

To live.

"Amelia." Jack's voice is calm but firm. Steady. "Let's not consider asking her to rewrite the book thirty thousand words in. It's July. This book will be not just completed but flying off the shelves in nine months. There's a firm publishing schedule, and it would be *highly* unadvisable to break it. And for what? Let's keep the kids. Bryony has her pulse on what her readers—your readers—want. Let's give it to them with all we've got. High sales. A win for *everyone*."

A pause follows and he raises his hand for the waiter. "Look, we finished the Q&A. I think we should take a beat, take a breath, get some coffee. Amelia, it'll be good for your speaking."

Amelia, who often downs a double shot of espresso to keep herself *sprightly* and to warm up her vocals, backs down a little at the suggestion, and for the moment the topic is dropped.

The conversation proceeds to shift, at Jack's subtle direction, to any topic besides that of writing (and, poor Susanna, kids), which with Amelia here naturally means it lands on what makes her happiest. Her. And for the next twenty minutes, everyone pretends to care an extreme amount about her latest flight to Sarasota and nods sympathetically at her latest crisis of losing her luggage for a sum total of four hours after her first-class flight.

Everyone, of course, has their personal reasons for drumming up puppy eyes while she drones on, and normally I'd make it my personal goal in life to ask targeted questions about her luggage situation, where her responses would be so egocentric she'd *have* to realize how self-centered she is and backtrack just a bit. But after the near loss of Theo and James, I don't have any fire in me.

These are the moments I'm grateful to have Jack at my side. He has never quite understood why I care so much for the content of my work, or how message always trumps money for me, at least any money not supporting The Bridge, but he respects my priorities. He respects me. And for that reason I'm ever grateful he is in my corner.

I'm just settling back down nerve-wise when Amelia turns to me. "So where specifically is the comedic aspect to this"—she waves her hand airily, then adds with some disdain—"*Beaufort* story?"

"Oh," I say, pushing my teacup around. "It's around. It's in there. In the nuances."

It *hasn't* been overt for some time, not that she's noticed.

Her forehead creases, and she narrows her eyes as if suspecting I'm lying about this fact. She could discover it if she read her books. "But my books are rom-coms."

"Yes. And they still can have their happy endings and laughable moments while centering around meaningful topics."

"My first book was *Party Girls in the USA*."

"Yes," I say. "And we're progressing."

"Which readers are loving," Susanna chimes in, but Amelia puts up a finger to silence her.

She frowns deeply.

"But the book covers are so colorful. They're stocked on the shelves under 'Rom-Com.'"

I nod. "Right. Well, I'd chalk that up to misdirection in the design department, except for the fact I did bring it up with them, once, and they said it was necessary for the sales trend."

"There are *literally* cartoon people on the covers," Amelia says, no less suspicious. As if I must have it wrong.

"I'm aware," I reply. "Apparently illustrated covers are 'on trend,' whether or not the initial main love interest dies brutally in a fishing accident during a family reunion."

"Kenneth *died* in *Smuggler's Paradise*?" Amelia stammers. And one point to her credit for recognizing the title by the fishing reference, although that point immediately must be retracted given his name was Gene.

"Brutally," I reply.

"I told everyone I wished my father could've had the same experiences Kenneth did at our reunions! Are you telling me I told everyone I wished my father was killed?"

"Brutally killed," I correct.

"Amelia, listen," Mona says. "Nobody caught that reference that time. You're so bewitching onstage, most people just assume you're giving an enlightened joke. Everybody throws their hands up when it comes to knowing writers all live in their heads. It's the universal excuse for all of you."

Cute. Lumping Amelia and me together.

"The point is you're doing *great*," Mona says.

"Incredibly well." Susanna snaps the laptop shut and slips it into her bag beneath the table.

"But *this* is what we are talking about. *This* is why we say we need to tighten up our responses to make sure, in the extreme event people start paying attention, they don't start questioning *you* as the writer."

"And I'd say we got a lot done tonight," Susanna adds, still nodding. "I just emailed you the interview, Mona."

"No more deaths," Amelia blurts out. She's directing her attention to me now. Looking me straight in the eye. "No more . . . *negativity*."

I purse my lips together.

"So what? You want to go back to the *great saga* of chipping your tooth at a party in LA?" I can't help spitting out.

Unlike her, I've read *her* book.

"Bryony's novels *always* end well." Susanna breaks in to defend me. "She brings witty and insightfully written, relatable trials to the table that people love. They laugh over each trial. And they *live* for every struggle. People *feel* it."

"I don't *care*," Amelia snaps, pushing her elbows out to force some room for herself and jabbing Penny and me in the ribs. "I don't want people *feeling* it. I want my books to be an *escape*. Move. I have to go."

I glance to Susanna and Mona.

The eyes of both women have changed. Susanna's eyes are large and round with an *oh no, we woke the beast!* expression. Mona's squinting, making to grab her purse and edge herself out the other side of the booth before it all breaks loose.

We did wake the beast. And now we have to be exceedingly careful to step around her while trying to spring out.

I hear an intake of breath beside me while simultaneously feeling Jack squeeze my knee beneath the table as if to say, "*I've got this.*"

"Amelia, the content that Bryony is writing is *working*. Sales are up—"

"I don't care—"

"Way up—"

She shakes her head.

"So far up you can't see the peak for the clouds blocking the view. Bryony has taken what worked and turned it into something *irresistible*. You don't want to lose that. And with you two working together—you doing the hard work of all the publicity, you being the face behind her brains—you two are a *mighty force* to be reckoned with in the publishing industry. Bryony has an eye for writing things that work for her. Let her keep on writing with full creative authority and don't squelch her spirit. It's what the people want."

It was a nice speech.

It's not often I get a direct compliment. Oh sure, there's the "Nice work!" and "She's done it again!" emails when I send in this or that. Whereas 90 percent of the time Amelia is getting praised and 10 percent of the time she's doing any work, I'm the opposite. It's fine. At least, I tell myself it's fine. I tell myself I write what I write because I actually like it. It actually means something to me. It is an opportunity to help people learn and feel something too. Lessons that I'm learning are organically woven in there, and I feel honored to share them around the world. Most importantly, it's a way to earn the money that allows The Bridge to carry on, but still. You never know how much you need an honest compliment until it has suddenly presented itself.

My cheeks flame.

And I'm almost entirely comforted, but for the fact that when I look from Jack to Amelia, I see in her expression that she has most certainly *not* taken his words to heart, cherished them in the palms of her hands, and taken to nodding with humility and grace. She is *not* looking at me now like one who has had an epiphany and realized, "We can do it, so long as we do it together!"

Amelia's looking at me as though I'm the *villain*.

The waiter walks up to the table, and wordlessly she raises a finger to dismiss him.

She presses her lips together. Takes her phone and slides it into Airplane Mode. Drops it face down on the table.

"Let me make this absolutely clear. Penny, put the pen down."

Penny drops it like it's made of fire.

Amelia resumes. "I have heard my fill tonight of what *I* should be doing differently. I've heard my fill tonight of all the ways that *I* am doing things wrong. And here I am, taking time out of my busy schedule to end up *here*"—she casts her eyes around disdainfully— "eating limp lettuce and *tomato pie*, two hours before I'm supposed to be onstage for over *three thousand* fans. *Hand* selling, if you will, *my* stories. That have *my* name on them. And began *with me*.

"These books would be *nothing* without me. And as such, I think you would all do well to remember that I could hire *anyone* in the field to be the backer behind my books while I'm too busy running around selling them. I could swap Bryony out *this second* for some high school kid on Fiverr tonight if I wanted to, and that book *would sell*. I could generate *AI*," she snaps, "at this point to create my stories. So when I say *I want perky*, I mean, *I WANT PERKY*.

"*I* am the author of my books and *I* am the one with final say over my stories! And to be completely honest with you all, I hope you realize that each and every one of you is equally disposable, and *I am the only one sitting here tonight who is not*. Is that abundantly clear?"

Amelia did it.

Amelia is the one person I've ever met who is so exceptionally arrogant, she will actually *say* her arrogant thoughts out loud without care. It's like she needs to make it absolutely clear that she cares so very, very *little* for the thoughts and opinions and general well-being of those around her that she has no problem informing them they are *disposable*. She is "nice" as a general rule merely because presenting herself that way in the public eye is most advantageous to *her*. But when the tiniest opportunity presents itself to be otherwise, the gloves come off. Amelia is the textbook definition of a civilized sociopath, lipstick and all.

Susanna, the most sensitive of the group, looks like she might cry.

Penny, at Amelia's rant, resumes her nonsensical note-taking like her literal life depends upon it.

I, however, am pushed to my limit.

People flee, freeze, or fight in the face of certain dangers.

And there are just some moments, particularly when targeted by angry people, when I find myself wanting to *fight*.

I've learned to do a lot of things in the past two years, ever since that fateful day I pushed open the conference doors and walked back inside that pitch room.

One being: taking my own opinions a little more seriously and those of others a lot less.

And with the look on poor Susanna's face, I'm just about to open my mouth and go *to town* in her defense.

Jack practically jumps out of his seat to be the first to speak. "Amelia, clearly we have gotten off on the wrong foot here and jumped ahead without listening to you. I thought we were all in agreement that the goal was sales, and we would be willing to pivot however necessary to ensure that goal was met. Given our previous conversations, I thought your ultimate goal was to skyrocket to the top of the bestseller list and beat your previous sales numbers. How long has Anne Sanderworth been at the number-one slot on the *Times* list, Susanna?" Jack glances over.

"Thirty-two weeks, I believe," she says quietly.

"Right," he says. "And Amelia's longest running at the number-one slot has been . . . ?"

Susanna's eyes swing wildly to Jack.

She purses her lips.

Jack waits.

"Never," Susanna puts in at last. "But she's been *on* the list at the number two slot for *plenty* of weeks—"

Jack shrugs. "Yes. So that's all that's going on here, Amelia." He swivels his attention back to her. "We just want what's best for you, for the publishers, for everyone. But if you want perky, even at the expense of that top slot, believe me, Bryony can *do* perky." He pushes down on my shoe to keep my temper abated. "In fact, Bryony would be *happy* to do perky. There's a lot less research for her, a lot less to do. In many ways, you would be doing her a favor."

I grit my teeth. Absolutely *claw* his hand with my nails.

"I can sit with Bryony tomorrow over her book, and we can come up with a plan to make it . . ." He pauses, then says, "Pure fun."

I'm pretty sure I'm drawing blood on his hand now.

Steam coming out my ears.

If this goes *at all* the other way from Jack's plan, I am going to throw a riot.

Never, not once in my two years of doing this, have I hated this job so much. I'm sitting here fighting for the life of a work I don't even get credit for but still can't keep myself from emotionally clinging to.

I'm sitting here being told casually to scrap an entire novel, an entire method of my writing, and just become a different person.

I can't *help* what I write. I can't *help* threading in the art of forgiveness or the sappiness of a mother sweeping her gaze over the ocean while holding on to her son's pudgy hand or walking with my characters through the pain of witnessing loss and having to rebuild their hearts and homes again.

The world is huge and multifaceted and fascinating and terrifying all at once, and the world collectively sits in my classroom every day telling me about it. And I, like a teakettle, have this need to let out the steam, to share the worldview-changing tidbits I learn every day. And yes, I can envelop stories with love and humor, big enough that the Brooks graphic designers get away with packaging them with cartoon covers and marketing them as rom-coms.

But the fact is, these books are *meaningful* to me. They're *meaningful* to readers. And I sit by my computer, day in and day out, living on crumbs of news about my own story. When on earth will it be my turn to write under my name? When *on earth* will I get the chance to reach readers with words *only* influenced by my mind and not dampened by Amelia's input?

Jack takes my clenched fist beneath the table and squeezes it, wrapping his hand around my balled-up fist tightly enough to break me out of my angry stupor. I look up from my boxed tomato pie. Look at Amelia. See what Jack has done.

It worked.

The name he dropped worked: Anne Sanderworth.

Mona, Susanna, Jack—even Penny has paused with her pen pressed to the paper, waiting for Amelia to respond.

The waiter seems to sense the tension, because he stands a few feet off, hesitating with the check in hand.

It was dangerous, using a bomb to defuse a bomb. Amelia is unreliable and easily provoked. She's happy one second, but if you say the wrong thing in the wrong moment, *bam*.

Throwing out the fact that Anne is twice as successful as Amelia and reminding her that she is second to the one who is sitting on some virtual throne called the "number one slot" will either make Amelia blow up entirely and flip some tables or, if Jack knew what he was doing—

"Fine."

Amelia has smoothed her hair.

Amelia is snapping open the little pink purse at her side and pulling out a metallic gold tube of lipstick.

"Keep the depressing book," Amelia says. "Keep Beaufort. Keep whatever guarantees this book will be a *hit*—except the kids."

I feel that hit. It feels like a punch in the gut, and yet no one around me notices the pain those three little words cause. They don't write, I suppose. They don't understand that she's choking me right here, right in public.

Well, fine.

The kids are too good anyway. She doesn't deserve to have them beneath her name.

I silently make a vow to write them into my next story—one that will see the light of day under my name.

"But if this one doesn't do it"—she waggles her tube of lipstick, its pointy red tip directed at me like a target—"if this one isn't going to get us to *the top*, then I'm going in and we're doing it *my way*. I'm done playing games here," she says, as if all of us have been absolutely incompetent while she, the sheer genius, has been waiting for us to step up. "I want *the perfect rom-com* this time around. I want it to be *perfect*."

I cannot help but hope, for the zillionth time in one thousand days, that I get my own contract soon. Get out.

"Is there anything else you want from me?" Amelia says, the sound of quiet disdain tinting her voice.

"Nope," Mona says, a tight smile on her face. "Susanna will tighten up the Q&A answers from tonight, and we'll shoot it off to you sometime this week. But there is one more thing." To my surprise, she turns to me. "One more thing we need from you, Bryony."

"Me?" Surprise quickly flares into frustration.

I'm already *plotting* the books. I'm already spending my nights and weekends *painfully* pulling the words out of my head, forcing myself to add layer upon layer of depth to these novels. I'm already shredding old scenes I spend weeks on for rewrites. I'm already giving it 110 percent and then watching it come out into the world to bring acclaim to *somebody else.* Not to mention most of the money. All for the hope of seeing my own little manuscript get its day.

I have already gone above and beyond in every way imaginable. I'm even writing out PowerPoints for the woman too lazy to *read* the book she's getting praised for!

"I am stretched to my limit, Mona." There's a firmness in my voice. A tight pinch because *they know this.* They *know* how hard all of this has been for me. "I can't work on *any* more PowerPoints."

"And we don't want you to. We just . . . need you to consider going on . . . a vacation."

"Of sorts," Susanna adds.

"What?"

Amelia and I speak simultaneously.

It may be the first thing we've ever agreed on.

"I have been talking to the rest of the team, and we just think," Mona says, her eyes shifting from Amelia to me, "it may be best if Bryony joins you on tour."

"*What?!*" we both say more urgently now.

"You want her *on tour* with me?" Amelia screeches. "What kind of game is this?" Her eyes shoot accusingly to Jack as if to scream, "*Fix this. Fix this NOW.*"

"Not to *talk,*" Susanna jumps in with a shrill laugh. Her voice drops to a whisper. "Not as the author."

"What is going *on* tonight?" Amelia cries, rolling her head backward.

"We just believe it's critical that you are prepared at all times for the myriad of questions you are going to face at these events over the next two weeks," Mona says. "Statistically speaking, we believe it would be more detrimental to your career at this point to accidentally reveal the situation going on behind the scenes than to cancel this tour altogether. We are open to you canceling—"

"*No*," Amelia spits out.

"In which case, we need to find a creative way to try to keep our ends covered. *This* is that plan. Bryony by your side for the tour— hearing the questions. You being fed answers to those questions that could trip you up. Maybe she'll look like she's your personal assistant. Nobody will notice. A win-win for everyone really. Bryony will *assist* you."

Why does it sound like I'm being kidnapped here?

"She will be there to *help you* however she can."

I cut my eyes to Jack. "You want me to just drop teaching for two weeks to be Amelia's lapdog? Jack, did you know about this?"

He shakes his head. "No, I know we discussed some changes and going over the Q&A tonight—"

"Consider it more like a luxury paid vacation with a sprinkle of work," Mona interjects.

"There are some lovely stops," Susanna chimes in softly with an eager smile.

I've seen Amelia's RV bus. The one wrapped in a giant picture of Amelia with her skinny arms crossed over her chest in a bright pant-suit, book titles sprawled over the windows, a three-foot-wide smile on her lips. I wouldn't step inside that thing for the world.

I stifle a cynical laugh. They've got to be kidding. "And how exactly does having me standing beside Amelia, giving her answers to questions about *her* book, prove to the world she doesn't have a ghostwriter?"

"Ugh, I hate that word." Amelia pinches both temples. "Don't use that word."

I press my lips together. I have had it up to *here* tonight. "What word?"

Her eyes become slits. "You know the word."

I shrug. "I don't know. You've just said a lot of words. To which word specifically are you referring?"

"The *G-word*," she says forcefully.

"Which G-word?" I snap back. "Ghostwriter?"

"I need to get *out* of here," Amelia hisses, eyes roving around for the door. "I have to speak in *twenty* minutes."

It's simple, really. I'm just not going to do this.

I can't stand forty-two minutes with her, much less two weeks. We'd kill each other.

I shrug again, forcing myself to release my pent-up energy. "I'm sorry, but I can't. I'm contracted to write the books, nothing more. You will simply have to come up with another idea."

There. It kills me to be the one to kill their plans, but I have to do it. For my own sanity. And believe me, were it *anybody* else, I probably would have said yes. The idea of jumping on a bus and getting away for two weeks sounds nice. The adventure, appealing.

I yelp as Amelia sprays yet another shot of her beachy perfume onto her neck and nails me in one eye.

But for *her.*

Mona gives a little cough, and with my one good, uncovered eye, I watch her shoot a message telepathically to Jack.

He rubs the back of his neck.

Gets up from the booth.

Motions for me to move out after him.

Ticks his tongue. Thinking.

"Well, that's the thing, Bryony. There's the whole part about publicity in your contract."

My brows shoot up.

"I'll have to double-check on it, but . . ."

To my absolute shock, he *trails off.*

I practically dive into the booth seat for my phone.

I'm just pulling up the old email with my contract when Mona jumps in. "It has just become abundantly clear that you are essential to our promotional services and the continued success of our partnership, Bryony. But rest assured, we want to make sure you see this as an opportunity for yourself as well. The higher the book sales, the more royalties *you* make as well." Mona flashes a bright, professional, and obviously rehearsed smile. "And needless to say, we will make this tour as fun and relaxing for everyone as possible. There will be great meals. Great hotels. We'll only need you to step in for a couple hours at a time. And even then, we're hopeful you won't even need to talk unless Amelia runs into a problem."

"All right," Amelia cuts in. Her phone drops into her purse, and it clatters loudly against other tubes of lipstick and metal objects as she snaps it shut. "I'm done hearing everyone cater to this woman. Stop trying to woo her with the promise of two weeks at beaches and hotels. Stop trying to help her get over her *woes* of getting the best job of her *life* selling books to the masses that she couldn't sell a hundred copies of by herself. It's two *weeks*, Bryony. If it's helpful to the cause, you're coming. And yes, there's food. And there are hotels." She directly spears me with a glare. "Just *do your job*, okay? It's *Not. That. Hard.*"

Silence cuts around the table.

I look down at my phone, my thumb scrolled down to section 3b.

Writer will perform Promotional Services, if any, at the times provided in Part 1 or, subject to Writer's prior professional commitments and reasonable availability, at such other times as Publisher may reasonably request and, if requested, as part of the Promotional Services, will sit for video- and audio-recorded interviews, which Publisher may reproduce, distribute, display, perform, and adapt for promotional purposes. All reasonable expenses incurred by Writer in performing Promotional Services will be paid by Publisher.

It seems I'm going on a book tour. With the most delusional woman alive. As her unwilling and unwanted ghostwriter. Who, apparently, is not supposed to call herself a ghostwriter but something more tasteful like, oh, I don't know, indentured servant.

My phone dings and I slide it open to see an email header from Gran.

I just found out. We need to talk.

Margaret Page
President, The Bridge Refugee Services
3395 White Spring Road
Florence, NY 13316

And isn't that just the icing on the cake?
After two solid years of anonymity, Gran knows.

CHAPTER 7

There is a *good* thing about all this, and that is, no more lies.

No more secrecy.

No more mysteriously rushing off in the middle of family dinner to talk (read: argue) on the phone with Jack about some insane Amelia-driven demand. No more looking like the most introverted person alive by shoving off invitations left and right so I can mysteriously "be alone in my apartment to water my plants."

Letting this little secret finally air out with Gran will release some pent-up tension. It will be a *good thing* to tell her what is going on. And, to be very clear, the absolute best thing in all this is that *I* have not broken contract. Somebody *else* told her (read: Gloria, no doubt); ergo, *I* am not responsible.

(Of course, the fact that I told Gloria roughly the second I got off the plane with Jack two years ago after specifically being told *not* to is, indeed, my fault. But she's my *sister*. The sister bond no doubt trumps a contract in a court of law. Everybody in the whole world knows all bets are off when it comes to your sister.)

I step up to Gran's office door.

Gran has always been a polite one, dignified despite the fact that the door is a textured hollow core made of primed composite with scratches all down its side. The brass on the knob has rubbed off in places. The commercial blue carpet has been trodden on for no less than forty years. The windows are single pane, and yes, in the winter the heat just can't keep up, and in the summers, like this one, we find it's better just to shove up the windows and our sleeves instead of asking anything more out of the old HVAC.

But Margaret Page has always held her head high, and from the way she dresses for work—the same single strand of pearls, her gray hair rolled up in curls—you'd think she was the president at New York University instead of some place like this.

Margaret Page is the one who puts the extra touches on the place. Making sure the halls always smell of citrus essential oils instead of cheap lemon spray. Making sure the bathrooms always carry a little basket of spare toiletries and fresh soaps at the sink. Bouquets of some sort always sit on the teachers' desks—a tradition that I discovered began in 1979 from bouquets selected from Gran's garden and has continued ever since.

These little touches lift the students', and teachers', spirits when they step inside. These, and the smiles, the conversations, and the reaches into each other's lives, are what make people lift their chins when they walk through the doors.

These touches are what set The Bridge apart.

One time I asked her why she goes to such effort, and she said simply, "It takes a great deal of courage for someone to come to this country, often with nothing, and make a new start for their family. They need to feel proud of themselves." And that was that.

So for the forty-year-old engineer who once taught at his university in Ukraine before the war took over and he fled with his wife and three children, the one who now works nights to clean the whiteboards as a janitor at a university here, the scent of the citrus essential oils is for him. To give him a burst of energy while he works so diligently to keep his eyes open as he finishes another test leading toward his GED.

For the young Somalian woman who fled an abusive situation and is now working to raise her two-year-old daughter alone, in a new country, the smell of the roses on the desk is for her. Along with the free lavender deodorants.

And it all began with Gran. I rap on the door lightly.

"Come in," she calls.

Gran is dressed in a blue suit today. Wrinkle-free down to the cuff links. Her ankles crossed over little white shoes. A window is open and the sound of the interstate floods through. It's not an ideal noise, but the breeze that's blowing in is a welcome addition to the hot July heat. A trade. The better of two options.

I begin to roll up my own blue blazer to the elbow and then pause at her slight frown. I push things enough by wearing tennis shoes. Let's not push her over the edge today.

"Shut the door, Bryony. Time for tea?" She motions to the little golden cart in the corner where her electric teakettle has taken a permanent post.

"Just a few minutes," I say, moving over to the cart. "I've only got about ten before I need to sneak back and finish up some papers." I pick up one of the little teacups and saucers.

There are, for the record, only real teacups and saucers at The Bridge. At the coffee station in the teachers' lounge. At the tea station here. Little unmatching porcelain cups with delicate golden curled handles and intricately hand-painted purple flowers. Little five-dollar finds found in any antique store in the whole of the United States. They carry such a reputation even the students sometimes discover one, buy it, and contribute to the supply.

One time an opportunity for a grant popped up, and an inspector tried to tell her the supply was extravagant when Styrofoam cups would do, to which she replied curtly, "Treat a stallion like a pig, and eventually you'll have a two-thousand-pound pig."

Needless to say, we did not get that money.

"So," I say, suddenly finding myself at a loss for how to start. I pour the hot water in the teacup. Reach for the tea bags.

"So," she returns, no more inclined to jump in than me.

I venture a glance her way and see she is frowning at me. The expression on her face is similar to when she discovered I had snuck out of the house at fifteen for a party.

Terrific.

Not intimidating at all.

"You emailed me that we need to talk," I say dumbly, as though that is new and fresh information to us both.

"How long, exactly, has this been going on?"

"Well . . . ," I say, dodging the question. After all, I don't know exactly *how* to answer it. How long has *what* been going on? The ghostwriting of books? The sending of money? Part of it? All of it? Something else entirely? "It's hard to say . . . What have you been told?"

"Is there *more* that I don't know?" She raises one brow.

"I don't know." I swirl my tea bag around in my cup. "Can you tell me what you *do* know?"

There's no way I'm going to tell her on the off chance she *doesn't* know about my little secret(s), so I might as well be stubbornly silent on the matter until she says something first.

There's the sound of heavy footsteps coming down the hall, and Martha, Gran's administrative assistant, talking in a very loud and friendly voice says, "Yes, Mr. Takahashi. I just saw her go down the hall, in fact. Let me see if we can get this straightened out."

"Ms. Page, I have a quick question." The door pops open, and Martha's eyes widen as she catches sight of Gran and me. More specifically, because of the expression on Gran's stern face. Flat. Unimpressed. I offer up a little wave to Hiroto. "Hello, Mr. Takahashi."

He beams a little and dips his head. "Good morning, Teacher. It's a . . ." He pauses before adding haltingly, "Very. Fine. Day. I have my head in the clouds to talk to Ms. Page."

My smile broadens. Nope. He's not even close with that one. But bravo for trying.

"I'm in a meeting, Martha," Gran says, her hands tensely crossed.

"Right, all right. But this man, Mr. Taka-"—she looks uncertainly at the man as if trying to read the rest of his name on his face—"hashi," she continues, then gives herself a little smile to prove she's proud of herself, "says he doesn't want to move on from Ms. Page's class."

He looks confused, and Martha points at me. "That one."

His face clears and he nods.

Usually I just go by Teacher. Or Teacher Bryony.

"He claims," Martha continues, "he's not trying to get the GED. He doesn't care that he's passed the test."

"He passed the test. He must move up," Gran says.

"Right. But—"

"No matter how much *fun* he has learning from Ms. Page."

"Okay then." Martha starts to spin herself toward the door. "But?" she says shrilly after a pause, raising a finger. "You know, I do wonder—"

"He must move up—"

"Of course," she says, again swiveling back toward the hall. Then her voice does a high-pitched warble yet again and she turns. "But just, you know, in this one *very special case* with his daughter in the same class, the convenience—"

"They are *all* very special cases, as you will soon learn once you have been here longer than a month, Martha. *Everybody* wants to stay in Ms. Page's class, and if *everybody* stayed in Ms. Page's class, we'd have three thousand students in her classroom and an absolute zoo." Gran pauses, and when it's clear Martha isn't moved enough, she adds, "Which, incidentally, also means we'd have no more graduates. And with no more graduates, we'd lose our funding. And teachers' *employment*. And close our doors."

"Right, so as I was saying, Mr. Takahashi," Martha says, grabbing him by the shoulders and wheeling him around and out the door, "Mr. Platt's class at level four is a wonderful, *lively* classroom environment, where you will have your head positively bursting with fun—"

Well, that's a stretch. Mr. Platt is a sixty-five-year-old man with sleepy eyes who reads directly from the GED ESL textbook and could take a job narrating for the sloth in one of those *Zootopia* movies. But c'est la vie.

I shut the door.

Turn to Gran.

Somehow she has managed to peer down at me with her blue eyes very seriously even while being the one sitting. "Bryony, let's get to the heart of the matter quickly before we get bombarded again. I know you are the Anonymous Giver."

Ah.

So I was correct.

She knows about *that* secret.

The Anonymous Giver has a reputation at The Bridge. Suspicions and rumors and interesting tall tales have been whispered among staff for the past few years about who this mysterious person is. Personally, I like the one about one of the students being in reality a prince from a distant land, of a wealthy family but small country, who came to America with humble motivations of learning the language and using the language to build relationships with politicians and create a mutually beneficial relationship with the United States. And in his time at The Bridge, he was so impressed that he pledged to donate silently for the remainder of his life.

The story of the Anonymous Giver has been fed like sourdough starter over the years, people adding interesting "clues" to it every now and then. Mrs. Platt remembered seeing one of her students stepping into the back of a tinted vehicle. Martha found a student's registration papers with curious redacted information. I always enjoyed that particular theory.

"I know. It's a letdown, isn't it?" I say with a smile.

But to my surprise, she's *still* not smiling. I mean, she's not a *smiler* in general, but still. Nothing.

She takes a deep breath. "Sit down."

"Good grief, Gran, you're acting as if I'm in trouble."

"You're not in trouble. *Of course* you're not in trouble. But we need to talk. Privately. And I don't want this to get out."

Ah. So words that are not conducive to paper-thin walls. Got it.

My teacup rattles in the saucer as I take a seat. I set it on the desk. Give her my attention.

She leans across the desk and, in a surprising gesture, grips one of my hands. Gives it a squeeze. "I'm very . . . proud . . . and very surprised . . . to find out that you have given so generously the past two years. But the fact of the matter is, I want you to stop."

"What?" I say, startled. "No. It's fine. I *want* to."

"It's a lot of money—"

"It's *fine*," I say again. "I have the funds. I'm not scraping by, Gran, I promise—"

"—because we're going to shut our doors regardless."

The funniest sensation fills my senses. It's like all the blood has just decided to slip out of my body and go through the floors. Except for the extreme pounding of my heart. And the fact that some blood *must* be remaining in my body keeping it going.

"But . . ." I flex my fingers, then push them to my lap. "I know we've had some financial troubles. Which is why you keep going to DC searching for funds—"

"There are no funds. And the funds we have will not be renewed for the next calendar year."

"But all your traveling—"

"I've hunted, yes. I've hunted all over. But the fact is, we are in challenging economic times. Washington's eyes have cut to other pressing matters that are also important. It's all important. It seems every facet of the government is sitting around a bed, and the sheet is too short to cover everyone all at once." She presses her lips together. Exhales. "They're cutting off our funding entirely. I plan to make the announcement to staff after Thanksgiving but before the semester starts. That should give them time to find other employment by January. As for the students, they'll just have to go to Corwick starting next semester."

"*Corwick!* That's a ninety-minute drive!"

Half the students at least would drop out entirely. It's too much money, too much transportation cost, too much time.

I don't know how Madih works all night for hospice care and spends three hours each day going through classes when she has three kids at home to clothe and feed. When does she sleep? When does she spend time with her children? She couldn't just cut out another three hours of each day for a commute.

"Bryony, calm down," Gran says, looking at me fiercely. "Lower your voice."

"I'm *lowering*," I hiss, but inside my nerves are all tangled together and setting each other off. "How much more do we need?"

Gran's shaking her head. "We are past that question. I've asked myself that question the past five years. Now it's time to realize it's done and go from here."

"But how *much*?"

"Six million," she says, and the number stills me. "Six million and we still wouldn't have enough left over to fix our AC."

"But . . . but surely *something* can be done?" I say, flustered. "You've kept this to yourself. Maybe with my help we can think of—"

"You have done *enough*. Believe me, honey, if there was any other way, I would have discovered it by now. The fact is, we are going under, and the very best thing you can do for me now, as your grandmother, is to hold on to your money—which is a whole other conversation we'll have at a later time—and not waste it on a dying program." She pauses. And then her eyes soften as she continues. "Despite how much we both love The Bridge, save it. Invest it." She throws her hands up in the air. "Spend it if you will. Just do literally anything else *beside*s dropping it in this fiery furnace never to be seen again."

I stare down at my teacup. The juniper-mint tea slowly circles the cup. A little puff of steam wafts upward.

Funny how quickly bad news comes.

My entire world has been flipped upside down and the tea hasn't even lost its steam.

"Fine," I say at last. "But tell me one thing." I flip through my mental files for the right words. "What would we need," I say slowly, my voice measured, "to stay open just one more year?"

Gran squeezes her eyes shut.

Her lips press together, and I see in this moment the unspoken pain that she's feeling too.

She opens her eyes. "A miracle."

Silence settles between us.

It's the most depressing thing I've heard in my twenty-nine years of life, outside of the most awful, dreadful day of Mom's passing.

The silence breaks as my phone beeps with a text, and I look up at the little clock on Gran's desk, telling me it's five minutes to class time. I move to stand as I slip my phone out of my pocket.

It's a text from Jack.

Have you talked to her about the book tour yet?

I purse my lips. Type back. Working on it now.

Geez, the man is pushy.

The reply is instant. What are you waiting for?

A miracle, apparently, I type back and then silence my phone.

I swivel toward Gran and pick up my teacup and saucer. The wheels are spinning as I turn at the door. "Hey, Gran. For what it's worth, I'm going to try to get this place back regardless."

She dips her head. "I know you will, stubborn child."

"And as for my mysterious money-making skills . . . I'll need some time off . . . pretty much immediately."

Her brow jerks up. "Can you tell me exactly why?"

I pause. Shake my head.

"Is it . . . legal?"

To which I laugh. *No, Gran, I've run off with the Florence mafia.* "Yes."

"And you need how long?"

"Two weeks."

Her eyes become saucers. Honestly, of all the things said this morning, *this* is what has caused the most reaction from her? I suppose to some extent it makes sense. I've never taken so much time away before and never on such short notice.

"Can I tell you no?" she says.

"Do we have subs available?"

"Yes."

"Then I suppose you can." I sigh. "But I'll have to go anyway."

And for the first time, Gran looks at me like I truly am some sort of secret agent for something mysterious. No, she looks at me like she's just realized there's more to me than plain, happy-go-lucky Bryony.

And to be completely honest, it looks like I've just gained some sort of respect.

"Wherever will you be going, with your mysterious money and your mysterious plans?"

"You know, Gran," I say, opening the door, "I'm not entirely sure myself. But I can guarantee one thing: I'm going to loathe every minute of it."

CHAPTER 8

"You told her you were going to *loathe* this? You are so dramatic, Bryony. Only you could declare you would loathe *this*."

Jack sits back, leaning against one of the many large windows where behind us the cars fly past. Pretty much every single passing vehicle includes somebody pressing their face to the window, angling up for a picture of the bus with Amelia's massive face along the side.

I am sitting just where Amelia's teeth are.

Jack is sitting on her hand perched on top of a load of books. At the center of the table is a cauliflower-crust pizza left over from lunch. Apparently, our stops are not dictated by the need for gasoline but by five-star gluten-free restaurants and how quickly they can deliver boxes of goodies inside. Whether or not it turns out that the restaurant is incredibly remote and the bus ends up having to see how far it can squeeze into one-way streets before hitting a parked car.

The food is, I'll grudgingly admit, very good.

Amelia is in the back bedroom. Lying on her massive bed. In a massive robe. Wearing some glowing red light mask on her face. The mask's box declares, "This revolutionary treatment is guaranteed to take off ten years!"

Apparently the "shocking reality" of having two more people on her giant tour bus led to a migraine only red-light treatment will soothe.

But where is *my* migraine-reducing, face-smoothing red-light treatment mask? Where?

Everyone around me is busy. Penny sits in a chair by the farthest back window, her face screwed up as she painstakingly practices slow loops on sheets of paper. Calligraphy, apparently, is going to be

Penny's homework assignment now because, as Amelia put it, "Your one single task is to write things down, Penny. The least you can do is make it *pretty*. If I wanted chicken scratch, I would have hired a *chicken*."

Garrett, Amelia's publicity tour manager, sits on the other side of the aisle, arguing in panic-level mode with somebody on the phone over misplaced book orders and declaring that if "we don't have four hundred copies of *The Seven-Year Holiday* on that table by four o'clock, somebody is going to get *fired*." Possibly (probably?) him.

Electronic equipment litters the table in front of Jack: laptops, phones, some electronic planner to track all the information on his laptops and phone. Even an electric sort of candle warmer to keep his electric-looking coffee mug at a perfect 132 degrees.

Jack is a frenzy of movement, making jumps from one electronic device to another, all with a phone pressed to his ear. I haven't caught all that's going on, but from what I can gather, the book of one of his newer clients, Tess Cray, has gone to auction and three publishers are in the game, fighting for it. Even his laptop has some sort of time-bomb clock on it, ticking down. Thirteen minutes and twenty-two seconds left. Twenty-one. Twenty. He's jumping from phone call to phone call, telling publishers, "Schmidt just offered exclusive World English rights on a two-book, 200 a book. Ben, you're up. What can you do?" and "Pennington just offered 230 each for three books. Where are you?"

I sip my cold coffee and watch him with mild interest.

Every couple minutes he pauses from his mad finger tapping and phone talking to look over at me and wink.

I can't help it.

He makes me smile despite myself as I watch him living for the adrenaline of this. It's responsible gambling, that's what it is. I bet he killed everyone on the block in Monopoly as a kid. He was definitely one of those kids who owned the bank and all the properties and gleefully loaned out money and kept tabs on their growing debts just to keep the game going.

"Look at you," he says, waving a hand at my stack of books. "Cheer up."

When I got on the bus earlier, Mona gave me an overly aggressive squeeze on both shoulders and slipped a company card in my hand, saying, "Take this. Spare yourself nothing—I don't care if it's a coffee mug or a chandelier in an antique store. You're a lifesaver to us all." When I told her I was most certainly not, she said, "Look up that interview from the other night on YouTube. Just . . . look it up. *Thank you*."

I was not, ever, going to sit on Amelia's bus next to her giant face, with her real face in the other room, watching her make a fool out of herself on YouTube. But I got it.

Susanna, in true Susanna form, placed in my arms a stack of books that she stole from the ARC room at the office and said in a small, soft voice, "Farewell."

As if I was on a brave journey toward certain death.

"You have hours to read." Jack, in a pause on his call, points to my books. "You *like* reading. *Read*."

"Can't," I say with a frown.

"Then write. You say you need to write."

"Can't. I have to kill off the boys from this book." Because, according to Amelia, I can no longer include terrible small human beings who make the world go round.

"Then for goodness' sake, call your Goody Two-shoes boyfriend," Jack spits out, waving his hand in the air.

Geez. I must look *quite* broody.

Jack never goes to such lengths as to mention I actually *call* the man he's never met.

"It's three in the morning in Russia."

"Then—" Jack's interrupted by the person on the line. "Bill? Yeah. Just got your email." His eyes jump to the timer and back. "No, that's not going to be high enough. We're going in ten-thousand-dollar increments."

I take another sip of my coffee and glance around.

Yes, I do need to get to writing. I do have an AMSI (Advanced Marketing and Sales Information) Word document sitting on my laptop about my current work in progress that Susanna begged me to turn in by the end of the week. And yes, I do have a stack of papers from students I need to go over and correct.

And yes, there is a phone call to Gloria I missed.

But the thing that's been at the forefront of my mind, playing over and over again, is the conversation with Gran. More particularly, how to make that miracle happen pretty much immediately.

It's an excruciating thing, sitting on a bus worth the cost of a year of programming, working with these magic fingers and yet completely stuck as to how to make them work magic in my own life.

I glance to the countdown clock.

Three minutes and forty-five seconds left.

To my surprise, Jack is actually speeding up. Wow. I didn't know he could operate this fast. For a man who ties his bowling laces at the speed of a tortoise, he looks positively manic.

He's quite the auctioneer, isn't he? Bouncing around to publishers reminding them of what a good deal this is. Typing into spreadsheets and spouting off stats about his author.

Meanwhile, I'm the sloth in the background, taking slow sips of my first cup of coffee for the day, the one poured six hours ago, with an untouched stack of books before me.

I don't really know how he does it.

"Time's up," he says happily, shutting off the clock and dropping the back of his head against the window.

He grips my hand and gives it an excited squeeze before tapping off an email to all.

"Happy?" I say.

"Extremely." His phone call to the winning publisher is jovial, as is his phone call to his author Tess, and soon enough he's winding down the emails with a big smile on his face.

Perfect.

I've been waiting for a moment precisely like this. When he's in a good mood. And this is a top-notch one.

"All good news?" I say in a light voice. A voice peppered with little red candy sprinkles.

"*Excellent* news," he returns, snapping one of the laptops shut and slipping it into his laptop bag. He rubs his temple with one hand. "Everyone at The Foundry will be *thrilled*."

"Great." I clasp my fingers together beneath the booth table, then power on in my most prepare-to-pay-attention-to-me-because-I-am-important voice. "Jack, we need to talk."

Then I realize that was a little *too* sober, so I flash him a bright smile—keeping optimism and self-respect perfectly balanced—and add in an equally bright voice, "I have some news."

Clearly I didn't nail down the balance, because a crease forms between his brows. "What's up?"

"Well," I say in an upbeat tone, "I want to talk about my book."

The way his shoulders droop tells me everything I need to know about how seriously he's planning to take this. Already his hand starts roving toward one of his laptops. A subtle sigh laces his voice as he speaks. "No, I haven't heard from her yet, Bryony. You know how publishing takes off for the summer."

"And in a little over a month from now, they'll be taking off in preparation for Labor Day, and let's not forget that the holidays are, at that point, almost upon us, I know."

I've heard it all from him before. The whole publishing world is off for Thanksgiving. They're off through Christmas. Actually, all of December. It's icy in January. It's too hot in the summer. Fridays are just hard. You'd think from his responses publishers *never* turn on their computers.

"Right, well, I think it's time we stop using bait to try to catch one fish. No more waiting on Florence Peters. It's time we cast out the whole net."

One brow tweaks up, evidence that he disagrees. "Bryony . . ."

"Jack!" Amelia calls from the back room. "Do you have a place to put all this *luggage*? I'm tripping all over these suitcases to get to the *bathroom*."

His attention shifts to the hallway, where his three gray suitcases of various sizes rest.

There's a *swoop* sound on his computer, informing him of an incoming email. His phone buzzes with a text, vibrating on the table. "Bryony, let's talk about this later—" He pulls out of the booth to stand.

"The Bridge is planning to close end of the year," I blurt out.

He pauses.

"We have a matter of months left unless, unless something happens . . . Unless we find some kind of, of miracle . . . Gran says it's over. And I just"—I throw out my hands—"*I can't* let that happen. It *can't* happen. I have to do *something*, and this is the only possible something I've got. So *please*, Jack. Let's cast the net."

His gaze holds mine for a long moment, his hand touching the table.

His eyes soften.

"Jack! *Seriously!*" Amelia calls in the distance.

"Bryony. You wrote a book. About your grandmother and this organization. And that was sweet. Honorable to her legacy. But have you considered that this is just too big a burden for you to bear alone? That this is just *impossible* to accomplish without something, somebody, else?"

"Of course I have. But I have you. I'm not alone."

Jack's lips press together and he squeezes his eyes shut. Throws his head back with an inhale. A particular vein in his neck is pulsing quicker now.

I'm driving him crazy.

I know I do, I know.

I didn't mean to make my voice wobble at the end like that. I didn't want to give away the earnestness of how I feel about it all. In fact, I feel like I've been found in the streets wearing nothing but a sheet and it slips off, and there I am—naked. Completely vulnerable.

"Fine."

I feel his hand on mine.

And with that word it's like he's handed me a coat. Tucked it around my shoulders with one single word. *Fine*.

"I'll do what I can, Bryony."

"Right away?"

"Right away," he says, and slips his computer into his arms. "But please, do me a favor. Two."

"What?"

"Don't get your hopes up. Like I say every time, it's not easy selling a book. Particularly a speculative, quasi–magical realism, quasi–women's fiction, fifty-thousand-words-too-long one like yours. Even with you at the helm of this story."

There is no way I'm not going to get my hopes up.

This is all I *can* do now.

Hope.

"And second?" I say.

And to this he points to my computer. "Go back and edit the manuscript."

I've done that. Three thousand times. Two years ago.

I looked at those words so many times I probably have them memorized.

"How many people will you message?" I call after him. How many people does Jack Sterling know? How many contacts does he really have in the world of publishing? Dozens? Hundreds? "Will it be today?"

There's a tightness in his jaw as he grimaces. It's obvious, oh so obvious, he is doing this solely for my sake, not really because he believes in this.

He believes in *me*, I know. Just not *the story*.

What will this do to his own reputation? I wonder suddenly. Sending off for consideration a manuscript he doesn't really believe in?

Because he doesn't really. It was obvious during that first pitch session. He liked my eye for *Amelia's* story. Not my own.

"I have to do something first." He avoids a direct answer to my question, a direct ask for a worldwide outreach. "And then I'll do what I can . . . today."

"Jack!" Amelia calls. "I'm about to pitch these out the window if we can't get this cleared out!"

He slips out of view and I open my laptop, feeling a breath of relief for the first time in ages.

My mouse slips over to hover on the folder for *Water Under the Bridge*. Something in me hesitates.

It's a nauseating feeling, actually.

The old, familiar sensation of opening that folder. How many times have I opened that folder? Thousands over days. Weeks. Months. Years. And with it the rush of those old, familiar feelings that came coupled with those days, weeks, months, years of waiting for an email back from agents that never came: Longing. Hope. Embarrassment. Shame. Second-guessing.

Oh, so much second-guessing.

Even fewer people knew about my writing then.

Writing was my little plan. My little secret.

They say you never forget how to ride a bike as soon as you feel the pedals beneath your shoes. Well, right now the mouse hovering over the folder is my little jolt back in time, to a cluster of chaotic feelings I'd rather forget.

My mouse slips over to my current WIP and I click it open. Click the "Welcome Back" bubble on the side where it drops me down to the four-thousand-word mark where I was six hours ago.

I highlight the section, a painfully massive 75 percent chunk of the page. Then tap Delete. Watch the whole beautiful section of the two boys disappear. A day's worth of work. Gone in a blink.

I take a sip of my cold coffee and begin tapping, all while the wheels in my brain begin turning, working to fill the missing dominoes I just deleted to get the story from point B to point D. Shifting the point of view from two parents of two beautiful children to two parents. Single. Painstakingly slashing through meaning to give what Amelia wants.

Fluff.

Still. It's better than revisiting the old folder and old wounds.

I'll go back to it.

Edit later.

But right now, it's time to reach the masses using Amelia's mighty pen.

CHAPTER 9

It's midnight.

Running lights line the length of the bus. Amelia's room is shut, although even the roaring sound of the ocean from her sound machine can't drown out her snoring. I'm lying down on the thin mattress, fingers tangling themselves up, fidgeting with the sheets. The whole bus is silent (well, except for me). The bunk beds Jack and I lie on are directly adjacent to the small bathroom. I'm on bottom. Jack's on top. They're sailor-ship style, at least as I have imagined, only a couple inches too short and a couple inches too thin.

And I *have* been trying to sleep. I have.

But every time I turn over, I find myself on the precipice of falling to the floor.

And then there's the tiny issue of . . . it's been hours.

And nothing from Jack.

Not one tiny little thing.

We've spent the afternoon and all evening riding on this bus, side by side as he shot off emails and made phone calls and gave his pep talks while I drowned out his conversations about "12 percent audio rights" and "fifteen-thousand-copy print run" to focus on slashing through my novel. I've effectively cut the kids out of a quarter of what I'd written. It was painful, heart-wrenching success today, made only a little bit better by the fact we dined on some shepherd's pie with the most incredible bouillabaisse of my life.

So when I hear the tiny *swoop* of Jack's email now, here in the dark, I pounce.

Just as I have through every single one of his no doubt normally maddening dings and swoops. (But honestly, what sort of *villain* keeps his phone on all night long? Who in their right mind doesn't put their phone on Airplane Mode or, at the very least, on silent? Workaholic literary agents named Jack, apparently.)

"Is it about the book?"

"Oh my *gosh*, Bryony, *go to bed*," Jack whispers tersely in the dark.

"Is it?"

"I quit. I'm sorry, I just can't be your agent anymore. We're parting due to personality differences. The difference being, you are annoying and I am not."

"So it's a yes? Who was it? Did you nudge Florence too? Oh! Did you tell her you were reaching out to others—that's what pushed her, isn't it? She felt the pressure."

"Do you *realize* you are the most annoying author in the world? None of my other authors badger me like you do."

"None of your other authors share sailor beds." I kick above me. "So tell me. Who was it? Was it a yes or a no? Or a maybe? But could you push it along? Did you send the whole manuscript? Honestly, should I just take over? Hand me your phone."

I reach up like a gremlin for his exposed elbow and grab it, scrambling down his arm toward his wrist.

"*Bryony, stop it!*" he cries out, fighting to pull his body back. He wriggles away and suddenly he's gone, no doubt cramming himself up against the wall. "You little creeper," he hisses. "You're going to give me nightmares."

"*The Things Desperate Authors Do When Left with Their Agents*," I hiss back. "Thriller. Coming next March."

Somebody in the distance gives a loud stop-it-you-are-waking-us-all-up-and-we-can-all-hear-you-except-for-Amelia-in-her-bloody-castle cough.

"Is that a yes?" I whisper.

"Does it sound like it's a yes?" he whispers back. "Do you think we editors and agents like to stay up after midnight just chatting about books? We have *lives*. It could be about anything." Five seconds pass. "Huh."

I push up on my elbows, alert. "What's the 'huh' about? What's happening? It was about my book, wasn't it?"

There's a long silence.

Long enough I kick at the ceiling of my bunk.

"This is *Amelia's bus*," he hisses below.

"Is it?"

"Yes."

"Yes, what? Yes, that was about my book?"

"Yes."

I purse my lips. Push myself as close as I can get to sitting. "And?"

"It's not the answer I wanted."

Someone passed.

My head drops back onto the pillow. It's the phrase they all give. Every last one of them.

A generic "I'm sorry, but unfortunately, we're going to have to pass" statement. And I ask, who? And why exactly do they *have* to? Why don't you just sneak this one through the doors, huh? Let it become a raving success and you can say, "See? No harm, no foul."

Several minutes go by and I stare at the top bunk, eyes peeled open.

My own phone has dinged over a dozen times today, students missing me in class, Gloria asking for updates. Like the rumor mill at The Bridge, word has picked up that I'll be out for a couple weeks and has morphed itself into a widespread rumor that I'm deeply ill. With pneumonia *and* strep simultaneously no less.

In the span of the day, my phone has become littered with messages from students recommending everything from rubbing my feet with onions and wrapping them in warm cloths (made of linen, not cotton) to cold showers and ice baths to reduce inflammation, to hot showers and hot tea to open the airways and release the phlegm. I have with grateful heart turned away offers of two homemade tinctures made from Icelandic and lemme sea moss, three actually very delicious-sounding soups, two loaves of rosemary bread, and a little homemade essential oil mixture of wild bark, frankincense, and myrrh.

Even Phuong offered to bring me a fresh meal. Phuong, whose apartment I wandered into once when I gave her a lift home and discovered she currently had no electricity.

All these extremely thoughtful well-wishes for my recovery today fill me up more than usual with a heavy, achy heart. Painful reminders of the world that is so big and so unbalanced.

I stare at the ceiling, thinking of them. Of Gran, who's back on the road despite her dire warning to me, quietly revealing how hopeful she'll be to the end. She put up a big talk about giving up, and yet not twenty-four hours later, Gloria told me Gran—at the age of seventy-six—was driving through the night to scout an opportunity in DC.

Thoughts stir like a pot of soup inside me, piping hot and unable to settle to a simmer. I can't sleep. I feel like I downed two shots of espresso, and now everything is whirring within me, my internal body humming with the humming of the bus as it drifts along the interstate. And yet, I have to. We have three events I'll be tugged along to like a rag doll during this forced "luxury vacation."

I'll be up in less than six hours. And if I'm lucky, on this thin mattress, I'll get four.

I force my eyes shut.

Take in a steadying breath.

Face the wall.

Wait as five minutes pass in quiet.

Ten.

And there's a small part of my mind that has started to wander. My thoughts are starting to swirl a little. Realism detaching from itself and starting to waltz into a space where dreams take hold. Gran, for starters, is wearing pajamas. While she stands on a box outside the Washington Monument, shouting for attention about The Bridge.

But then a voice speaks in my periphery that draws me out—a voice I admit lingers in my dreams probably more than it should—and my eyes flutter open.

When I see Jack, seated in the booth we spent the day in, adrenaline knocks the dream right out of me. I close my eyes quickly.

"Yes, but things have changed. I just feel we're at a point where it would be unfair to—"

Jack's voice is blocked out by the hum of a passing truck. I crane my ears to catch more words but hear only, "Yes, but Bryony doesn't care about that—"

Slowly, painfully slowly, I inch my neck toward him.

What is he talking about?

Who is he talking to? About *me*. At this time of night?

For the man who claims he's not a workaholic, it's half past midnight and here he is, whispering. Is it the editor he emailed with before?

It has to be.

But of course it has to be.

And yet? I lift open one tiny sliver of my left eyelid to see him again. He's facing me. More than that, his eyes are directly on me. Obviously thinking ahead as always. Making sure I'm asleep.

Jack's arms are pressed tightly over his chest. He looks so stiff his biceps are bulging, which, to be quite honest, isn't the natural look for bookish Jack who is more prone to picking up organic sheep cheese to pair with some wine from the nearby French market than any kind of actual weight. A permanent frown rests on his face as he stares down in the general direction of the table.

It gives me an uneasy feeling.

Everything about this moment does.

"I know it's late. But I'm on this forsaken bus—no, I know Amelia didn't want me to come. I came for Bryony—"

My sake?

He didn't *have* to come?

The liar.

"No, it's not like *that*— Well, she's going to try to eat her alive. Don't you *think* somebody should be here to protect her? I get that, but Bryony deserves her own— No, of course she's grateful—" He drops his voice even further as he leans forward, resting his elbow on the table and dipping his head down to protect his voice even more.

There's no way to catch whatever he's saying now. All I can go off is the tone of his voice before he dropped his head. Meek. Pleading. Desperate, even, knowing he's not getting his way.

And what exactly is his way?

I crane my ears for ten more fruitless minutes until he eventually clicks off the phone. He stays in the same position for some time, head facing the laminate tabletop of the booth, hand rubbing his temple. His shoulders are hunched. And I have a momentary temptation to get up with a smile, put my hands on my hips, and say, "Okay, *buddy*, what the heck is going on?"

But I don't.

Some feeling deep down is hushing me. Stilling me.

Telling me to wait. Watch. See what I can learn in this quiet.

Stay within the camouflage of these woods, behind these bushes, before giving up and presenting myself to hear whatever information he'll give.

Because Jack does have a secret.

A few, it seems.

And I don't know anything yet about them.

I just know they are about me.

· · ·

I dream I am back at The Bridge.

People are on the other side of the doors. A mob of angry people rolling impossibly large metal cans, crowding the doors, standing on one another to get in. Yelling. Screaming. Lighting things on fire.

Jack's blocking the doors. He's wearing a gray suit, and yet it's ripped in multiple places, exposing skin at the wrists, legs. And for all his useless efforts, I stand in the crowd and feel something there, looking at him, that I've never quite felt before.

Never allowed myself to feel before.

Never in all my waking hours.

A swell of pride in him, in who he is.

My heart leaping out of my chest at this man who puts up a good front with all his luxury watches and colorful macarons but in reality is standing in the gap, holding on to the building.

He's fighting for this, for me, and it's all useless. The crowds are swelling, the building begins to take hits, bricks begin to crumble and fall. And still he stands there.

There's a flash of white as a towering column falls to the ground beside him, and with legs like cement I yank myself desperately forward. It's hard, as dreams are, but eventually I reach him. Feel the quick relief of grabbing him by the arms. Pulling with all my might. "Come on, Jack! We've got to go!"

And I tug and I tug, but he won't move. He's rooted to the spot, urging people to turn back, to save the building.

I scream and scream and yank and yank, but he's like a statue, my efforts useless to move him even an inch.

He won't look at me. He doesn't even hear me.

Does he even know I'm here?

"Come on, Jack! Leave it, *please*!"

Another column falls around us. An explosion hits the side of the building and a window crashes in.

And then I do something in a flash. The most illogical urge known to man.

I kiss him.

Press my arms tight around his shoulders, his tattered suit shirt, and kiss him with all my might.

And it's . . . time-stopping. The hammering in my chest, my heart slamming with adrenaline as I hold him for dear life while columns crumble around us.

So earthshaking, so electrifying, that I jolt awake, my eyes bursting open to stare into the darkness above me.

My ears pulse even as I lie motionless, my heart still pounding.

And then I jolt, seeing Jack off his bunk bed and beside me, his hand giving my shoulder a shake. His face hovering beside me, so close I can see the bristles of his five o'clock shadow on his chin. Jack's eyes glint with pure concern in the dim running lights.

I must've been making noises in my sleep. Clearly he's been trying to shake me awake, maybe even causing the earthquake in my dream.

"You good?" his voice whispers huskily beside me.

"Yeah . . . Yeah," I repeat, but the words are slow. Forced from my mouth. I want him to stay, I realize. I want to linger in this moment. The bus is quiet but for the hum of the tires rolling on into the empty interstate ahead.

He seems to feel the same way, because he doesn't move.

Stays.

Looking into my eyes.

I swallow. Force a little laugh. "I didn't say anything out loud, did I?"

And at this a tiny smile twists up one side of his lips. He inches closer, ratcheting up my heart rate. "Why? Any secrets you trying to keep?"

I say nothing but just look at him, temporarily seized by an inability to think. To be clever. To do anything beyond look at him with a confusing and overwhelming amount of emotion in this moment. He *was* in my dream. And while the picture of him is fading, the feelings remain. Intense feelings. *For him.*

After a few more seconds he blinks and pulls back. Grins and—meaning to or not, I don't know—drifts his fingers over my hair as he moves to standing. "Don't worry, Bryony. You didn't say anything. At least, nothing I didn't know already."

And suddenly he's gone, pulling himself back up to the top bunk, his bare feet the last thing to slip out of view.

"Sweet dreams," he whispers in the darkness. "Kick me if you need more saving."

I wind myself tightly into my blanket and roll over, the haze of this bizarre night lingering all around as thick as the Deep South's humidity blowing through the vents. And sleep.

CHAPTER 10

"What are you doing?" Jack says.

"Nothing."

The bus is one giant top of a flashlight, sun streaming in from both sides in the 8:00 a.m. light. The whole bus is awake, has been awake since six thirty, actually. I bleakly remember hearing an alarm go off in Amelia's room somewhere around five. Penny is out somewhere, tasked with coming back with gluten-free, sugar-free, fat-free organic pastries homemade in the Himalayas and brought by donkey here to Seaside, Florida. Garrett is off racing around town in panic mode because apparently they are still more than fifty copies short, and the first event of the day starts in two hours. The bus driver, Trina, whom I've become quite fond of after a happy little discussion in regard to her short-haired terrier, is nowhere to be seen. If I had to guess, she dropped herself into the PetSmart store I spy across the parking lot. Amelia threw herself into the only tiny bathroom in the place with two armloads of hair appliances an hour ago, and we haven't seen her since.

Which is fine.

I have to go to the bathroom desperately and I'm in my pajama pants, but I'm fine.

Fine.

I flip my phone over while my knees knock against each other, bouncing beneath the side table. I'm twisted up like a pretzel in the booth seat, trying to relieve myself from the reminder that I desperately need to relieve myself by flying through tabs on my browser.

Jack and I have both been dodgy this morning. Our eyes glued to anything but each other as we woke up inches from each other, sat in the booth inches from each other. As Jack slipped me a coffee word-lessly, inches from each other. As we both pulled out our phones and computers quietly, inches from each other.

He looks guilty, to be honest.

As he should, I suppose.

I have no clue what he was on about last night, but whatever it was was about me. And he isn't telling me. He's actually keeping a *secret* from me. Possibly to protect me? Although from what, I can't imagine.

And as for me, well, I had almost forgotten the dream, but then I saw his face. And those bookish biceps beneath his gray T-shirt as he slipped off the top bunk that weren't so *entirely* unappealing. And those green eyes cutting to mine as our gazes met.

And then that dreamlike feeling came back in a whoosh. A strong gust of wind that whipped through my bones and flipped me upside down.

A powerful, tantalizing whoosh.

I have come to a realization: This is all because we are stuck on this bus together. People who are stranded on deserted islands are *bound* to end up together; it's just what happens. And Amelia's bus is my proverbial island. If it wasn't him, it would be fifty-three-year-old stressed-out Garrett.

I just can't take something like that seriously. I can't take *anything* about my life too seriously right now. I'm stressed. And I am annoyed, yes, that Parker told me last week that he potentially won't be coming home for a visit until Thanksgiving at the earliest. Long-distance re-lationships are never easy in the short term, and here we are halfway through year two with no end in sight.

So I am making a decision and the decision is simple: When in an extenuating circumstance such as this one, with temptations out of the norm, I just need to be particularly vigilant to stay the course. Stick to the reality of the situation: As of right now I have a *boyfriend*, and I have absolutely no intention of ruining *anything* I have going with my *agent*.

Sure, somehow in there the waters have become a little murky, and I suppose I've done that to myself with all the dinners, the bowling, and the phone calls, but that's just because I have a giant hole in my life under the label of "boyfriend filler," and without Parker around I have let convenience win and had Jack fill it. I can't help it. He is *always* around.

I mean, that's what agents do after all; they are always in every facet of their authors' lives.

I gulp, realizing even as I think it how absolutely, universally untrue that statement is.

I can't even lie to myself in my head.

Fine.

That's it then.

In situations of unusual temptation, such as sleeping approximately three feet under your male friend you start having dreams about, you need to do the extreme.

And that means, in this case, messaging Parker my plan at 1:00 a.m. his time.

Which, as I learn five brisk minutes later, Parker is not super in favor of.

No don't do that yet.

I flip back to the two tabs on my computer and begin to type. I just see there's this deal on the airline tickets right now. I could get to Auckland with only three layovers, but it'll get me to you at your 4am.

Bryony, let's talk about this later.

I take another sip of my coffee—my third cup of the day. Right, but the deal is not going to last. You know how it is with tracking and browsers. I'm thinking I should go ahead and grab tickets now. Could you get off that week? August 4-10?

I press Send and before I get an answer add: Actually, don't worry if you can't. I'll just work during the day solo, maybe sightsee a bit if I need to. It's totally fine if you can't! This would be great!

I press Send again and wait. Actually, force myself to wait. Force my hands to stay still by clutching my coffee mug like a lifeline.

"Bryony." Jack's voice is cautionary. I steal my eyes toward him for just a moment. They're too green. Too concerned. Too intensely looking into mine as if to figure out what's going on. Too much like that vision I'm finding myself uncomfortably clinging to during that walls-down kiss. "What's going on?" he says.

I force my eyes back toward the screen. Toward *Parker*. My loving and devoted, if painfully distant the past two years, boyfriend.

I know it's late, I add. Sorry. You're sleeping I know. I just saw this deal and wanted to tackle it. Finally do something. Finally get a flight on the books. It's been too long.

Ridiculously long.

How it is possible to be apart from each other *this long* and still be together is somewhat mind-blowing. But every time it seems that I'm free, he isn't. And every time I find out I'm free, he isn't.

Wait, I said that twice. It's supposed to be the other way around.

I know it *looks* bad, but the reality is, the organization he's with pays him less than I make teaching, and it takes a lot more than what I make teaching to casually book a flight from Auckland, Russia, to JFK. Even his parents haven't seen him except via laptop screen for holidays. But his work is vital to the area. His patience in teaching in a not-particularly-warm climate admirable.

And I'm just keen to tell him so.

In person.

"You look like you're a horse-betting addict waiting on results."

I ignore Jack's painfully true remark and continue staring at my screen.

Even his voice sounds more . . . more rugged and handsome this morning.

I tap on Pandora.

My patented classic *Vince Guaraldi Trio* instrumental album blasts from my cell phone, faithful and true.

He rolls his head back. "*Bryony*, can we please play *anything* besides the same playlist you played the last thirty times yesterday?"

"It's soothing," I remark, not looking up.

"It's insanity. What about . . . oh, I don't know . . . anything else?"

"Peanuts music is my muse. Charlie Brown is my muse."

"Make something else your muse. Make me your muse."

His cheeky comment jolts through me, though. I can practically hear my overcaffeinated heartbeat coming to a screeching halt as I look at him.

He's so taken aback by whatever face I give him that he laughs and gives a careless wave. "Fine. Keep your music. Far be it from me to deny you women what you want."

Ex . . . ex . . . excuse me? Has he *always* done this?

I down the contents of my mug and all but growl and stand. Well, stand and bounce a little from one foot to the other. I *really* need Amelia to get out of the bathroom. "Who wants another?" I start toward the coffee machine.

"Halt, Prancer," he says, and before I know it, he's snatched the mug right out of my hand.

"I need coffee."

"Are you always this—"

"What?" I challenge.

"This growly in the morning? The real you. Bryony, the little angry prancing reindeer with a caffeination problem."

He looks amused with me.

No, worse, he's sitting back in his seat, looking up at me with his arms crossed around his very flattering chest, admiring me. Like I'm *cute*.

In my pajamas.

With my hair done up in a side bun that has more than a few hairs spiking out in all directions. (I can feel it. I cannot *look* because that requires a mirror, and the mirror is inside the bathroom Amelia refuses to open.)

Some people are actually cute when they wake up. My roommate in college, for one. Penny, who crept out of bed somewhere around four in the morning to freshen up whom I got a view of as she slipped off the bus, her bronze curls bouncing and gorgeously waving back at me, for another.

I am under no delusion being morning cute is any trait of mine.

No. I'm just a tired, angry, desperate-to-go-to-the-bathroom, very confused woman who is now having dreams about my coworker/boss/agent/undiscussed-and-never-stated-but-quietly-understood best friend. While trying to get my two-year long-distance boyfriend I've just woken up to agree to let me fly across the world on a whim to see him.

Honestly, it's not *that hard* to say yes.

I wasn't asleep.

Oh.

My brows furrow as I take in the text. My hopping side to side stops.

"What?" Jack says. "Lose your bid?"

"I . . . I don't know."

If he wasn't asleep, if that wasn't the reason he was so hesitant to get with it at this moment, to snatch up the phone and say, *Why yes, absolutely, please, Bryony, come! Come at last!* If that wasn't the hiccup right now . . . if it wasn't him jumping up, looking through his calendar trying to make sure we can get a trip finally tied up, then . . . then what was it?

What was the cause of his hesitation?

Who was the cause of his hesitation?

And then, just as I'm trying to get my thoughts to organize themselves nicely so I can properly address them, his second text comes through. We need to talk.

I feel Jack beside me at some point, the touch of his arm against mine as we stand in the little walkway of the little living room of the bus. He's eavesdropping. Rather, eyedropping. Reading the message on my phone without care or hesitation. And I let him.

I'm too stunned, really.

No, not stunned, I suppose.

A curious feeling is coming over me. Adrenaline peeking through as I feel myself settling into a new reality. We're breaking up, aren't we?

We're breaking up.

The rope that we had been clinging to as we stepped farther and farther apart is so long now it's weak, the center so far from where I now stand that I didn't even feel it breaking in two and dropping to the ground.

This is what's happening, isn't it?

And sure enough, my phone rings. Parker's name and face—a big smiling face pressed cheek to cheek to mine over a bowl of tonkotsu ramen on one of our earliest dates—comes on-screen.

I look to Jack. "I . . . have to take this."

Jack's face is equally surprised by the round of things going on as well. His brows are screwed up. He's put his hands on his hips. His eyes are soft. Concerned for me in this moment.

Only concern there.

Just . . . concern.

I wheel toward the back of the bus with my phone but spy only a closed door to Amelia's bedroom, a closed door to the bathroom that is currently occupied, and a bunk bed. No place that will give me privacy. I wheel around, facing the front of the bus. I'm going to have to go outside. To stand in the parking lot in my pajamas on the side of the interstate next to an outdoor shopping mall. Where cars slow down every few seconds to stop beside the bus and take selfies.

"Here . . . I need"—Jack scoops up his laptop—"to stretch my legs. You stay here." He pauses at the door of the bus. Turns back awkwardly. "Want me to pick you up anything? They have a nice"—he scans the rows of strip mall signs—"Dick's Sporting Goods."

Yes, that's exactly what I need right now.

A volleyball.

"I'm . . . good." The breath is starting to expel from my chest. My head is starting to feel . . . fizzy.

The doors shut on Jack and I spin around to check the bathroom once more and answer with a tentative and semi-inquisitive, "Hello?" The kind of hello one gives when they step inside an abandoned house and wonder if somebody is living in the attic and might reply.

"Hey, Bryony," he says, and I hear it right then in his voice.

The sound of an era coming to an end.

• • •

The conversation went entirely as I'd feared.

No, *fear* isn't the right word, is it?

More like . . . well, I suppose I can't explain it. A jumble of emotions were mixed in there, as with most big things in life. There was some sadness as we spoke, a hole as I heard him speak to me just as he had for hundreds of days. A moment of silence to honor the good times we had, both of us knowing the sincerity of it. How we shared and will forever share in those memories. My first glimpse of him when he was hired to teach the level below mine. Our first conversations. Our first hopes. Our first flirtations. Our first date, followed swiftly by more dates. They were good, those times. Cherry on top of a cherry cupcake good. And to think of those moments and those moments alone would be enough to break me.

But for the anger.

The confession that he wasn't quite so honest about his delays in coming home to visit. About Katia. About the woman he'd been seeing, oh, roughly the last six months behind my back.

And I could remain civil through that, almost entirely, *except* for the moment he used Jack as an excuse for his behavior. The moment he tried to announce his innocence by saying, "And it wasn't like I'm entirely alone in this, Bryony. You have Jack."

"Jack is my *friend*! And Jack has *never*, not *once*, done anything below board!" I cried out, a flare of anger that he *dared* compare a person who I happened to kiss *once*, in a *dream*, as anything *remotely* the same as one you are *actually* kissing behind your girlfriend's back.

And really, what is a dream? I've had entire dreams devoted to me panicking because I discovered I had a third leg and there were no stores that had the right pants for three legs. Does it mean *anything*? No, it just means I ate something weird before falling asleep.

And then, when the call was done and I pressed the red button, there was shock.

A gaping hole in my heart.

In my life.

And the realization that suddenly I was single. Entirely single.

Which brought a new bundle of emotions buzzing inside me.

I look out the window to see Jack walking across the parking lot, walking with purpose. There's a little baggie in his hand—smaller than a volleyball.

I take a couple steps toward the window and watch him from my private view through a tinted window as he stands at the bottom of the bus when he gets to the door.

He stops.

Then moves alongside the bus.

Pacing.

Slowly.

Back and forth with the little baggie swinging from his side.

Not on the phone, but deep in thought.

Kicking a little asphalt pebble as he pushes his hands into his pockets, his laptop still under his arm at his side.

What's he doing?

Is he . . . waiting for me to finish?

I stand there for some time, watching him, wondering. Exactly how long does he plan to pace around?

His phone rings and to my surprise he doesn't even answer it.

He turns it to silent.

Keeps pacing.

His hand moves to the back of his neck and he rubs it, continues walking.

I ignore the flutter in my stomach, ignore the whisper of what he's thinking of, daring myself not to think about it because, of course, *it cannot be true*. It just can't. Gloria's gotten into my head is all. This is what happens when you have a sister filling your head with the same narrative over and over.

At last I push the door open. Drop down the steps onto the sidewalk. "Hey."

He jolts up, and I see him move hastily from his lackadaisical walking, doubling his steps to get to me. Suddenly looking like he was doing something terribly important. "Hey."

And it's funny, his tone is the exact one I used but half an hour ago with Parker. It's funny enough I find myself smiling. Throw my hands out. Drop them again at my side.

"You know what's always surprised me?" I say. "You can spend a million hours filling up a suitcase—all the days and weeks and months and years carefully picking out the blouses and organizing neatly your set of toiletries and lining up your shoes. All that time and preparation. But it only takes a second to snap the suitcase shut and toss it into the ocean."

"Well, I think you should probably get a better organizing system if it takes that long."

"Shut up, it's my analogy. What's in the bag?"

"Oh," he says, as if remembering what he's holding. "Nothing much. I just saw it in passing when I dropped by the CVS and remembered you were out. Here." He holds out the little plastic bag. It dangles lightly from his hand.

I take it.

Open it up.

It's a little package of pens. The little five-dollar six-pack bundle of white ones I really like. The ones that write so smoothly. The ones he's seen in my little disaster of a junk drawer beside my refrigerator on Friendsgiving Day when hunting for a lighter for the candles. The ones I keep in the bun in my hair sometimes when I'm in the middle of teaching. The ones that always end up on the floorboards of my little car and roll around beside the takeaway bags when Jack gets inside with his knees hitting the dashboard and says for the millionth time, "I hate this car."

And it's ridiculous, but I feel myself tearing up a little, clutching the little bag. "Thank you," I say, with a little warble in my throat.

And then I reach in and hug him.

In my pajamas.

In front of, yes, probably some random Amelia-obsessed photo takers.

So tightly there's a possibility I heard one of his ribs crack.

"It was nothing," he says with a surprised laugh. "I mean, literally. Nothing. You just went on about that other pen yesterday and—"

I squeeze tighter, because he says all the right things. Always does.

"Bryony, you're cutting off my oxygen," he chokes out.

But even in that moment, I feel him sinking into the hug. Not peeling me off but tentatively lifting up his arms. Wrapping them around my rib cage. His hand resting ever so tenderly on my shoulder. Resting his cheek against my very unwashed, very tangled hair.

I don't know if I'll ever speak to Parker again. Or see him. And he was wrong, so very wrong, about so many things.

But he was right, to a degree, about one thing: I always have had Jack.

CHAPTER 11

Penny needs a new job. That's all there is to it.

Nobody deserves to be doing this.

I have spent the past three of the last six hours wearing an earpiece to send subtle voice messages to Amelia all while serving as a human tray, holding random items as Amelia hands them off to me because, as she says, "I can do a better job if you're close." Always without looking. Always with some big, flashy smile through massive glossy pink lips. Always in near hysterics of giggles with some mob of fans as she laughs like they are children at a sleepover sharing great big jokey secrets over extremely insignificant things. Laughing together over a comment she made about the rain. Laughing together over a joke about spilling bottled water (after which somebody dropped a pack of napkins in my hands—I'm currently cleaning it up, on hands and knees, while she carries on).

I have saved her butt twice so far. Once when she started to go down a terrible road of saying that Roman's interference with his daughter was *unintentional* (massive "no" eyes from me there, followed swiftly by a corrective snap through my earpiece) and once when she started to say there was no meaning in the baseball cards. (Of course there is meaning in the baseball cards! The baseball cards are *everything*!)

Oh, and then once when she said she would be interested in writing a spin-off from Daniel's story in *A Room for Rose*.

Absolutely.

Not.

I will not be revisiting that story again.

I can see why she loves going on these tours. It's just one massive group of fans swooning over her every smile and begging for autographs.

She's the ... the Narges Mohammadi of Nobel Peace Prize laureates. The head of the debate team at the state competition. The Taylor Swift of the book world.

And it's all jokes and champagne and frosted cookies in the shapes of books until three-quarters of the way through the event in Seaside, Florida, when things fall on Amelia's head.

"No, I'm—I'm sorry." The girl is speaking at the front of a long line during the Q&A.

The girl clasps her hands in front of her awkwardly.

"I just, you know," she continues, fumbling for words. "It's just, I'm an aspirational writer myself, and I've been told how writers grow as they write, so, I mean"—she casts her eyes desperately around for fellow comrades, causing everyone to stare down at the books in their laps—"I just thought it was really interesting in the class I took, where we compared your first and latest novel, and how you've grown as a writer—"

Oh, the pain.

I drop another paper napkin on the floor. One of the flimsy napkins I was handed when the bottle was tipped over. Which are absolutely useless for soaking up even a teaspoon of water.

"—from your character depth—" she continues.

I wince as I drop another napkin on the puddle. It disintegrates immediately.

"—your subplots. Actually, *Party Girls in the USA* didn't seem to have a subplot at all."

I drop a couple more. Somebody stop this poor word-vomiting woman.

"I just, I mean, it's obvious"—she throws a hand out wide—"*The Seven-Year Holiday* is just worlds above. I mean, *Party Girls in the USA* was fine, but when you really look at them side by side ... clearly your talent has grown exponentially. So would you say, maybe, you have some tips for the rest of us? You know, maybe just . . . some insight"—she gives a strangled laugh—"into what you'd recommend to skip the *Party Girl* stage of writing and get straight to *The Seven-Year Holiday*? For us newbies?"

The room is entirely silent. The woman herself looks like a blueberry, her cheeks so inflamed and swollen it looks like she's about to cry pink tears of humiliation and stress. She clutches the lanyard she has on over her shirt with about thirty book-related pins tacked on. Her skirt, featuring colorful watercolor books, quakes at her knees.

I drop the rest of the napkins on the floor, move them around a little, and scoop the whole soggy mess in my arms. It's time to get off this stage before I jump in to relieve this poor, panicked soul.

I step off to the sanctuary of the side of the stage, dump the load of napkins in the bin, and give Jack a look that screams a sarcastic, "*Isn't it just so wonderful I was here to pick that up?*"

But his eyes are glued to his phone. He looks lost in thought with brows furrowed as he scans something on his phone and hastily begins typing a response.

His phone rings and he picks up as he's wheeling himself toward the outside doors. "Hey. Well, I know I'm annoying you, but I wanted to finish the conversation—"

I belatedly realize that the room is *still* silent as I turn back to the scene before me.

There is Amelia, looking at the woman with that vulture-on-a-branch-waiting-for-you-to-die expression. I've seen that look on her plenty of times. Behind closed doors. Away from the public.

But here?

I take a deep breath, feeling both anguish for the woman but also a sense of justice. "*See?!*" I want to cry as I throw out my arms. "*See who she really is?*"

But then, like a pebble dropped into a pond, there is a ripple of movement and Amelia's face clears. She smiles. Nods, as though she knows and agrees with exactly what the woman was trying to say.

"What tip would I give to help you"—her voice wobbles almost indiscernibly—"*skip* the *Party Girl* stage and go straight on to the good stuff? Well, that's a good question. And if I told you, I suppose I'd have to kill you."

She starts laughing, a high, utterly innocent laugh, and the room joins in because what could possibly be more delightful than your favorite author pretending to be mad and then pronouncing murder on anyone who dares to compete with her?

"No, no, but in all seriousness," she adds, not sounding remotely serious as she raises her champagne, "hire a ghostwriter."

She continues to laugh. They continue to laugh with her.

"They're a dime a dozen." She breaks off to continue with more laughter and takes a long sip of her champagne with a smile. The tension in the room has exploded like a popped balloon, the audience members even happier than before at this comedian who isn't just brilliant with her writing but can joke.

But as she lowers her glass, in the midst of a distracted hum of conversation around the room, her blue eyes lock on the woman with the lanyard. And between the two of them, a little silent signal is passed as Amelia's smile slips from her face. A tweak of her lips. A look that somehow says, "*But seriously, mess with me, and I'll make your life a living nightmare.*"

The woman's face goes white as a sheet and she turns, gathers up her purse and books, and rushes out the door.

And then Amelia does something that surprises me. Her eyes slither my way and she smiles. She knows. Knows I alone was watching the interaction all along.

Wordlessly she raises her glass as if to say, "*Well? It's empty. Do something about it.*"

My nostrils flare.

And *nobody* sees it. *Nobody* sees the extent of her evil like this, those little manipulations that would scare the living daylights out of psychologists in their easy chairs. She's just stringing me along. Getting her vengeance for that woman's comment. Trying to push me back in my place.

And ruffling my feathers without having to so much as say a word.

Penny looks at me with a frantic look of *"Are you going to fill it? Somebody needs to fill it!"*

The overeager bookstore owner is now looking at me, a little frown forming a crease between her brows as if to say, *"What is this PA doing? Stop just standing there and fill it!"*

I take a step forward, my chest pinched tight as I bring the bottle over, pour the champagne in.

Yes. Here I am.

Another person moves to the front of the queue and asks her what the inspiration for the book was, and several people subtly roll their eyes at the unoriginal question. It seems that there is some sort of game going on at these events. People are racking their brains to get in line, feeling some sort of group pressure to make their question unique. Witty. Memorable. Proving how well-read they are by making it painfully intricate and well-researched. Cross-referencing multiple books. I don't know if this is some new trend or has been this way all along, but more than one person in line has their book flipped open to a page and roughly a hundred rainbow-colored tabs highlighting pages. They come *prepared*.

I'm starting to see why I was prompted to come along.

"And so, when you referenced the eighteenth-century word *hibernacle* on page 220, were you referring symbolically to a winter retreat with regard to Harriet's soul needing refuge after the losses in her life and emotional meandering, or were you speaking more specifically about the haven she's discovered at the Magnolia Bookstore and she and Nate's yearly meetups?"

I swivel round. Take a few steps backward into the dark protection of the staff hallway behind me where I was strategically set up. With one raised finger I tap the back of the earpiece as I face the stack of cardboard boxes spilling over with books.

Actually, the answer is: It was neither. I referenced hibernacle because I came across it on a defunct-word-of-the-day calendar Gran gave me for Christmas, and I liked it enough to slip it in. If I *had* to pick an answer from the two choices, however, I'd go with Magnolia Bookstore and Nate being a haven for Harriet. One could easily make a case for it.

And I *should* go on and make a case for it, I suppose as I look down at the dozens of copies of a political book release from an open box, a black-and-white photo of a man smiling a little too brightly up at me with his arms crossed over his chest. I *should* use the earpiece and feed this heartfelt answer to Amelia as I stare at this lovely cerulean-colored wall right in front of me. And this champagne glass in my hand that I've just picked up.

But wouldn't you know it, this book looks *fascinating*.

I pull out a copy. Swivel around. Take a sip of my champagne.

Amelia, from her seat just ahead, shifts a meaningful glance my way. "Oh. You know, I *love* that question."

I flip the page.

Take another sip.

"I'd have to say . . . ," Amelia begins, fluttering her exceedingly long lashes toward the ceiling as though thinking deeply.

Another painfully long span of seconds elapses, and then I look up.

Our eyes meet.

I smile.

Flip the page.

And raise my champagne glass her way.

CHAPTER 12

"Bryony, you *cannot* go around *trying* to irritate Amelia. She's irritated enough by life as it is."

"All I did was get lost in a book on this 'luxury' getaway I was promised. What is possibly wrong with reading? I'm an *author*. It's a universal vice of ours. We can't withstand the temptation of good literature."

"It was a nonfiction book about reducing the corporate tax rate from 21 to 15 percent."

It took one look at Amelia's screwed-up face onstage, then one look to me standing there in the corner with a smile on my face, before Jack was grabbing my hand and steering me out the door.

It's a welcome change.

The view of the ocean opposite the strip of rainbow-colored shops is perfection in a shot. Tanned children racing along piping-hot white sand, giggling with boogie boards in hand. The sea a bright blue-green aquarium of colors. My face immediately warmed by the sun and the wet, salty sea air.

Even Jack's hand, still holding on to mine, seems to fit inside this moment.

The pressure and intentionality as he holds it clasped protectively, all while eyeing the inside of the store in distraction.

I clasp my champagne glass and fight a little rise in my stomach. I find myself unwilling to be the first to let go.

What is wrong with me?

What in the been-single-a-sum-total-of-four-hours is wrong with me?

That's a very good question to ask.

Later.

Jack turns his attention back to me when we're out of sight and then swivels me around to face him, looking down at me like I'm his misbehaving puppy.

He looks down at our entwined hands.

And for one long, deep moment says nothing. Does . . . nothing.

Just stands there with me on this wind-beaten shopping board-walk as we listen to the sound of waves and children, holding on to each other in a moment of surprise.

"Let's . . . take a walk." Jack's voice is different than it was a moment ago. He begins to walk and slowly lets go of my hand. He takes a few more steps. Stuffs his own hand into his pocket. "Bryony, I can't protect you if you *try* to sabotage Amelia."

"I wasn't *trying*. Okay, fine, I was just a tiny bit. But she *looked* at this poor woman," I say accusingly.

There's a pause.

"And . . . ?"

"She did that *look* of hers! That evil look!" I cry out. "You know the one."

"Look. I know she can be—"

"—a cold-blooded, man-eating dragon—"

"—but she—"

"—makes you loads of money with her schemes—"

"—and I—"

"—don't want to have to start wearing off-brand Polo—"

"Stop." His fingers are on my lips to shush me. The touch is elec-tric. "No," he says softly. "What I'm trying to say is, I know she can be impossible to deal with, but she has afforded you an opportunity to do something about something you love, and I refuse to let you lose it."

My heart has stopped.

My brain, stopped.

I'm suddenly stuck in this moment, this seagull-overhead, sea-breeze-all-around, surreal moment.

"So can you please do me a favor and try to step back to see the forest *and* the trees here? I'm only watching out for you."

I press my lips together, unable to break myself away from his fingers on my lips and the intensity of his gaze.

"Well." I clear my throat. "Well," I say again. "You are good at your job, aren't you? Is this how you win over all your clients?"

His eyes twinkle. "Why do you think old Mrs. Hastings has stayed with me so long?"

We share a grin.

But it's different now. Oh *gosh*, is this what Parker was referring to? Have we been *like this* all along?

Gloria's words are splashing around me now. Parker's. But I never *did* anything about it. I still *haven't*, and that *counts*.

Not to mention, there are stakes here. Jack may not feel this way about me at all. In fact, I remember with a mental thud, he doesn't, of course. There's Claire.

Or is it Chloe?

Whatever. There's Claire/Chloe.

We turn back around, make it until we are in sight of the bookshop, and stop again.

Jack turns to me. "I know things are . . . tough right now. In lots of ways. We're heading to the Keys tonight. But how about we stop in town and I take you out? Just . . . you and me. To get your mind off things."

Is he asking me out?

Out out?

And am I okay . . . actually, quite fine . . . with him asking me out?

"Do you think . . . Claire would mind?" I venture. "Or . . . I mean . . . Chloe?"

He lets out a noiseless exhale of a laugh. Takes a little step closer. "I think we landed on Chloe."

"Oh. *Ha*," I say as bells are exploding in my head. We've apparently been dating figments of our imaginations. Terrific. "Right." I snap my fingers and point at him. It's pretty much the dumbest thing I've ever done. "Great. That sounds like a perfect idea then. Dinner. You and me. *Not* new. Although—"

His expression shifts warily at the word, and his reaction almost makes my heart burst then and there. And all of a sudden I see his confident mask slip off his face, just a little, revealing he actually *does* care quite a bit about my response.

He's asking me out.

I think.

"I am two thousand words behind in my writing today. I'll be counting on you to keep me awake and writing when we get back. Maybe prod me with a pencil every time I start to doze."

And there the old, confident Jack is. His eyes shift up to some-body in the bookshop snapping for our attention, and he puts a hand behind my back, gliding us forward.

"Sure thing. I have just the white pens you go all weepy over for the task."

CHAPTER 13

The only thing more unnerving than having first-date jitters while preparing for a first date is having first-date jitters while preparing for a secret first date with your agent and best friend in the confined space of an RV bathroom you share with him. An RV bathroom that actually manages to be smaller than that of an airplane. As in, my elbow is hovering above the toilet and one foot is in the shower as I race a brush through my hair.

"Just a moment!" I say in a cheery voice through the paper-thin bathroom door. I rapidly unwind my hair from the curling iron—and ram my elbow into a wall. Everything inside this bathroom is exponentially smaller. And fragile. Knock your knee on the toilet paper and the whole thing falls off. Tap your elbow on the wall and it sounds as though you're trying to punch through it.

"You all right in there?" Penny says.

"Super! Thanks!"

"You sure?" Penny says in that bright, listen-you've-been-in-there-a-*long*-time-but-I'm-Southern-and-too-polite-to-be-direct way. "Anything I can . . . do?"

"Not a thing!" I reply brightly. "I'll be right out!"

I decided the safest plan of action for tonight was to wait for Jack to be on a call (not the hard part), sneak into the bathroom (a little more challenging with Amelia's eight-hour-long beauty "routines"), and get ready as quick as humanly possible, on the off chance I am overthinking all of this.

Which is why I don't change my outfit from the plain blouse and simple black flats I was wearing all day. The only thing I've changed is from the black leggings I wore this afternoon (the same I crawled all over the floor in to sop up Amelia's spilled water) to a plain brown corduroy knee-length skirt. A nod to the Kathleen Kelly style of nineties fashion. Simple and understated class that says, "Oh, why, I fit in here!" whether we end up at a high-end restaurant or a pizza joint. I am prepared.

I am calm.

I am collected.

I whisper under my breath through the phone cradled in my ear, "So. What do you think?"

I've filled Gloria in on every single *possible* detail over the course of the past ten minutes. Touching on every single detail quicker than Jack, even when he played auctioneer a few days ago.

And Gloria, like the truly efficient court reporter sister she is, gathered in all this information wordlessly and responded with meticulously organized, rapid-fire responses.

The breakup speech with Parker. *"Oh, how could he?! You know what? I told you he didn't deserve you!"*

The grief that he was cheating on me. *"I never liked him. The man always was looking for the next thing, wasn't he? Couldn't just be happy knowing one language. Had to learn two. Couldn't be happy in one country. Had to fly off to live in two."*

The gaping hole in my heart from the sudden loss after such a long and complicated relationship. *"Oh, hon, you are so brave though."* And subsequently, the new incident with Jack: *"No, he DIDN'T?"* Even the dream. *"Are you serious?! Why have we wasted the last twenty minutes talking about, about—you know who—given this inspired news! Forget Parker! It's agreed, then—Parker ceases to exist in our brains. Tell me more about Jack."*

"Right, well," Gloria says, when I've finished and I'm now hastily dotting my cheeks with blush while simultaneously continuing to curl my hair, "to answer your question, *no*, I do not think this is all in your head. If you'll recall, I've been telling you he's had feelings for you for years."

"Yes, but—"

"As evidenced by the fact he's been making up names of females to pretend to date the past year. A *year*, Bryony? You have to ask yourself, why? Who's he waiting for? And maybe think, *Oh, I don't know, perhaps he's waiting on the girl he has dinner with every week under the guise of 'friendship.'* And no, I don't think this is all just a case of temporary insanity because you're stuck on a bus—even if Amelia does make you crazy."

My eyes jerk toward the door as I notch the volume down two more levels. Even her name in my ear in this place is loud enough to echo.

"And *no*, I do not think this falls under the category of rebounding. The law of rebounding clearly omits instances of long-distance relationships where one guy is a cheating idiot. But you know what? *Who cares* if it is? *Who cares?* You've wasted two years waiting for this guy across the planet, turning down dates left and right—"

Well, that's a stretch.

"—throwing aside every guy who's turned up at your door—"

Which would be none.

"—and you have a *lot* of time to make up. *A lot.*"

I sniff. I mean, I wasn't like some knitting lady glued to the sofa all these years. I had a laptop. I was a laptop lady glued to the sofa all these years. Which is categorically much better.

She slathers on layers of compliments, as she does, and for a few more minutes I listen while managing to wind up a few more strands of hair while burning myself on the arm twice.

When she hangs up, I uncurl the last strand and stare at myself in the mirror. There is a crazed look in my eye. It's all so very adrenaline kicking, uncertain. So very . . . scary, not knowing what my next step looks like, or even if I want to go there.

What if this date goes wrong?

What if this date ends horribly, and instead of getting to run back home and hide in my apartment, in another town, for a few days until the awkwardness wears off, we both end up back here—*together*—

where we continue to see each other every second of the day? And night? Would we ever recover? Would we damage anything beyond repair?

Is there a case study I could turn to? Somebody else out there in the world who has done anything just as weird as this and has a recovery story to tell?

I wince at the very obvious display of shimmery golden shadow I just added across my eyelids and rub it out as Penny knocks on the door. "Bryony? D'you know how much longer you'll be?"

Perfect. I'm turning into Amelia.

I open the door. "Sorry, Penny."

"Wow," she says, taken aback. "Don't you look nice." Her eyes cut to my outfit and then a look of alarm runs across her face. "There's not an event tonight?" She scrambles for the electronic planner glued to her side.

"No, no," I say hurriedly. "I just . . . wanted to get some fresh air. Take a breather from the bus."

"Oh. Right. The *bus*," she says knowledgeably, then slides her eyes toward the closed back door where Amelia has been busy doing "manifestations" the past hour—which basically amounts to her declaring all the things she wants like a child on Santa's lap while listening to ocean music.

The rest of us have taken to referring to Amelia as *the bus*.

Sometimes *the bus* is acting uniquely punchy.

Sometimes *the bus* needs to refuel and it'd be wise to let it have the last doughnut.

Sometimes *the bus* needs to take a nap or else the rest of us will lose our ever-loving minds.

Frankly, it's incredible how much attitude *the bus* has.

"Good for you." Penny gives me a look that screams, "*Help! I'm a captive here. Please take me with you!*"

"Do you . . ." I hesitate, but her brown eyes are so big and hopeful I can't help myself. "Want . . . to come with us . . . in a little bit? We could swing back and pick you up later?"

The RV door opens and Jack steps back onto the bus and up the stairs to our little living area.

"Hey." We lock eyes. And I hear it, my own little surprised intake of breath. It's not that he's changed clothes. His shirt actually bears a tiny mustard stain neither of us noticed after lunch. Even his expression is one of carefree ease.

But he's put on his watch. His father's lucky watch.

The one he reserves for only the moments that really count in his mind.

It's a funny thing, going on a date with a longtime friend. You can't mask your true feelings, I guess. You know each other so well that you give yourself away even without meaning to.

Were I a girl off the street, I never would've thought he was anxious about our dinner. In fact, I would've mistaken that easy, open expression on his face and the way he's resting his hand on the back seat of the leather captain's chair as almost *too* easy. *Too* nonchalant about how we plan to spend our evening. Almost as though, well, if we end up at a burger joint with a bunch of other acquaintances and then split ways, fine! Who cares? Certainly not me. We can chalk it up to a nice time between friends.

But I'm *not* a girl off the street, as it happens.

He hasn't ever had to say the meaning behind his lucky watch; I just know. He wore it on the day I went with him to the German book conference, and he was particularly anxious about securing a conversation with a specific foreign rights company. He wore it when I ended up at his fifteen-year high school reunion (heaven knows how) and he was anxious to show the world he grew into an entirely different man than the (*quite*, I learned) immature youth he used to be. And he puts it on practically every time he's called up for a special meeting with his CEO father.

His watch represents moments in time he wishes to mark as his best.

And apparently tonight, with me, is one he wants to mark as his best.

Penny's eyes slide from Jack to me and she slowly moves backward, back toward her chair. "Oh, *shoot*, I just remembered I'm supposed to be finishing up Amelia's newsletter."

One of her six that come out every week, I've learned, and always begin with: *Hi, My Beautiful, Creative, Talented Babes.*

"Let's shoot for a group escape tomorrow night," I say. And I mean it.

We have to get this girl off the insanity train sooner rather than later.

The sky is cotton candy with puffs of pink, sunset-bright clouds set against a blue canvas sky as we step off the bus and march our way through the parking lot. It's another strip mall we've landed beside here at Rosemary Beach, and a high-end one at that. A Tesla dealership bookends one end of the strip, a commercial bookstore the other, with an REI and a Williams Sonoma featured prominently with their large block lettering, wide-open doors, and shoppers peeling in and out with large shopping bags. Smaller mom-and-pop shops dot the rest of the landscape, small but mighty with their bright blue facades and swirly green palm tree signs.

"Okay." Jack stops and waves a hand panoramically at the long row of stores. "Take your pick."

I scan the names on the shops, my eyes sliding over everything from La Carreta to Rai Lay Thai and in between. They land on a little white restaurant just off to one side. A black-and-white-striped awning hangs over the front window, with black Parisian umbrellas cluttering up the small sidewalk to the curb. Light flickers from heavy lanterns on both sides of the wooden doors, and a man dressed in a white button-up and black slacks puts out his cigarette and rushes in with an accordion, of all things.

"That one," I say, pointing, but he's already walking in that direction.

"I know." He turns and pauses for me to catch up. "As soon as I saw the man with the most annoying musical instrument possible, I knew."

I feel pretty good about my choice, however, as we get settled in our seats and look around. The small black-and-white bistro chairs are comfortable and quaint in our little patio setting. Live music streams out from the open doors, but with the band at the back end of the restaurant, it sounds lively. Pairs nicely with the sight of flickering flames from electric lanterns and white votives all around. Our bus is in view at the end of the parking lot—Amelia's big, bright smile leering at us from a hundred feet away. I scooch my chair around to face Jack without Big Brother watching.

My stomach is seizing up with jitters again, with so many unknowns swirling around this moment, and my brain goes into overdrive as it questions every single little thing.

What was that look he gave me as we sat down?

What did he mean, *"No, we'll take somewhere quieter, if you have it"*?

Why exactly did he order a basket of bread for the table?

Is this just a basket-of-bread-for-the-table type of meal between friends? I mean, bread is not stereotypically romantic.

Oh. And there he goes. Ordering champagne. For what?

WHAT DOES THIS ALL MEAN?

Not to mention the equally overwhelming thoughts regarding the way *I'm* doing things.

Sit up straight, Bryony! Why is it so impossible to sit up straight in these chairs? This is all your fault. You should've made use of that posture bra Gloria bought you for Christmas last year. You went on and on about how you wanted it, and she went on and on about how it would give you the grace of Audrey Hepburn, and yet did you use it? Noooo, you found it all too "inconvenient" and now look at you. You've spent all your time hunched over your laptop and now you're a hunchback over your plate. This, THIS is what happens when you haven't gone on a proper date in two years—

"What are you doing?"

Jack stops me in my self-loathing anti–pep talk. "What?" I look up from the bread roll I've been shredding into little bits.

"You're sitting like a telephone poll. Stop it. It's weird."

A look of deep contempt comes over the face of our waiter, who has hitherto been standing over us.

Then, with an entirely *different* look, he turns to me. "Perhaps *mademoiselle* would care to start off with something a little nicer than 'free bread rolls for the table,' hmm? Perhaps our famous seven-hour beef tongue in a nice potato mousse with gravy?"

"Oh," I say. Well. That's quite honorable, isn't it? He's trying to save me. "Well . . . absolutely." I nod emphatically. "Beef tongue sounds just lovely. Thank you very much."

He gives a little bow to me. Pointedly ignores Jack. Moves off.

It's not until he's back inside that Jack addresses me, all while slathering up a roll with butter. "Are you happy? This is what you get when you sit like the queen of England. Beef tongue."

"Dipped in potato mousse," I add.

I look at the butter on his bread. He seems to be spreading on an extra layer. I bet it's salted too. With honey. A nice, lathery honey. This seems like a lathery honey kind of establishment.

He slathers on some more butter and then sighs, handing it to me. "Here. Unless you'd rather I sneak the pathetic 'free bread roll' under the table to you?"

"That won't be necessary," I say, but snatch it quickly before the waiter comes back.

And the butter roll breaks the ice.

Somewhere between sampling the dinner rolls, prodding the beef tongue together like some science experiment, and eventually daring each other to try it (Jack fares far better than I do; it goes straight from my mouth to the napkin), we end up in the course of dinner as we always do.

Talking about work. Talking about the little noticed nothings of the day. Talking about bowling and wondering if our team misses us. (We text. They don't.) It's all just . . . normal.

I look into his eyes as he tells me about the latest news in his apartment hunt and . . . nothing.

He looks into my eyes as I give him bite-by-bite commentary on the tarte Bourdaloue and . . . nothing.

Now I sit back in my chair, stuffed to the gills, slouching and slightly regretting the after-dinner cappuccino sloshing around in my stomach as the waiter comes by with the bill and Jack lifts his hand to take it and . . . something.

Something.

All of a sudden I'm aware of my ankle so casually resting on his the past half hour beneath our tight quarters.

And the way his hand so casually reaches out with confidence and gathers up the bill for the both of us.

And the way he—*oh my gosh, what is wrong with me?*—holds his pen as his signature slides over the bottom of the bill.

And here I am, lounging like a couch potato, having gorged myself on words and food without another thought.

"You're doing it again."

Jack isn't even looking up as he speaks. No, he's snapping the pen shut. Setting it on the bill. Sliding it to the end of the table.

Then he looks up at me, and as our eyes lock, it's like a hole has suddenly opened up beneath me and I'm dropped through the concrete.

It's as though a current of electricity zips between us as our eyes lock. It feels so loud that people around us *have* to notice. *Have* to feel the change in the atmosphere.

And yet in my periphery nobody's head is turning.

People are carrying on in their own conversations. Numb to the seismic shift between us.

A slight smile lifts his lips, and I feel a hundred more pings as it does. His eyes soften. He speaks softer. "You're sitting like a telephone pole again."

And there's a slight tease in his voice. But also . . . something else. Something with more intimate force.

"Sometimes," I say, "I wonder . . ."

I haven't got anything left to say.

I can't say it.

I can't open up something like this. It's a tin can. Once opened it cannot be resealed.

He waits for me to finish, but when I don't he just nods slightly. Stands.

We walk around after dinner and in our wanderings end up past the massive bookstore and the bustling groups of people and cars, past several smaller businesses, and finally onto a quieter neighborhood street.

They are older houses, lined up side by side with perfectly manicured lawns of St. Augustine grass and zoysia. Palm trees and scrub oaks. Stained glass features of seagulls and wind chimes swept up in the salty breeze.

Night comes upon us.

And we continue on, talking about little nothings as all the while my mind is preoccupied, my thoughts elsewhere.

Who knows? Maybe for him too.

Nobody can be *that* intrigued by the location of a piano through a windowpane into somebody's living room, right? Nobody can be *that* interested in talking about concrete turtles in a yardscape, surely?

And yet, there he goes. Perfectly content it seems to walk alongside me. Strolling along beneath a clear evening sky, dim stars twinkling above, hands in his pockets without a care in the world.

"Do you think that's an addition they added on above the workshop?" he begins.

"What exactly is *happening* here?"

I've done it.

I've blurted it out.

I clap my hands over my mouth. And yet a part of me is relieved.

Perfect, Bryony. Looks like you can make it roughly twelve hours before you need to have a talk about the status of your next relationship.

He looks away from the workshop in mild surprise at my outburst.

Stops.

Turns.

Studies me.

"Well," he says after a pause. "We just went out to dinner. I told you you were acting bizarre, the waiter became smitten with you and decided to loathe me—nothing new—and now we're walking off the three-pound cheesecake you made me eat because you said it was blueberry, and you went on about how I love blueberry cheesecake, but it turned out to be raspberry, and you made me eat it anyway. So here we are. Cue"—he waves his hand at the house opposite—"palm trees."

He says it like it's the most casual thing in the world.

"Right, I know that, genius, but"—I look around me—"just, I just, well, I just *feel* like something is different."

"Nothing is different."

I shake my head. "*Something* is different. Do not challenge me on this, Jack. Something is different. I want—I need—to know what it is."

He cocks a brow. "Do you really, Bryony? Do you really *need* to know what it is?"

I hesitate. Take a breath.

Do I need to verbalize it?

Tackle it, right now?

Against all Gloria's (and usually my own) wisdom? "Yes."

"Fine. The fact is, nothing has changed. For me." He puts his hands out. "And everything, it seems, has changed. For you."

"*What?*"

"Bryony. How often do we go out to dinner?"

"I don't know. Maybe . . . once a week."

"Three. Four if I'm lucky."

I feel a little zing in my chest with his understated word choices. The way he says "if I'm lucky" as though, well, this is something he hopes for. Waits for.

"How often do we see each other?"

I shrug, my anticipation rising. "Well, every other day or so, I suppose. But we've got a lot in common. Work, like on this tour."

"Which I chose to go on with you."

"Bowling."

"Which I signed up for, for you."

"Mutual friends."

"Your friends. Your friends whom I've made my friends." He must see the electricity in my eyes and adds, "I'm actually far less needy than you and can exist happily with only two or three important people in my life. All of which proves my point."

"Which is?"

"That for all intents and purposes, up to this point, we have been dating."

"*What?* No, *sir.*" My ears flame at the boldness of his suggestion. "I think I would know if I am *dating* someone. And I was dating someone." I clarify with an indignant air, "I was dating Parker, and I was very loyal."

"You were indeed. Maybe I should clarify then," Jack says, and there's a bemused grin on his face as he looks down at me.

He slows the moment down.

Lets silence rest between us, so that only the sounds of humming HVAC systems and cicadas whisper around. He takes a step toward me. "You weren't dating me. But I was dating you."

The world is swirling around me now.

I feel such a rush of confusing emotions at his casual attitude toward this moment, this revelation. Gloria was *right*. *Gran* was right. *Parker* was right. *Everyone* was right.

"There's just one little detail I've been missing in the past year and a half, and if it's all the same to you, I'd like to go ahead and capture it and take it home with me."

My breath is coming shallowly now.

The world spinning around me slowly, not like some swooping roller coaster but like the gentle movement as you sit on a sailboat in a bay. The slow rush of excitement is taking over me, and despite all my plans and goals, despite all my orderly aims, I find myself asking in a whispery breath, "Which is?"

"This." He closes the gap between us and kisses me, there with the onlooking concrete tortoises and clapping palm trees. His lips brush against my cheek first, sending a shiver up my nerves, and before he even has time to reach my lips I find myself rushing to his.

His kiss breaks into a smile, then a kiss again, as he takes me by the elbows and draws me in, more impatiently now, more eager. Fingers gripping me more protectively now, delight clear in the way he holds me, touches me. Draws his fingertips through my hair. Me. His Bryony.

His girl.

And it feels, well, it feels like home.

CHAPTER 14

"What are the odds they'll send a search party out for us?"

"Pretty low. I think if Amelia actually steps away from her five-hour nighttime skin care routine and notices we're gone, she's more likely to seize the opportunity to leave us—me—in the dust."

Jack's arm has been wrapped around my waist the last hour. We've walked until the neighborhood peaked at a set of concrete yard art manatees, at which point we declared the house the winner and decided to turn back. Everything and nothing has changed in the past two hours, since that first kiss beneath the stars. The conversation continues on companionably about our normal shared lives, yet now there's a fizziness to it that keeps my heart racing.

Maybe this'll be my new heart rate.

One hundred and twenty beats per minute.

But even in the midst of our casual chat, a part of me slows things down every few minutes, says something regarding the subtle change around us that seems too good, too perfect to be true. "I know you were just exaggerating when you said that bit about dating me for ages. I remember Marilyn."

He grins and tugs me a little tighter to his side. "That was before the Friendsgiving party. Everything changed the day before Thanksgiving."

Thanksgiving Eve. The night I had Jack and his then girlfriend, Marilyn, over, force-fed her pigs in a blanket, and dragged them into playing that awful murder mystery board game.

They had met at the gym a few weeks prior, unironically, and I knew it was something when he texted that day that he wasn't going to make it to dinner with me after all. That they were going with some of her friends to some trendy spot where everyone wore only neon items and there were no bowling balls in sight.

And I wasn't *jealous*. Of course I wasn't jealous—I had no right to be.

And it was *fine* on that first date when he bailed on me to choose something lame like twenty-five-dollar appetizers and music that didn't make you pay a quarter to play.

And it was *fine* the second week when he was suddenly busy.

But it was not fine on Thanksgiving Eve, when he just casually skipped. Just. Skipped.

Bowling. The thing that was principal in our lives.

Date on Sunday. Date Monday. Date every other day of the week for all I care. But Wednesdays were mine. *(Ours.)* The Pin Pals needed him *at least* that one day of the week.

I needed him.

So, yes, technically, I had been morosely strolling the aisles of the grocery store at nine o'clock at night after bowling, and when I came upon the little box in the clearance aisle with the Christmassy cartoon figures—the leering Frosty the Snowman, a self-righteous little elf holding a toy hammer quite viciously—all looking suspiciously at one another, I snatched it up. *Who Stole Rudolf's Red Nose at the Karaoke Party?* it asked.

Well, we certainly needed to find out.

I pretty much spam texted him into coming over to play, and everyone else for that matter. My conversation with Jack went like this:

> **Me:** We need to cling to our youthful roots.
> **Jack:** No.
> **Me:** Do something spontaneous. You know, they say that's what helps the fight against Alzheimer's. It's never too early to start considering optimizing our mental health, Jack.
> **Jack:** No.
> **Me:** Not to mention, you are the reason we lost

tonight. It's the least you can do to show up after that morale-shattering loss.

Jack: The Ballbarians (still the worst name) are undefeated. We both know I would've done nothing to bolster the team.

Me: I'll make my special nachos.

Jack: Be there in 40.

Marilyn showed up with him.

She stood in the corner of the living room, pushing tortilla chips around on her plate in her slinky black dress for half an hour. She smiled and nodded uncomfortably as Emiliano spoke to her, emphatically, about something she could only partly understand in his budding English. But when she was handed a Grinch face mask along with her character card, that's when she snapped. Suddenly had a terribly important email she'd entirely forgotten about that just *had* to be sent via her desktop, at home, and called an Uber.

Jack stayed.

"Ten thirteen p.m.," Jack announces. "Everything changed at 10:13."

I laugh. "You can't know the *exact* minute."

"You were standing on top of your coffee table, that huge trunk of wood, in your swinging reindeer antlers and pajama pants, singing—horribly, I might add—a bluesy 'Santa Claus Is Coming to Town,' when I decided."

"My character was Rosie, the jazz-singing ex-girlfriend of Rudolf with a chip on her shoulder. I *had* to be bluesy."

"And the bluesy did it." He squeezed my waist. "That's when everyone else was off the table." He pauses. "Ah." He grins at his little joke. "See what I did there? Because you were on it."

"Why?" I say incredulously. I remember my pajama pants. I remember the horrible singing. "Why then?"

"Because that's when I saw in your eyes there was a chance."

And I know, I know we have just kissed. I know his arm is around my waist right now, but it feels exposing realizing he knew the truth about that night. Like he's opened the very secret medicine cabinet in my bathroom and perused the bottles.

Warmth rises in my cheeks that's immediately cooled by the July breeze. Even I haven't fully acknowledged what happened to me that night. I had made some tiny rash decisions, then put the experience and memory behind locked doors and thrown away the key. After all, I was *in a relationship*. And jealousy was not allowed when you were *in a relationship*.

My worldview is easy to manage in black and white. I'm a rule follower.

You have a boyfriend and a declared mutual relationship? Stay loyal. Loyal until one or both agree to terminate the relationship.

You have a job? Be there when the clock starts.

You have a deadline? Get it in by midnight.

The world is simple to comprehend when you follow the rules.

But that night was different. I was feeling just so . . . so . . . down that he had deserted us for that beautiful, perky Pilates gym rat. Seeing the empty chair beside me at bowling. Feeling the gaping hole in the evening in his absence. I *wanted* him there. I *wanted* to hear his little satirical jokes. I *wanted* him to show up with two Cokes and slide one over to me without speaking. I *wanted* to feel the brush of his knee in a casual way against mine as we sat huddled so close together, too many of us on the seats. I *wanted* to hear about the tiny stuff, the little details of his day. I *wanted* to tell him about how I broke the letter *A* on my keyboard and spent two hours writing things like "the glss cndle ws centered on the tble."

I *wanted* to live in his nothings and him to live in mine.

And I felt it so strongly, so urgently, that yes, I all but dragged him to my place for an excuse of a party.

And yes, when the inspiration struck and it was time to show off my character, I did use it as an excuse to grab his hand. To pull him—not Chen, not Jose, but him—up on the table with me.

I wasn't beautifully dressed. The one thing slinky about my outfit were the reindeer antlers that bounced as we danced.

"But you gave me the most stunning smile I'd ever seen," Jack says. And I know I did.

Because Marilyn was gone. And he was all mine again.

And I guess the feelings that I thought were so cleverly shrouded by party games and hat tricks were not so cleverly shrouded after all.

I guess . . . even though that night I went to bed and vowed to forget what I did . . . I guess he remembered.

"Oh," I say, squeezing my eyes shut at the memory, "don't remind me. I was just terrible that night."

"No, you weren't." He squeezes my hand reassuringly. We're at the entrance to the parking lot now. The bus and Amelia's face peeking out in the distance. "You didn't betray Parker, Bryony. You just . . . couldn't fool me. There's a difference."

Wordlessly our hands break apart as we step onto the parking lot and start toward the bus.

We both know and don't have to say it.

It's best if we keep this between us.

At least until we get off this bus tour.

Light emanates from the humming bus as we reach it, and we pause just before getting to the door.

I look up at him. Cock my head. "So . . . that's it? You were waiting all this time for me to break up with Parker? I gotta admit, Jack. It just . . ." I shrug. "It doesn't seem like you. You're not a waiter. When you see something you want, you go for it."

"It wasn't about Parker." And to my surprise, he sounds solemn. "There was something I wanted to take care of first."

"Did you? Did you take care of it?"

"Almost."

I laugh. "How very Edward Rochester of you. What? You've got some secret certifiable wife stored in your attic you gotta figure out how to ditch first?"

The laugh he gives is only half-hearted, clearly concealing that whatever it is isn't a laughing matter. "Something like that. It's all water under the bridge now—"

"I see what you did there—"

"But let's not talk about it tonight. Tonight's perfect, and I want to remember it this way." He stoops down. Brushes his lips over mine in a way that makes the tips of my toes tingle.

"Fine by me," I say, and kiss him again.

Amelia calls from inside the bus, asking why we're not moving yet.

Time to *go*.

I give the door a couple raps.

"So," I say, tucking my hair behind one ear. "I'll just, um, see you tomorrow then."

"Tomorrow?" he says with a laugh, gesturing at the door after it opens. "Bryony, I'll continue to see you for the next million hours."

Million hours.

And that sounds . . . wonderful. That sounds right.

Sure enough, all night he does stick by me, refilling my coffee and scrutinizing his own emails as we both work. Keeping me company, encouraging me as I slash and write. Slash and write. Following my usual rhythm.

Eventually I can see the weariness in his eyes, the slow drags of his typing, like a clock winding down.

"Go to bed, Jack. I've written the last six books without you by my side. I can manage to do this one too. I'm in the zone."

He doesn't need me to say it a second time. His laptop snaps shut and he grabs his empty coffee mug. Checks his watch as he stands. "Top you off?" He gestures to my empty coffee mug.

It's one thirty.

I shouldn't have more coffee.

But then I remind myself of that article taped onto the coffee shop wall with the "statistics" of all the ailments you relieve by drinking more coffee.

A fifth-cup level solves dementia. Might as well go for a sixth and enhance my brain cells to solve world peace. "Please."

And when I hold up my empty coffee mug, eyes on the computer screen, I feel the surprise of a kiss on my cheek. Turn toward him. Make the second one count.

"You're amazing," he says in a hushed voice. "You know that?"

My whole body is still tingling as I take in the first sip of the new mug and the door to the little bathroom shuts as he moves with his toiletry bag inside.

What a whirlwind of a day.

My entire life just changed, didn't it?

My fingers type despite myself, one half of my brain on the story and the other half still trying to process the elation of the past twenty-four hours.

Love lost. (But can I really call Parker *love*? No. Whatever that was cannot compare to this. *This*. *THIS*.)

Betrayal. (Gutting, of course. But more importantly, how selfish of him. *How selfish* of him to hide his new relationship for *so long*, to deny me from moving on.)

And then, of course, Jack.

The date.

The waiter.

The bread.

The walk.

The kiss.

The revelation.

The . . . well, the everything.

I am in love.

Because of course, *this* is love.

And I've been in love for quite some time.

I just didn't know it was with him.

· · ·

The bus is pitch black at 3:00 a.m., all but for the glow of my laptop and the dim running lights. My typing is still going strong.

I don't know why, but my best work happens this way, when the world is silent. When the world is calm. It's probably what Gloria dubs my "fear of missing out" syndrome. How I can't turn down any activity during the day that looks remotely possible with other human beings. (Grocery store to get bananas? *Absolutely.* A post office trip to buy stamps? *Immediate need. Christmas card time is only nine months away.*)

I don't think I could be like other writers, tucked away at a desk somewhere in their home, all alone but for their cats and the occasional mailman. *Wanting* to be alone.

Who *wants* to be alone?

No. This is why I teach.

I thrive amid busyness. I love the clamor of people and languages around me. I love to feel the whole world surrounding me. And at night, I love to write.

I love living with one foot in both worlds.

It's the loss of Mom. Part of it, at least. I was an extroverted child to begin with—I would always end up turning strangers into playmates when we went to parks and libraries in my early years. Gran said it wouldn't take but ten minutes in a new place before I was parading around with my new friends—and then when Mom passed, it was earth-shattering. My heart split in two right there in the hospital room. The grief felt so big that the floor seemed to open up and swallow me whole.

In that moment Gran went to take Gloria to the hospital room's bathroom. I think it was an excuse, really, because I could hear Gran's stifled sobbing through the bathroom door. Gloria was only four then.

Besides that one deeply sorrowful moment, Gran never cried, at least not that intensely, in front of us again.

But then a janitor accidentally came in, loaded down with buckets and mops, clearly thinking this was another room. I remember how particularly bouncy her backside was as she backed into the room, wheeling in her mop bucket, humming to herself a little song.

And when she turned, the shock registered on her face when she saw my face. And the tears streaming down my cheeks. And Mom's body. Still there.

She plucked those earbuds off her ears and dropped down to her knees. And opened her arms.

And I don't know who she was or her name, but I'll never forget stepping forward. Running forward really. And the smell of jasmine perfume on her neck and the total envelopment of her arms around me. How her arms seemed to be trying to keep me in, protected from the brokenness outside.

And I don't remember her words, but I do remember the tone of her words. The soft hush of them. The way her soul reached out and wrapped around mine for just a moment in hopes of easing my pain. Telling me I was not alone.

She was an angel in a critical moment for me. My gran, of course, too. Of course.

But the janitor lady reminded me that while one soul moved on from this earth, separated from me for a time, there were millions, billions, more just as beautiful, just as intricately made and perfectly rare, who remained with me and who would step in to carry me through.

So. It comes as no surprise that I write at night.

Sacrifice a little sleep, drink caffeine to supplement, work my days surrounded by beautiful souls.

"Coming along?"

I'm not going to say I scream, but there is a real temptation to as Amelia's voice rises from the darkness and interrupts my thoughts.

And then I look up and that's when I really *do* give a little scream before clapping my hand over my mouth.

There's nothing but blackness at the back end of the bus. Blackness, and the glowing red outline of a face hovering in the air.

Then the glowing face moves toward me.

Her robe is cinched tight around her, huge round curlers surround her head, and a wire runs down her side to a pocket connected to what appears to be a lasery, fancy-gadget face mask covering her entire face. All I can see are the slits of her blue eyes as she approaches the coffee and tea station at the little kitchen. She reaches for a mug, misses, putters around, and finally grabs it.

Good grief. I can't even see nose holes.

How is she breathing?

She looks like Darth Vader's lover.

I keep on writing as she mumbles complaints under her breath about the fact the teakettle was turned off (heaven forbid we don't start a fire at 3:00 a.m.) and fiddles with the sink until she gets it turned on and the water begins to pour into the kettle.

I try my best to ignore her and keep on writing. But it's a little challenging to do when somebody in full glowing mummy garb is standing in the shadows, watching you. Out of boredom, no doubt.

She's like a toddler. Has no problem just staring at people.

I only zero in on typing faster. It becomes my new goal to get to the end of this page before I slip off into bed. I'm at thirty-eight thousand words now, made a wonderful dent in the manuscript this evening. Two thousand words. *Good* words. I have fallen in love with the way my character stumbles into the resident hermit of the town when he's in the backwoods of his house, following the sound of the lost dog. The shortcut back as the two men talk.

I can't help it, this falling in love with my own story.

There is no bigger fan, I think, than an author over her own narrative. Sometimes I pity readers, to be honest. I remain in this world for months, day and night, breakfast, lunch, dinner, and midnights, always thinking, always living partly in this made-up world.

Readers, if the book is good, get to see the marsh water. If the book is great, they get to touch it. Smell it. Hear the sound of the ripples. But the writers? We have dived in. Submerged ourselves. Touched the clay bottom. Felt the wet earth squeeze between our toes. We drink it. Swallow it. We live and, for a thousand reasons, love our fantasy worlds.

"I don't like that."

I startle and look up.

"Cut it," she says.

I lift my eyes to see where Amelia stands over me. Her finger is pointing at the page on my screen.

A small ball of fire swirls in my stomach. Every muscle in my body tenses up.

"Amelia," I say, my tone measured. "If you keep asking me to cut my story to ribbons, I will eventually take the pieces and make them into a flag of my own."

And then she laughs.

But the laugh is choked and stifled sounding behind her mask.

She pats me on the back. "Oh, Bryony. It's my story. Never forget that for a second. These are *my stories*. And I'd like—I really would like—to see you try. If that day ever comes, make sure to tell me. I'd love to be one of the five people to buy it." She gives my shoulder a friendly—and creepy all the way to my toes—squeeze. "I'll be your biggest supporter. Guaranteed."

CHAPTER 15

The following week is one dizzying event after another. Days of traveling from one palm-tree town to another, slightly different palm-tree town. Feeding lines to Amelia through the earpiece while she tosses back champagne. Jumping back on the bus to peel off dresses for sweatpants and ride along the interstate again.

Jack and I, meanwhile, have been in a state of bliss, keeping our new state of things to ourselves as we sneak off for nightly adventures and steal kisses when no one's around. Which is, for the record, virtually never.

"I really don't like to say *hate*, Jack. It's an unkind word."

"Mm-hmm." His hands are stuffed into the pockets of his light gray slacks. He leans against a car. Whose car? I don't know. But he's been standing here, with me, the past twenty minutes. "But . . ."

"But you know what? I just—I just—" I start pacing. Again.

In my long black dress.

More specifically a long black gala-suitable dress.

I borrowed Penny's wretchedly high heels from her last night, just after we'd come back from our third group outing of the week.

As it turns out, the poor girl's nerves are completely shot. But like me, she carries on. Her reasons are different. She stays because, as she says, on repeat, and usually while tracing cursive letters into ketchup on her plate (because Amelia has broken her, and now she practices her calligraphy on everything from food to shaving cream on the bathroom mirror), "I just need to make it to a year of working under her. A year is respectable."

Penny repeats that phrase often to herself. *A year is respectable.*

She's under the delusion that everyone will come rushing to her offering employment in publishing if they see "Personal Assistant to Amelia Benedict" on her résumé.

Of course, she also would need to garner a positive recommendation from Amelia. Which itself would be a miracle.

It's been a week since Amelia told me to cut down my chapter in her Darth Vader's bride getup.

A week of visiting bookstores and helping out at signings and eating more lobster bisque and crab cakes than I have in my entire life, of drinking champagne and taking evening walks and sneaking little kisses with Jack—and yes, becoming quite fond of Penny and our little trio sneak-outs—but I still can't get what Amelia did out of my mind. The whole thing still boils me up.

"For goodness' sake, Bryony." Jack rubs the back of his neck and gazes up to the night sky. "*Keep* the page. It's not like she's going to read it."

He fails to see my struggle.

Which comes down to two facts. One, Amelia is really quite evil. And two, she has decided to zero in on me and make my life miserable.

It was tolerable before. Now, it's just beyond.

Of course, I don't believe Jack has seen the full wrath of Amelia Benedict. And to be fair, he's sort of in the business of managing fussy authors.

I honestly think he's a little immune to it.

To some extent, that's what makes him a good literary agent. He doesn't take entitled behavior to heart. It's like he wears an invisible shield of armor, and anything slung at him just slides right off.

Me, on the other hand . . .

I can't help it.

"It's not *about* whether she reads it or not." My pacing speeds up to match my rising anxiety. I'm getting myself worked up too much.

I know. But it feels *necessary*. "I just . . . I just don't know how much longer I can take doing this. I can't *for the life of me* imagine doing ten more books for this woman."

"And our goal is that you won't."

I rub my forehead as I pace. "I know that. It's just . . ."

"Waiting is the cross in publishing we all have to bear. Nobody likes it, Bryony. It's not for the faint of heart. And most people, to be brutally honest, can't take it. *That's* what kills them off in the end. That's what separates the wheat from the chaff. Not the roller coaster of book sales going up and down. Not the rejections. It's the waiting that'll get you. But—" I swing back in front of him, and he reaches out suddenly and grabs my hand, halting me. I look up at him and feel the shift from the wobbly vision of cars and telephone poles to the steadiness of his clear green eyes.

He takes a breath, then resumes in a measured calm. "But things are looking up for you. I have a feeling it won't be too much longer."

My heart skips a beat. "You heard back from Florence?"

He hesitates. Then shakes his head slightly.

"Anybody else?"

His eyes shift to my shoulders drooping further and further by the moment. "I did have some positive conversations."

"With who—"

"And I think it won't be too much longer until I have them convinced. Patience, Bryony."

He leans in, kissing my temple as though to smooth away the tension throbbing in my head. "Rest assured, I have you top of mind in everything I'm doing."

"I bet you say that to all your authors," I mumble.

"And you have every right to be frustrated. About everything. But . . . what if we got *on* the boat instead of hanging out here in the parking lot, considering they leave in ten minutes and I've promised to keep your plate loaded down with hush puppies and Amelia on the opposite side of the boat the whole night?"

I chew my bottom lip. "The whole night?"

"Whole night."

I eye the cruise boat waiting just on the other side of the little boardwalk.

It's a beautiful boat, and a beautiful evening in Charleston.

Sailboats bob everywhere in the water, bells dinging from them as they pass by. The riverboat floats large and proud, gleaming white with a giant red wheel at its stern. Lights are strung along the front of the boat, where people are already gathered. Mingling.

It's the first event that isn't *just* about Amelia in the spotlight. The first event where Amelia is sharing the limelight with two other well-known authors for a sunset book-themed cruise.

My stomach growls. "I suppose I can table this conversation until after we try out their lobster bisque."

"*More* lobster bisque?" He grins slightly as he takes my arm. We turn toward the gangway.

"It's an obsession at this point. I feel compelled to try it in every restaurant we end up at. Do you think it's possible to poison yourself from too much lobster?"

"Compared to your previous life of eating too many ramen noodles? I think you'll make it another week."

And as we step onto the riverboat, a lightness comes over me. It's very possible I over-romanticize my life, treating the dialogues of my day like I do on the page, but there's something symbolic to what he says as we finish our words on the subject of my struggles and move on to the festivities around us. I *can* make it another week.

That's all I have to do here with this launch.

Amelia may be out to ruin my happiness. Amelia may be exhausting my patience. But as often happens in life, the greatest joys and greatest struggles tend to be delivered to your doorstep in the same basket. And it's up to you to dissect the two and embrace the good without letting the bad overcome. That's been a hard-won lesson after losing my mother and getting a front-row seat to the true hardships my students face every day.

And honestly, if everything that has happened with Jack only would have happened if I lived with Amelia, then I would move into this bus all over again. Sure, I might be tempted to kill her. But I'd make the move.

CHAPTER 16

True to his promise, Jack has stood by my side the whole evening. He also, to his credit, has kept the hush puppies coming—though after the fourth trip, I was cut off.

The riverboat cruise down the Charleston Harbor was a glorious mix of both peaceful and energizing. The wheel slowly churning and pouring water from one bucket to another. The hum of readers and industry pros chatting about all things books. The serene beauty of the surroundings. And occasional input about the current ranking in the PGA John Deere Classic from some husbands sneaking looks at the game on their phones.

I find myself settling at the front of the ship. It's quieter here, tucked away from where the authors are set up talking with readers. They don't technically have a designated meeting spot—their role is to mingle—but the second Amelia stepped on board, she spoke quietly to Penny, who rushed quietly to Garrett, who dashed quietly to the person in charge with the news that, essentially, it wasn't her job to do the walking. That *her* doing the work would be self-deprecating and desperate. No, if people were so eager to talk, they would need to come to her, not the other way around.

So they quickly found her a chair.

It was a folding chair and, evidently, too "foldy" and cheap looking for her rosy backside.

Penny was tasked with informing someone that it was not "on brand." You should've seen her face swallowing that one.

Anyway, they threw a crisp white tablecloth over it and tied some bows around the back of the chair, and that's where Amelia is now.

There's a pleasant drift of people around me now, and the saxophone from the live band lifts a little melody nicely into the air. A number of couples have taken to the dance floor not too far off, twirling slowly and whispering sweet nothings before stepping off again.

But for the fact that it took an act of Congress to get it through Amelia's brain that I am *off* tonight and officially unavailable for carrying out any of the silly little duties she so likes to hand me in the name of assistant, I can almost forget entirely why we're here.

I can almost believe this is just a romantic date for two—work thrust far, far aside.

"Isn't that the editor you were talking to earlier today about Pat's marketing plan?" I say, looking past Jack's shoulder to the man standing in a cluster beside one of his authors.

Jack turns and looks. "Huh," he says after a moment, his voice less than amused at the coincidence. "So it is."

I can see it.

Clouds are forming in his eyes.

The man has been ghosting Jack's emails for three weeks now. His team modified the marketing plan for Pat Henderson's next release, and apparently it is quite a bit *less* impressive than the efforts they made for his previous books. Which Pat's marketing person knows. And Jack knows. So Jack has informed this editor and put in a request for more help. Multiple times. And the editor has dodged each request.

"Go on." I elbow him in the side. "He's stranded on a boat. You got him now."

"You sure?"

"I've got a dozen seagulls to watch. And if that gets boring, I'll go find Penny," I say with a smile.

He hesitates. Looks into my eyes to make sure it's absolutely fine. Sees nothing there to indicate otherwise. Then that little work-loving smile slips up one side of his face as he sets his glass on a nearby table.

"Need both hands to pin him down. Good thinking, babe!" I call out after him, grinning a little too gleefully at the remark I'm not too proud to admit I find hilarious.

The man's face when Jack comes up behind him and gives him a hardy slap on his shoulder is priceless. Jack is all smiles and friendly words, you can tell, and from the look of it, it only seems to terrify the man more.

Fair enough.

I imagine the only thing more terrifying than Jack being stiff and unfriendly is Jack being just the opposite . . . friendly.

It's actually quite the stroke of luck—bad luck for the editor, naturally—for Jack that Pat's editor is here tonight at all. Most publishing teams don't show up to author events, really.

Now that I think of it, it's probably because of that big conference event here this weekend. SIBA. The Southern Independent Booksellers Alliance. Wouldn't be surprised if the other authors for Amelia's event tonight are piggybacking the weekend by doing double duty both here for release and there. Which, actually . . .

My breath halts.

There she is.

Editor Florence Peters in the flesh.

She's standing off to the side of her author and the little mingling cluster, staring at her phone. She looks quite a bit grayer than the website photograph, the brown of her short hair replaced by silvery-gray strands tucked behind her ears. But the glasses are the same large, round, friendly frames that scream, "*I read books for a living, am highly intelligent, could beat you in a spelling bee any day, and most definitely bring my own reusable bags to the grocery store.*" All facts confirmed when I perused (stalked) her meager rows of photos on her socials. I went all the way down to 2011.

I'd recognize her friendly face anywhere, even here.

I take a step forward.

Then stop.

Another daring step forward.

Stop myself again.

I shouldn't do it. There are no stated rules, but the unstated ones about author to agent to editor relationships are just as concretely laid down as the stated ones.

You do *not* talk to the editor your agent is querying. You do not hire a middleman and then meddle in the situation by reaching around the middleman to shake hands.

You don't.

Agents get furious, which in itself isn't the problem in my case. It's Jack. And anyway, dating your agent is top of list of those unspoken things one does not do, but here we are.

The frustration part on his side doesn't scare me. I can handle a little, "What are you doing, Bryony? I am in the middle of a very fragile conversation here."

No, what makes me nervous is her reaction. Florence Peters. Will she take kindly to an aspiring author jumping in to talk potential business without the gatekeeper around? Or is she one of those old-fashioned types who'd scratch me off just for trying?

Will it make me look too desperate?

Possibly.

Will she get angry?

Maybe.

Do I have to try?

Absolutely.

This is my opportunity.

I feel the double angst as I carefully maneuver forward, keeping one eye on her and the other on Jack. It's not like I am *hiding* this meeting from him, but if he sees me, he will probably stop me, and if he stops me, I will probably die. I have waited for two *years* for a moment like this.

I end up halting just off from the drink area, and wait.

This must be what a mountain lion feels like sitting in the shadows beside the watering hole, waiting for the deer after what feels like *months* since having a decent meal. My wait really has been that long. I've been waiting on her response after her request for the full book for literal *months*. I've been living off crumbs of hope from Jack. Hearing she liked the sound of my book proposal. Hearing she found it *intriguing*. Hearing she was looking forward to reading the book on holiday and getting back with him. *Holiday*. As in *months* ago.

Forget all the people Jack has reached out to during the past two weeks.

She's the dream.

She's the big kahuna of publishing hope-fors.

She is the metaphorical deer at my metaphorical watering hole.

And looking at the way her glass is empty, it's only (*please, oh please!*) a matter of time before she goes for a refill.

Five minutes go by.

Amelia is laughing loudly now as she smiles gayly (i.e., maniacally) and clutches a gaggle of ladies closer for a picture. I bite my lip as the staffed victims of the folding chair incident watch in the distance with mildly disturbed frowns.

Ten minutes pass.

I start to flip through backup plans of ways to meet.

Nothing is coming to mind.

I mean, how exactly can you not rudely interrupt a tête-à-tête between two strangers to introduce yourself? Especially when your goal is *not* to look like a stalking, desperate aspiring author preying on the editor in question?

Conveniently trip into the conversation? "Oh, I'm so sorry. I slipped right on my dress there. Oh, hiiii. Is that you? I'm that wannabe author with lots of potential. Let's shake hands."

Pretend to be on staff and offer a refill? "Sorry to interrupt, miss, but can I refill your drink and discuss my manuscript?"

"Those crab cakes are so salty, right?" I feel myself trying to send a telepathic message, zeroing in on Florence's plate with my eyes. "You know what would be nice right now? Oh, I know. A nice big glass of water. Or tea. Or coffee. Or champagne. Or decaf coffee. Or lemon water. Or this very spritely looking strawberry water. Really, *anything liquid* would be *such* a good idea right now, wouldn't it?"

I almost startle myself when she says something in parting and actually moves forward, *toward the drink table*!

This is my moment!

My *moment*!

I rush forward, then slow my steps just in time to line up with her.

We reach the table at the same time. This part is going to be tricky.

I keep my eyes averted, straining, waiting for her to make her move.

What is she going to go for?

And more specifically, *whom* exactly was the sunset cruise trying not to offend by offering precisely *this* many drink options?

Nearly every square inch of the white tablecloth is covered with bottles and punch bowls and carafes with various little labels. There's a carafe for black coffee. Carafe for organic black coffee. Carafe for organic, single-source, fair-trade black coffee that is mold free and tested for authenticity in three countries. (Serious question: Why not just use that one?)

My goal is to wait until the *millisecond* she moves toward one of the drinks and then move my hand toward the exact same thing at the same time. It's a tricky thing, though. Wait too long and I'm just strange and bad-mannered. Too early and I may misjudge which one she's after.

I have to be surgical about it.

Neurosurgeon level.

She's made her move!

Out of the corner of my eye I see her reach toward a glass water jug (that, or it's a speck in my eye, but it's a gamble I'll have to take) and I casually, decidedly reach for the jug as well.

"Oh," she and I say at just the same time.

I grin (although what my cheeks *want* to do is grin like a madwoman, which I'm forcing down with all my mental ability). "Sorry. Go ahead."

She says something similarly polite at the same time, then gives a breathy little chuckle when I wait and says, "Thank you."

I take in a "surprised" breath. Put a hand to my heart. "Wait a moment. Are you ... Florence Peters?"

A subtle respect permeates my tone. One that says, "*I, too, am distinguished and have self-respect but am here to offer you respect as well.*"

The best kind, not too groveling.

She looks a little taken aback.

Wow, she really doesn't know aspiring writers all over the world have her face on their computers and would buy her baseball card, should it exist. "Yes. And I'm sorry, I'm not too good with faces. Have we met?"

"Oh no," I say, giving a little laugh while trying to temper my internal response of *Oh, I wish, I WISH. I wish we were best friends and had a standing coffee date every week to walk to our favorite shop together to buy croissants and drink black coffee like cool adults and talk books and you would lean on my wisdom about where you should plant your windowsill cilantro, and I would be granted goddaughter privilege at your granddaughter's birth, and ...*

"I'm Bryony Page. I believe you've been chatting back and forth with my agent. Jack."

She pauses.

What is that?

The light in her eyes dims. Just a little bit.

"Jack ...," she says.

"Sterling," I finish.

And *oh the relief* I feel as it comes back again. The recognition in her eyes. "Oh, Jack. Yes, I've worked with him plenty of times over the years. Is he here tonight?" She glances around.

"Yes," I jump in, redirecting her attention to me. "But as for my book you two have been discussing ..."

"Oh. Well. I'm not ... recalling any recent correspondence ..."

My fingers are beginning to wind around each other in front

of me, poor immature habit, and I pull them back to my sides in a mature manner. "I think you've had my manuscript, *Water Under the Bridge*, for a few months now. You received the proposal. Asked for the manuscript to read over the holidays. I believe it's been"—I pause, pretending I don't know exactly how long it's been—"about a year since his first email."

Three hundred and eighty-two days.

Florence's eyes give a flash of pity. "Oh. Hm." She presses her lips together, thinking.

"No . . ." Her eyes drift away from me again, searching for him, and I have a sinking feeling in my chest. "I think I would remember anything from Jack. He has such talented authors"—she throws a hand out at me, as if offering up a consolation prize—"no doubt such as you. Are you published?"

"I—" I feel a growing sickness coming over me I don't understand. "No, well, a bit . . ."

How does she have no recollection of any conversation about me?

I've talked with Jack a hundred times over the past year about his conversations with Florence Peters. A *hundred* times. How could her memory of something so *vastly* important to me amount to *nothing*?

"What's your genre?" she continues kindly.

"It's—um—" But I'm finding it hard to answer. Not only because saying, "It's magical realistic, semi-biographical women's fiction," is incredibly confusing, but also because the conversation isn't anything like I imagined. This *isn't* how this conversation is supposed to go.

This is why I have an agent. *He* is the one with the talent who understands how to pitch.

"I'm just, I have to say, very surprised. Are you . . . are you *quite* sure you haven't gotten anything from him?" I tiptoe with my words.

"Maybe it was another editor at Brooks." Her eyes are even softer in pity. In fact, she's going off and filling the glass I've been holding numbly in my hands with water. Somebody draws her attention from the corner of her eye, and she gives me a little *I'm sorry about this* smile. "I'll be sure not to forget this conversation though. Have Jack email me. I'll look forward to your—well—whatever it is you write," she says with a light laugh. "It'll be a little surprise!"

She turns and moves off into the crowd.

And I continue to stand there at the table, dumbfounded, so long that someone asks me to move aside so they can get in.

People are chatting around me.

The hum of people laughing gayly in their shiny sequins with their hair in clips.

Someone in a conversation to my right is stoking Amelia's ego with gushing compliments about how *The Seven-Year Holiday* helped her get through her reading slump.

Amelia is responding with shock and thanks as though nobody has ever said anything nice to her in her life, leading to a sudden on-slaught of a dozen women throwing compliments.

But one thing sticks out in all of this.

One thing that sticks me to this spot, unable to move.

Unable to think.

Jack never emailed Florence Peters.

Never.

And slowly, painfully, I'm watching the columns crash around me and dust kick up into the air, considering the domino effect on my life of that one, oh so important fact.

If Jack never emailed Florence Peters, maybe . . . Jack has never pitched my book.

CHAPTER 17

I don't have a solid plan.

Nothing makes sense, except for one fact that is abundantly clear in all of this: I'm leaving the second this boat docks in the harbor and the event is over.

I'm leaving all this madness behind, and I'm never turning back.

Jack is *good* with words.

Dangerously good.

It's why people want him on their side, doing things like *representing their books to those in publishing*. He is a professional at winning people over to his side.

Which he will try to do with me.

And so I must not give him that chance.

My eyes are glued to the unloading dock in the distance as I grip the rails at the front of the boat, begging it to hurry up as it moves to shore. The last thing I want is for Jack to see me like this. I can't fake my fury. And sense of betrayal. And really . . . just humiliation.

What else is he lying about?

Our relationship, a lie?

His friendship, a lie?

I knew he was money hungry, and maybe not even that, just obsessed with his work. I thought it was dedication. Before I had found it admirable that he'd found something he loved so much, that he was passionate about. In a world where so many people loathe the thing they dedicate such a great portion of their lives to, he was always excited. His passion for his work was something about him I *liked*.

I'd seen enough half-hearted agents snatching up far more clients than they could handle just to give them no attention unless their books "went somewhere." I always liked that Jack didn't do that. That while he seemed tough and unfriendly at the front end, it turned out his rejection of so many aspiring authors was really a kindness in disguise. And he was willing to be misjudged as that villain; he wasn't off trying to please everybody because, as he said, "There are only so many people one person can please."

These were the things I had *liked*.

But what I didn't see, the dirty little secret that has been hanging over my head this whole time, is the truth. I've been, from the very start, the naive little girl who can be manipulated to work her heart out and give her words away in exchange for a little attention. A little hope.

I am *exactly* who Amelia thinks I am. I'm nothing more than their prized little ghostwriter, sitting up in a castle turret tucked away from people. Slipping words through the cracks in the door by day while typing away all night.

And all this time, the only difference between the two has been that Amelia is the one who said it, and Jack is the one who thought it. The craftier one.

And *he* is on their side.

Her side.

He really is Amelia's puppet.

That's what his job is, isn't it?

Amelia reached her success, and then he was tasked with keeping me from succeeding on my own. All this time he has said he's making progress. All this time he has said he's reaching out, but *Water Under the Bridge* needs work . . .

Well.

I've been a fool.

I've given him all this grace. I've shrugged off the times he missed dinner meetings in the past. I've always said yes, been agreeable, as he's talked me into pushing forward another deadline. Working faster. Writing harder. Dropping scenes to suit Amelia's wishes. Adding scenes when she wanted. Tasked with creating for somebody else an impossible goal of writing "the perfect rom-com." Even going on this *stupid, stupid book tour.*

I don't even realize my cheeks are wet with humiliated tears as the riverboat employee unhooks the lock from the railing and I am the first to step off.

"You need help walking down, miss?" he says, concern etched across his face. He points down to my heels as an excuse to help me. A *good* person. A *decent* person.

"No. Thank you." I wipe at my cheeks and pass him a little smile.

"Okay then. You have yourself a good evening, okay?"

I can't muster a reply and just nod.

The first time I hear Jack's voice calling me is when my feet are on dry ground. "Bryony!" he calls from the boat.

I hold the hem of my dress tightly in my hands as I walk across the parking lot, not slowing. Not turning back. The heels are unable to keep up with my pace and I'm wobbly on my feet, my stride awkward as I push myself forward to the bus in the distance.

For the hundredth time tonight I wish I had taken my phone. My wallet. Anything to make this transition quicker. I could've had an Uber ready to go by now.

My head is whirring, trying to rapidly think up a plan.

"Bryony!" I hear Jack's voice a bit more urgently now. I speed up.

Thankfully I don't have many belongings. Another one of the benefits of being an indentured servant in Amelia's rodeo.

I'm out of breath as I rap on the door of the bus.

It's humming quietly. The lights on low as it rests in the congested parking lot.

I can see Trina sitting up in the driver's seat. She jumps in surprise, drops her feet off the dash, and slips her phone back on the dashboard. Pulls the handle. The door opens.

"Honey?" she says in surprise. "You all right?"

"No," is all I can manage to say as I get up the stairs, crudely pull off the heels, and drop them on Penny's seat. Penny's gone. Everybody's gone, except for Trina. "No, it seems I've been a bit delusional, as it turns out."

She's up from her seat now. Standing in the walkway. "About . . . ?"

I drop down on my knees. Pull out my little suitcase.

Begin grabbing odds and ends that are still on my bed.

I hear the question in her voice. *Is this about that young man you've been seeing on the top bunk? Or the crazy lady who lives in the back?*

I throw it all into the suitcase. Squeeze it shut. Throw my purse around my shoulders with my phone inside. "About everything. About it all. And now"—I glance out the window, see Jack halfway across the parking lot, striding quicker now, a stream of people disembarking the boat behind him—"I just need to get out before they catch me and make it worse."

"On it." She's back in her seat like a pilot given fresh orders.

I feel a jerk as the bus turns on and shifts into gear.

Before I know it she's peeling the bus forward, toward the entrance to the parking lot.

"Trina?" I say.

To be honest, the whole peeling-out-of-the-parking-lot thing takes me by complete surprise. I had hoped, at best, to duck out and dash out of sight before Jack reached the doors. But to escape in a *bus*. Well.

"You always were my favorite." She glances over her shoulder as she turns the big steering wheel and gives me a big smile. "The rest of 'em I wouldn't take a dollar for."

"No. Stop. You can't put *your job* at risk here—"

"Worry about yourself for once, honey. I'm not worried about me at all. Believe me, I can handle myself. Now, where do you need to go?"

I stumble to reply. Where *do* I need to go? I don't have a clear answer to that. "Home," I say simply.

"How about the airport then? The airport will have to do."

I nod and sink back into a seat.

As we get onto the main road, she adds, "And I know this'll be novel to you since you haven't been able to get in that bathroom because of that vanity hog all week, but you might want to consider changing into something a little less Cinderella for when you get on that plane. Unless you're going for a girl-running-away-from-the-ball feel."

The bathroom.

Changing.

Right.

I gather up some jeans and make my way to the bathroom. The tiny bathroom is cluttered with hair spray bottles and lotions and dozens and dozens of bottles of this and that—vanity creams and foundations and serums and prep sprays, heat sprays, setting sprays. The room still stinks of chemicals dispensed without care earlier this evening. I barely can move without tripping over some French label of this or that.

I pull open the door.

Squeeze myself out.

I'm going to Amelia's room.

I can see Trina looking at me from the big rectangular rearview mirror as she wheels us down the expressway. "Even better," she calls out. "You go, girl."

I open the door and can't help the sound that escapes my lips.

We have been *crammed* into pint-sized bunk beds when Amelia's room has been *this*?

Wall-to-wall windows surround a king-sized bed. At least a dozen pillows are strewn all along the bed, swimming in the sea of duvets and waffle blankets and soft, welcoming white sheets. A white leather couch rests against one wall, covered in clothes. A *kitchenette* sits on the other side of the room, also, miraculously, covered in clothes.

And—I gasp as I peer into the cracked door of what I had assumed was one of the many, many closets—she has her own bathroom. *Her. Own. Bathroom.*

Curling irons and straighteners and motivational Post-it notes stuck along the mirror and, again, clothes covering the bathroom so thoroughly it looks impossible to step in. It's like . . . it's like she'd rather just leave the mess she made and take over the feeble one we use than deal with the hassle of *putting her things on a hanger.*

Which, for the record, we didn't even have the option of.

I unzip my dress and quickly work on changing into the holey jeans and loose graphic T-shirt I've owned for so long I can't remember. It all slips on like a glove, a welcome, cozy glove that wraps around me and is the first reminder of home. My cozy little world I left behind.

I look at myself in the mirror as I unpin my hair and let the pins drop to the floor. *Amelia will never notice in this mess*, is my first thought. And then, of course, comes the second: *Who cares?*

Who CARES?

I need to *stop* caring.

I flick the pin on top of a heap and a large strand of brown curls drops to my shoulder.

Penny did up my hair this afternoon. It was a sisterly moment between the two of us. I will miss her.

Eventually I take a look at myself in the mirror, finished.

My hair is still all curly at the bottom of my strands. Dandelions, peonies, roses, and lilies curl up out of little pots on my T-shirt, each flower labeled in dainty little cursive below the pot. My jeans sag a little lower on my hips—unsurprising given the number of calories I've burned in stress and anxiety over the course of the trip.

I look at my frowning, weary face in the mirror, all surrounded by Post-it notes declaring, THIS IS YOUR MOMENT! and FUTURE #1 *NYT* BESTSELLER and REESE WITHERSPOON BOOK PICK and an eerie large X over the name ANNE SANDERWORTH replaced by AMELIA BENEDICT.

It's pathetic, really.

These are her goals.

The messages on these Post-its are her life aspirations, the "manifestations" she speaks over herself.

This, this longing to take the glory for words she didn't produce is the best thing she can come up with to hope for in life.

Honestly, it makes me wonder what her childhood was like.

Bryony, please call me.

I see Jack's text on the bathroom countertop. Consider ignoring it, but the question burns.

I snatch it up. Text like my fingers are on fire. Did you ever email Florence Peters?

There's a long pause.

The longest pause in eternity as I watch the text bubble go. Then stop. Then go again.

At last the phone vibrates.

No.

Followed swiftly by, But there's so much more to this. Please call me. Let me explain.

I stare at the chain of texts. Read the sentences again slowly. Slower still.

Jack has just confirmed that he has lied to me. For a year now. Lied straight to my face.

And the reality is, I don't care what his explanations are.

I don't *care*.

It *doesn't matter*.

No excuse to justify this *matters*.

Because he has broken my trust, and mark my words, he will *never ever* gain it again.

The bus jolts and I lift my chin as I look at myself in the mirror.

Staring back at the girl with the pale face and heart-shocked eyes.

And find myself gripping a little nugget of truth deep in my gut that drives me toward home.

I may not be rich. I may not be powerful. I may not even be wise enough to discern the difference between honest and dishonest people.

But I have people who love me back home.

And people at home who appreciate me for just who I am.

Who live good, honest, hardworking lives.

And I am smart enough, apparently, to write things people find worth reading.

And I *will* find another way to get my words out there. For them.

CHAPTER 18

Bryony, please. Call.

I flip the phone over and slip it into my pocket, but not before Gloria sees who it's from.

It's a slow Thursday afternoon on Broadway (at least, as slow as Broadway can be), and a week since I left Jack and all the chaos of the tour bus behind. I've spent the week at Gloria's town house. Showed up out of the blue as soon as I stepped off the plane, and without a word, she welcomed me in.

We haven't talked much about it. She got the shortest version possible—just enough to appease her desperately curious mind— and then we left it like yesterday's egg salad sandwich on a concrete patio.

Her pink, tufted yard-sale couch is firm but still a hundred times friendlier than the tiny bunk bed on the tour bus, and a thousand times friendlier than the loneliness of my own apartment. She has more cats than is reasonable (of course, that definition varies by person) and more plants than she can possibly keep up with, so when I sleep it smells like I'm in a conservatory, and when I wake up, it's usually because a paw from a passing cat has ended up on my ear. And when it's not a cat, it's the display of her indoor wind chimes as they jingle in the morning breeze. Gloria always keeps her windows open. It's absolutely a safety hazard, but she claims her cats will protect her. And to be honest, they might.

I've always liked the way Gloria keeps up her life.

She's a carefree spirit, always has been.

She let me wallow in wind chimes and cat fur and down covers and magazines and takeout and a never-ending stream of emails typed madly to every editor and agent in town (it's a maddening work of type and wait, type and wait) up until yesterday afternoon, at which point she returned from a deposition, dropped her stenographer bag on the floor, and declared cheerfully, "It's time to get up!"

So here I am.

En route to 200 West 45th Street on Thursday afternoon for a matinee show of *The Lion King* because, as Gloria declares, "*Nobody* can stay down with *The Lion King*."

This is the show Gran took us to after Mom passed. Right when we'd first arrived in the city. I remember the moment Timon and Pumbaa cracked their first joke. It was the first time I'd smiled in weeks. I remember seeing Gran watching me out of the corner of her eye, and as it happened, I could see her body sink into the plush red chair with her exhale. Like she was taking her first breath after too long as well.

The Lion King was the first reminder that we could get through this.

That life, while at times terrible, hard, and unpredictable, could never keep goodness from poking through the ground too.

So.

I said yes to Gloria.

Before heading to the show we ate at The Watchtower, one of the—according to Gloria's *fun* facts—23,650 restaurants in the city. We ordered a full English breakfast and stuffed ourselves until we couldn't eat a bite more.

"You in pain too?" Gloria asks now, pointedly ignoring the message from Jack that just flashed on my phone. We stop at the crosswalk to wait for the passing stream of taxis and buses.

"I should've kept the leggings on." I tug at the waistband of my faithful corduroy skirt. "I feel like I've swallowed a whale."

"The body knows what it needs," Gloria says in one of her little quips, as though this solves everything. She often likes to say, "The body knows what it needs," to justify everything from three pounds of mashed potatoes in a sitting to a gallon of ice cream. "Cravings are just urgent messages" is another.

"So," she says.

Then she leaves off.

Lets the word hang in the air.

Waiting for me to grab it.

I purse my lips together.

The flow of traffic eases and I begin to walk with the crowd across the street.

It's not until we are pulling out our phones again to scan the tickets—and we see two more messages—that she breaks. "How many times has Jack messaged you?"

"I know no Jack."

"But what? Has he called you five times in the past week? Ten?"

"I don't know. I don't keep track."

Twelve calls a day. Every hour on the dot after eight.

The texts come less frequently, and when they come they are in spurts.

I do my best to keep my wits about me and not read them. Any of them. And the voice mail filled up after the first day. I haven't listened to those either.

"Aren't you even a *little* curious? Just to hear him out . . . for a moment?"

"No," I reply firmly, more firmly than I intended, actually.

The topic isn't up for discussion.

It's why I haven't gone back home. On the chance he does drive over to my apartment, he won't find me. Or at work. Considering Gran is expecting me to be off another week anyway, for those suspicious undisclosed reasons she didn't trust (rightfully, as it happened), he won't find me there either.

I make a mental note to tell Gran the whole thing tomorrow.

Gloria looks a little chastened, and I add, a little softer, "I can't even let myself entertain the thought I could talk to him, Gloria. This is what he does. He's a master at persuasion. But the facts are laid bare. He lied to me *for a year* with a straight face. No doubt the whole two years. I can't imagine what he's capable of."

"I know. I just . . ." Gloria's voice trails away as we sit in our seats. "I just . . . can't imagine *everything* he's done the past two years was because he was trying to use you. I've seen a thousand bad guys in court, Bryony. And let me tell you, none of them joined bowling leagues."

It's painful to hear her speak like this, in his defense. It actually physically hurts my heart.

It's best *not* to think. To keep the world in straight lines, black and white. To keep to the rules of common sense. And rule 1 is: People who care about you don't lie.

Surreptitiously I check my email a dozen times during the show.

While the giraffes are walking on stilts.

As Rafiki makes everyone laugh with her antics.

During the great, horrible scene of the final battle.

Nothing.

Not a single email from anyone.

Over the past week I have been spending half my time in self-loathing on the couch with a bag of chips and the other half emailing every agent and editor under the sun.

That part has been . . . challenging.

Half the respectable agents in the world seem to be at Jack's agency, and the other half seem to declare they are "not taking on representation at this time" and follow the general "don't call us, we'll call you if we really want you" rule. Makes sense. The world is crawling with writers, and with social media being so popular, all they have to do is plug in "person with a million followers whom we can convince to write a book—or smile while we hire a ghostwriter," and there you go.

And yes, I read and reread my contract a few times, and the most frustrating part of it all is, mum's the *absolute* word on the only short-cut I could possibly take. I could be sued for every penny I have now and henceforth forevermore for revealing to *anyone* (*particularly* in writing) that I am Amelia's ghostwriter.

And believe me, I've tried *alluding*.

But the challenge is, it's nearly impossible to sound humble and successful at the same time with vague words. Without being able to give specific figures, I just sound ridiculous.

It's gone more or less like this:

> Dear so-and-so,
>
> My name is Bryony Page, and while *my name* is un-published, I write in the genre of romance and there is a high likelihood you have read my books. And seen them on billboards. And at the top of certain lists. For long periods of time.
>
> I have a special project I'd love to discuss with you regarding my own manuscript. I'm pressed for time, so could you please message me at your earliest con-venience and we can discuss?
>
> With warmth and thanks,
> Bryony Page
> *No socials.*
> *No website.*
> *No backlist of books.*

So. As you can see, I'm a real winner. I waffle back and forth in my methods, half of them like this, the other the opposite, just in case.

> Dear so-and-so,
>
> My name is Bryony Page and I write books. I did have an agent up till recently, but he broke my heart

and has proven to be a lying, cheating pig. But rest assured, I am capable of making you proud. I hope.

Please give me a chance.

Please, please, please please please.

Bryony Page

Again, no socials to refer to.

No website.

No backlist of books.

I mean, it's really a *wonder* they aren't pounding down my door.

As the curtain falls and the applause tapers off, Gloria looks over to me with hopeful eyes. Hoping to see that yes, *The Lion King* has cured everything. Every single problem in my life.

I fake the biggest smile I can muster for her sake and carry on clapping longer than most.

When she finally reaches for her purse, I do the same. Honestly, I feel like the couch is calling me.

"How about we pop by that little store that has all those candles before we head home? I've been wanting to get a few more beeswax tapers."

Gloria does not need more candles. No, Gloria needs a label maker and a storage bin so she can remember where exactly she has her hundred tapers at home and no longer "pops in" to buy more candles once a week.

Honestly, though, I'm pretty sure she just likes having a reason to shop so much that she would just "forget" where the candle bin was anyway.

I agree for her sake, and we make our way to Glow. Gloria insists we walk, despite the fact that it's at least a forty-minute stroll, and I'm fairly certain she's masterminding the whole plan just to get some vitamin D on my face and fresh air in my lungs.

The stretch does feel good, however. I'll give her that.

My legs welcome the movement after the hibernation that has lasted the week and, honestly, most of the week before that. All those hours on the bus were constraining. People romanticize road trips, but the long hours confined to sitting or pacing the narrow five feet are enough to make the average person feel anxious and an outdoorsy person absolutely feral.

It doesn't take too long to get off the beaten path, and once we tuck ourselves into the quieter strips of the city, I can feel myself taking in deeper breaths. Letting my thoughts wander from the topic pressing on the forefront of my mind for the first time in a long time.

Gloria turns us onto Mary Street, and I know she's done it on purpose. I always love this street. Rows of townhomes in various colors of brick with grand arches over bay windows and concrete decorations on front lawns. Little pots with lemon trees sitting out for the summer by front doors and window boxes on second and third levels covered in dangling ivy. Ivory curtains pulled back to showcase impressive living spaces. Artwork in big, gaudy golden frames.

These are the kind of people who wrap their TV in a golden frame and hide it among a wall of framed art. I'm certain that half the people on this street end up going to the Boston Marathon each year, because every time we walk here tenants are either going for or coming from a jog. Maybe it's part of a clause on their HOA contract. Maybe below the section about mandatory wrapping of TVs in gold frames it says: *Must run twenty miles a week.*

Gloria and I like to have conversations about the rooms, deciding which homes we'd take for ours. Critiquing the expensive interiors as if we ourselves weren't living in flats with electronic keyboards tucked underneath our beds. Considering quite seriously if that color of oak around their banisters was the right choice when carpet covers our own floors. It's always a fun game.

Sometimes, after we've picked our own homes, we play the game again, but for others.

"Gran would absolutely pick that one, no question," Gloria says fervently, pointing at the door with the golden squirrel knocker.

"She would not. She'd never go for that color brick. It's *pink*."

"It's *salmon*," Gloria says.

"Just another word for pink."

An older man at the house two doors down locks his door and descends the steps. "You're both wrong," he says, passing by. "She says it's strawberry gelato."

"Thank you!" Gloria calls after him, and without turning, he drops his hand to his side for a little wave.

I imagine he gets this kind of thing a lot.

No doubt the pink versus salmon debate is a hotly discussed topic down on Mary Street.

I'm smiling slightly when I feel the vibration in my pocket.

And it jolts me back to reality.

To the angst.

To the reminders of what all is going on.

To the world outside debates of pink brick.

I pull out my phone, bracing myself as I pull up the notification. *Calm down, Bryony.* It's probably a spam email about some "vital eye cream discovered in the algae of a mysterious lake." Or a reminder that "with only four payments of $650, you too can own this deluxe water desk with real goldfish!"

But then my heart stops beating.

It's from Florence Peters.

Dear Bryony,

I'm so sorry for rushing off the other day and thank you so much for reaching out—I was just thinking about how I wished I had your contact information to do just the same thing, so your message is convenient timing! It was lovely meeting you, and of course any client of Jack's is a welcome friend of mine. Would love to talk more about this intriguing manuscript of yours. How about the three of us set something up? I can email Jack if you prefer we discuss through him. I'll be traveling for a work conference at the end of next week but

am fairly flexible until I leave on the 6th. Would you be
free to squeeze in lunch beforehand? If not I can make
myself available after the 12th.

Looking forward to it!
Florence Peters
Senior Acquisitions Editor
Brooks Publishing

"Make myself available." Those three key words tell me everything
I need to know.

Shift the power holder in the conversation.

Put a wonderful, terrific spin on it.

She *wants* to work with me. No doubt because of Jack and the
clientele he picks up. We are little commodities to the world. Or perhaps, better yet, he is a finder of unique and uncommon goods, and
his job is to scour the earth picking up special little trinkets full of
possibility. All his trinkets (clients) are usually snapped up by publishers before the ink has dried on the author-agent contracts.

I must be a rare find.

Florence must think that.

Heart racing, I'm whipping out a reply as fast as I can as all the
while thoughts rip by in the back of my mind. *Please don't email Jack.
Please don't pause for a moment and decide to email Jack.*

I know it's unconventional talking directly to the author. Informing the agent of a meeting instead of working through him to get
something set up.

Agents get very particular about these kinds of things.

And editors tend to be very careful, at least in the beginning before contracts are made, to follow suit.

So all I can do is *hope and pray* she doesn't go ahead and send Jack
a respectful "heads-up, I replied to your author" email.

I feel Gloria over my shoulder shamelessly watching as I type. It
takes me four rewrites, along with Gloria's frequent "you missed an

s there—oh, I see now, never mind" backseat commentaries before I finally get it how I like.

"What d'you think?" I let Gloria look it over before I press the definitive Send.

She puts on her most serious face and gives it a long look. Honestly, if she had them, I'm certain she would pull out glasses and put them on just to look intelligent. "I think it's perfect. And perfect timing too. Send." She blows out a happy breath, beaming at me. "What a relief, huh?"

"Well, we still have a few months before Gran announces closing, but agreed," I say, my eyes going down the lines one more time. "It's such whiplash in publishing. All slow, slow, slow until—*bam*—things move at the speed of light. To be honest," I say with a jittery chuckle, "I was a little worried it would take much more time than we had. I mean, of course I know this is all still a long shot," I add, seeing Gloria's face. "I'm not deceiving myself—too much. But I really believe *this can happen*—"

"No, I mean I'm glad it's happening for *you*, Bryony."

Frowning, I look up. "What?"

"Because I couldn't bear to see you out of both jobs simultaneously," Gloria says, her voice softer.

I pause. "Well. There's still hope. *This* is hope." I point to Florence's name on the email bar. "This is Florence Peters. She's one of the best. If we can get a contract to happen—"

"It'll still be too late for The Bridge."

I am so startled by her, dare I say, traitorous words that are delivered so calmly.

Of *course* it's not too late. "No, if we just speed this along—"

"What do you think will happen? You'll become a zillionaire overnight?" She smiles softly.

"No." I frown. "I was hoping for something much more reasonable. I only need a few million."

Gloria gives a choking laugh. "Right. Just a few."

"Not from *me*. Not an *advance*. But if we had a spread all about The Bridge on the back, and an author's note where I explain everything at the front, and I really dig into it during publicity and marketing tours, then maybe *word* will spill around and enough of the right *people* could come forward, caring about the project, and—"

"Bryony." Gloria puts her hand on my arm. Stills me. She takes a breath, letting the pause clear my head. "I'm happy Florence is reaching out, but not because of The Bridge. For *you*."

I can't believe her there. I'm shaking my head. "See, I just can't believe that. If you think that way, you lose. You lose before you give it your all and really *try*—"

"Gran made the announcement." Gloria presses her lips together. Eyes me solemnly. "She made the announcement last week while you were gone. She said she didn't think it right to wait any longer when everyone could start trying to get new employment plans going."

"But . . . but they're still not closing until January."

"October."

"*October* now?" I say with a sinking heart. "October?"

"It was the best she could do, she said. The building owner said he can't let it for any longer than that. He said he could let them have it for a few more months, but that's it." Gloria pulls a face. Drops a hand on my shoulder. "I'm sorry, Bryn. I told Gran not to tell you."

"*Why?*"

"We talked and . . . she heard that you were back and . . . well, we agreed that it would be best to wait a little while. Recover from one blow before you get hit with another."

"And if . . . and if all the teachers leave before then? If they find other jobs now?"

Gloria shrugs. "You know Gran. She told everyone to take care of their families. Themselves. She understands if anyone finds somewhere else they can go and goes there. Actually, she's already started writing recommendation letters."

"And if enough teachers go?"

"Then I guess The Bridge will have to shut down early." She sees my blanched face and throws out a hand. "Or I don't know. Knowing you, you'll end up trying to one-room schoolhouse it and take all the students under your wing."

An image of two hundred students stuffed inside one classroom, every level from the 1a, fresh-off-the-boat newbies, to the 5b, GED-prep students working on their essays, all listening to my words—some with zero comprehension, the others bored. I'd have to work overtime, triple, maybe quadruple on the lesson plans. I could do it.

I could make that work.

For the semester.

But then . . .

I shake my head with fresh determination. Return my attention to the email I'm almost ready to send to Florence.

Delete the final, fuzzy words and switch to a new plan. A simple question.

What luck! I'm in the city. Are you free this afternoon?

I press Send.

My hands are sweaty.

Heart racing even as I try to calm myself down.

This. Means. Nothing.

So *what* if Gran demonstrated her thoughtfulness by making sure all the staff got themselves as prepped as possible for the changes to come?

So *what* if the deadline for a miracle is now pretty much *immediately* instead of *almost immediately*.

So *what* if things have gone from almost impossible to exactly .00001 percent chance away from impossible?

There's still time.

She can just . . . eat her words if my plan turns out.

That's all.

And she'd be thrilled to do so at that.

They'd taste like cake going down.

The kind of cake people in these townhomes buy, the ones with fondant icing in intricate shapes of bouquets of roses.

"Bryony?" Gloria is looking at me with a dubious expression, half-wondering from the looks of it if she's broken me. I suppose that's fair.

After all, I'm smiling slightly.

Smiling as I picture (*yes, perhaps a little bizarrely*) the thrill on Gran's face if—when—this glorious news comes to fruition.

Because *I* have a date with Florence Peters.

Now all I have to do is convince her that this book is a once-in-a-lifetime opportunity.

And above all, keep Jack out of it.

CHAPTER 19

Bryony,
    Terrific! As it stands, I have this afternoon wide
open.

I grin as I type a quick reply.

The email conversation moves at a text-like speed as we go back and forth, each sentence relaying new information regarding her hopes and thoughts about the potential of this meeting. And with each new tidbit of information, my grin widens as I translate.

I have this afternoon wide open.

Translation: Either I am at all times swamped under a pile of emails and papers and can use this as an excuse to get out of anything I want to, or I am "free as a bee," which means absolutely *nothing* will stand in my way to stop this meeting. Meeting with you has become top priority because I see something of potential value in you.

I'm free until 5.

Translation: I'm not even going to bookend my afternoon with pretend obligations that could become useful as an excuse for skipping out early. I believe you to be so normal and such a person of interest to me that I have no fears that you will suddenly terrify me with a secondary personality or prove to write one-dimensional plotlines with puppetlike characters.

3pm at The Terrace work for you? My son has violin practice at 5 I'll need to scoot out for.

Translation: I'm sharing randomly-thrown-in personal details with you in hopes of proving to you I am a normal person and we are close. Look how close we are now. We're *connecting*! We're practically friends! And friends *absolutely* want to work together. I'm *so* much more wonderful than any other editor out there with zero personality and zero connection.

Can't wait, Bryony.

Translation: You are not just a random person to me. You are *Bryony*. We are first-name-basis people. And we are *close*.

See you soon!!–Flor

I gulp at the last line.

"She used a double exclamation point. A *double* exclamation point, Gloria. Do you *know what this means*?" I'm shaking her elbow excitedly as she looks at the phone in bewilderment.

"Um . . ."

"She's *completely* thrown down all barriers," I say. "I mean, the *vulnerability*. She's just laid it *bare*. Right there. She's practically *begging* to sign me."

"And you get all that . . . ," Gloria says dubiously, "from . . . two exclamation points—"

"And then she says *Flor*!" I cry, jabbing my phone with my finger. "*Flor!* We're already on *nickname* basis! She's dropped her official titles entirely! We're practically *best friends*!"

"Ooookay." Gloria takes the phone from my hands. "Terrific work, Bryony. You've got that meeting all set up. Time to put the phone away before you do anything drastic. Like, I don't know, invite her on a friendship cruise for two."

She's right. I know she's right, which is why I tuck the phone back into my pocket and nod fervently as we walk across the street. Gloria has agreed to walk with me all the way to the restaurant, partly because she is afraid I'm "emotionally unstable" after everything that's happened and partly out of morbid this-is-why-I'm-a-court-reporter-I-want-to-hear-everything curiosity.

The jitters nearly take me over as I stand in front of The Terrace and spot Florence's back against the glass.

I turn to Gloria.

"Don't be getting nervous on me now, Bryn." Gloria gives my back a little push.

"I know." I inhale a breath. It's crazy to get the jitters to this degree *now*, but I can't help it. Seeing her—it just cements that what's happening is real. The truth is, as best as I can see, *this* quite literally is my last chance. For The Bridge. But also, more than likely, for me. A chance like this won't come again.

This *interview* hidden beneath a thin veil of croissants and sandwiches is truly at its core an interview. And quite frankly, it's all I have from my years of service to Amelia Benedict (et al.). I don't have more contacts I can lean on. I don't have more emails I can send. I don't have more information I can give.

It's reminiscent of that first pitch session with Jack and a reminder that all of what I do, this entire life of a writer, is insanity.

If the road to publication means going back to square one and doing all that I did at that pitch table, then writing feverishly for two more years, to get to this moment . . . I'll just give up. I'll quit.

Choose a path more sane.

More feasible.

Maybe law school.

Med school.

Aerodynamics.

My fingernails claw into my palms as I ball them up at my sides.

This is *it*.

And I feel myself on the brink of an all-out panic.

Florence is going to see me like this.

She's going to see me panicking and then everything really *will* be lost.

I hear Gloria behind me.

"All right, Bryony. It's your big interview and I *know* this is the one. So *buck up*. Pull yourself up by those bootstraps. Slap that proposal—more or less—on the table. And get back on that horse because you are going to have a rootin' tootin' good day, ya hear? This is *it*. I can feel it in my bones. If the creek don't rise, I reckon you're fixin' to be in high cotton any moment now, and whatever anyone else says about that don't make a hill of beans a difference."

I turn around. Gloria has her phone out now. And with a grin, she's reading off some old iPhone note from two years ago. Despite myself, I feel the ice breaking, the anxiety cracking within me as I let out a jittery chuckle of disbelief.

Turns out she did it again.

She nudges me toward the doors. "Now go on," she says in her exaggerated Southern voice. "You did it once. You became that 1 percent. All on your own. And you can do it again."

CHAPTER 20

"Ms. Peters?"

I move around Florence Peters's chair (no matter how casually she types her name, she will *always* be known as the formidable, amazing Florence Peters in my head) and peer at her as if very casually wondering if it's her. Of course it's her.

I've been staring at the back of her head for five minutes.

I pretty much have her head memorized from all my stalking social media research.

"Bryony, hello again!" Florence moves to stand and, before I know it, is leaning forward and extending her limbs in one of two things. A hug or a handshake. It's impossible to know which. And, of course, I'm immediately crippled with indecision while being forced to make one.

An unwanted hug when she meant to give a professional handshake makes me creepy and is immediately undesirable.

But an unwanted handshake when she was moving forward to give a friendly hug makes me pointy and sharp edged and is immediately undesirable.

So I do what we did at our first meeting. Try to match her moves to my moves by the millimeter.

We end up hugging. With limbs awkwardly at our chests. Hands weirdly touching. Like two Tyrannosaurus rexes.

I quickly step back with an overbright smile. "Well!" I exclaim, throwing my gaze around the table. "They've already brought water. Wonderful!" I sit down quickly.

Take a sip.

Pretend I *don't* sound like a person with a hyperfixation on common commodities.

To her credit, she doesn't seem fazed and sits down like the class act she is. Classy Florence Peters.

My editor soulmate and future best friend.

"Have you eaten yet?" she says, peering over her menu.

"I had a bite a couple hours ago, but I could *absolutely* eat again." No. That doesn't sound right either. I have *got* to tone down the enthusiasm.

We both peer at our menus for a bit. Get down to ordering when the waiter arrives. Make small talk until the meal arrives. It's decent enough. I successfully prove I *can* be normal.

And then, precisely when her lentil soup has hit the halfway-gone level, she speaks. There's a new tone in her voice.

I can't put a finger on it, but it screams, "*Now down to business!*"

"I'm sorry Jack wasn't able to come."

I pull a face, then set my napkin down. "Yes. Too bad. He's just so busy . . ."

"Of course."

"Of course," I echo.

"But he won't mind if we have this little chat, I'm sure—"

"Oh, I'm sure," I echo, quietly kicking myself for repeating her words.

What is wrong *with me?*

It's tenth grade symphonic band recital all over again. I am the absolute *worst* under pressure. I morph into some bizarre other human who is incapable of using her brain cells.

It's just so *hard* dealing with all these intrusive thoughts like, *You know what would be the absolute* worst *right now? What if you spit out your soup* all of a sudden on her face? *Wouldn't that just be crazy?*

And then I'm staring at her face, telling my head to *shut up and let me listen* while she talks, all the while feeling incredibly anxious because *what if* I suddenly clicked my brain off and something *awful* like that happened and I missed everything she's saying?

Again, I am *horrible* under pressure.

And that's when I realize she's looking at me expectantly. There's a smile on her face as she's just finished saying something.

What was it again? "I'm sorry. Could you repeat that?"

"Oh, of course. I was just saying, do you think you have your manuscript on email? If you could email it over to me now, I could take a look while we talk."

I whip out my phone so quickly my hand knocks the little table between us and ice quakes in the glasses. "Yes. Absolutely. Here it is," I say, ignoring the new throb of my hand. I email the manuscript over to her and hear the *ding* a moment later.

"Perfect." She settles glasses on her nose as she pulls out a tablet and sets it on the table. Already she's beginning to look at it and touch various points on the screen as she says, "So how did you and Jack get started working together?"

"Well . . . we met at a writers' conference in Nashville a few years ago."

"Oh?" She glances up in surprise, her brows knitting together briefly. "And you're still unpublished?"

"Well . . . yes. Technically speaking. Under my name."

"Ah." Her brows rise even higher toward her hairline. "So you do some extra work then, I gather. Under another name."

"I have. Yes."

Good. This is *good*. She's connecting the dots and doesn't seem put off by any of it.

"And you . . . work for one of Jack's clients, perhaps?"

"I do. Yes." I grin. *Finally*. The relief of getting to say what I need to say without having to break any rules is incredible.

She mistakes my smile for nervousness and says, "Don't worry. Jack has had hundreds in his time. I'll never guess your little secret."

She reads another few pages in silence, and then, just as I'm distracted by a stream of passersby out the window, I hear the snap of the cover over the tablet.

The definitive movement as she slips the tablet into her purse beside the chair.

Looks at me.

My stomach falls.

Rises again.

Then falls again.

There's something definitive in her expression.

"I can't work with you on this."

"What?" I exclaim. "Wh-why?" I find myself peering down at the floor in the direction of the tablet in her purse, as if it'll give me some clue as to what, exactly, just went wrong.

"Is it that I'm unpublished?" I ask, groping for clues.

"No."

"I know I don't have much of a following—"

"You have no following," she corrects. "But no, it's not that. I feel confident we could make it work out despite that. We've done that plenty of times with the right author."

"Was it the thing about echoing you? Because I *can* be normal. I really am. I have a whole list of references who'd back me up. Tell you—"

Florence laughs outright. "No. You are *quite* normal. Endearing even. You remind me of myself starting out, and it is absolutely normal to be nervous."

"Then what?" I say, completely at a loss.

And then it occurs to me.

"Have you talked with Jack?"

"What? No. Bryony, for the sake of your nerves, let *me* do the talking for a moment. It's not that you are just starting out, or your platform numbers, or your *personality*—for the record there, I think we'd get along swimmingly. It's because this manuscript isn't your genre. This isn't where your heart is."

"What? Of course it is. This is the first manuscript I ever wrote. My heart is solemnly there!" I point in the direction of the tablet. "I spent more time on this novel than any of my other works!"

"Hence the 149,000 words." Florence smiles slightly. She clasps her hands together on the table. Leans forward a little. "Bryony, I know you must be very talented. Jack doesn't take on clients who *aren't* talented. But this"—she waves a vague hand at the tablet— "this manuscript needs work. And lots of it. From the very little I've seen, it seems clear to me that you possess potential, but now you just need to take some time to hone that."

"But I don't have time."

"Then make some." She presses her lips together. "Take out forty or fifty thousand words. Change the start. Your story doesn't begin there. It *begins* at page 20. And on that point, succinctly *define* your story, your plot, where you want it to go from page 1. Clarify your craft. Make it *special*. Make it your *own*. And then"—she shrugs— "let's talk. I don't know about you, but I'd be happy to revisit this conversation when you get those matters shaken out."

Craft.

She wants me to hone my craft.

When *I write Amelia Benedict's books*.

I *have honed*.

I just don't have the reputation behind me to back me up.

The bill comes, which Florence graciously insists on paying. My chest is a ball of knots and all the while I'm thinking, stewing, trying to come up with a plan for how to convince her.

I *want* her to accept this manuscript right now.

I *need* her to declare, "Why, this is exactly what our esteemed CEO has been looking for since our company's inception in 1952! President Otis is going to be *elated*!"

"You know, I have to admit, I'm a little surprised." Florence gives a flourish at the end of her signature. "Jack told me you were in contemporary romance."

Jack's name coming from her lips strikes me like a splash of ice water across my face. "Wh—you spoke with him?" I try to say casually, though to my own ears it comes out as anything but.

"Oh, sure," she says, as though *of course* she would be corresponding with the agent. In fact, *Jack* and her professional, successful relationship with *Jack* is the only real reason we're having this conversation. At all.

Then she sits back and, to my surprise, gives a dreamy little chuckle to herself as if remembering something quite special. "You know, I believe this is where I met with him last time we had a business lunch. I don't know who's more of a fan of the lentil soup, Jack or—" She looks up. Her brows tweak up at the sight of my face. Or rather, the way my eyes are casting about, searching for him. "Are you all right, Bryony?"

"Me?" I point at myself. "Yes." My eyes are darting around frantically. Searching. "Although I'd like to throw my own name in as a contender for loving the soup the most—" Oof. There he is. Through the doors. Coming straight for the table.

It's too late.

I'm trapped.

Trapped by the need to be pleasant for the sake of any—slim though the chance may be—relationship with Florence Peters.

"Sorry I'm late," Jack says. "Traffic was murder."

"Running all the way from the Strand, were you? I hear Terry Mills is signing over there today. She's been phenomenal on the charts this past month," Florence says and stands, leaning over the back of the chair to give him a hug.

He pats her shoulder lightly—and eyes me while doing so.

There's a little dimple in one corner of his mouth as he says, "Her release has been doing very well, yes. And I was a little bit farther away than that, actually."

Again, while looking at me.

"I was in a little town out in the middle of nowhere you've probably never heard of. Been on the hunt for something the past few days."

"Never heard of? Try me."

"Florence."

"Florence?" she says with a laugh. "Now that is a commute—but I *do* know it," she says triumphantly. "You know, I got lost there once. Thought I'd never make it back out to civilization."

She laughs.

Jack laughs.

I die a bit inside.

"Now where were you all on the manuscript?" Jack takes a chair from the table opposite and swings it around to sit. "Catch me up."

You know what? I can't do this.

I'm *not* going to do this.

Even at this cost.

"I think we got everything covered here." I rise so quickly the chair behind my knees threatens to tip over, and Jack grabs it, steadying it.

"You know, I was surprised, Jack," Florence says. "This project isn't normally your . . . style."

And there it is.

Plain as day in the way she says it. *Style.*

The truth.

She doesn't like my work at all. She has had this entire conversation *solely* because of her relationship with Jack. I imagine it now. They pass a steady stream of clients back and forth over the years. He's the one standing at the gate while she sits on her throne, slipping through the really relevant ones.

He's her bouncer.

That's what he is.

She's the member of the exclusive club.

And *I* am the surprise girl strolling in with the 149,000-word novel looking entirely out of place.

His eyes stay fixed on hers now as he answers. There's a confident smile on his face.

"Oh, Bryony is *nothing* like my style, believe me. She's doesn't hold a candle to my other clients."

I feel a punch in the gut at his words.

Then he adds, "She's got the whole cake."

Florence's brows shoot up at his words.

He nods in my direction, again with his eyes on her. "Bryony's the future of the industry. I give it a year before you can't go anywhere without seeing her name."

She blinks a few times.

Looks over at me with fresh interest.

"With . . . ," she says with a hint of dubiousness, "*this* manuscript?"

"With some tweaks, it'll start with this one. But with them all." He leans forward with dead seriousness in his eyes. Lowers his voice. "I promise you this, between you and me, I'd trade all my clients in a blink to hang on to her."

He lets the silence linger after his words, ensuring we absorb their power. The weight of them.

I ignore—*staunchly*—the river of shock that runs through me. Refusing to let them go to my head. Refusing to let them twist my opinion of the truth about what he's done.

But I can see the whole Rolodex of his blockbuster clients scrolling across her eyes.

Incredible.

She blinks.

And her entire attitude toward me has melted out in the micro-expressions of her facial features. In the tiniest creases on her forehead. "That so?" she murmurs, looking at me as the wheels churn inside her head.

We all sit in silence for a long moment.

And then Jack takes in a breath. "It's just unfortunate that this conversation must come to an end."

"What?" we say in unison.

He holds up his hands. "Florence, who's on your nix list?"

Her back jolts up. "Nix? I don't know."

"The company nix list," he continues, unfazed. "Can you do me a favor and pull it up real quick?"

Florence's eyes flash.

It's clear Jack has stepped voluntarily into dangerous territory.

"Did you know," Jack says casually, "Bryony and I just had the most wonderful time touring down to Seaside, Florida, with one of my writers? Amelia Benedict. It was so great to get away for a week, get some fresh air."

And then, to my absolute shock, she slings her purse strap over her shoulder and reaches for her to-go box. "It was such a pleasure to catch up." She faces me now. Looks at me with her warm, gentle eyes. "Bryony, I wish you all the very best. Your manuscript isn't a good fit for us, but"—she gives my hand a little pat—"if there's one thing I know, you have the very best at your side. Jack can't steer you wrong. Good luck."

Then, before I know it, she whisks herself out the doors.

I'm . . . flabbergasted.

Completely and utterly shocked.

Having Florence turn me down was saddening.

Having Jack show up unannounced was enough to throw my heart into overtime.

But *this*.

What is *this*—this secret little ring in the publishing industry?

Everything.

Every little thing I feel like I've known about the publishing industry is being turned on its head. It feels . . . otherworldly.

I push myself to my feet.

"Bryony." Jack stares at me like this is too much to bear.

"I don't want to talk to you. You sabotage *everything*, don't you?" I throw my hand out. "You sabotaged this!"

"I did not sabotage this—"

"You could've kept my identity private—at least till the ink dried!"

He throws back a humorless laugh. "Do you really think a contract would've stopped Amelia Benedict from ripping your book to shreds? The only thing worse than *not* signing a contract with Florence is *signing* one and then Amelia finding out—which she would. She would've halted the publication of your book the second she found out. Or worse."

"She couldn't. She doesn't have *that* kind of power—"

"Her uncle is the CEO of Artemis Publishing. She *absolutely* has that kind of power. It'd happen quietly and indirectly too. It'd happen under a thousand excuses. She'd stop you at the editorial stage when Florence gives you a twenty-page letter and demands total rewrites again. And again. And again. Until your book is unrecognizable, and it's not even about The Bridge anymore. And if you didn't comply, she'd call you uncompliant and forfeit the contract. Your book would never publish.

"They'd stop you at the marketing stage, and they'd put no money toward it. Throw up a five-cent advertisement on some site nobody would follow and call it quits.

"They'd stop you at the publicity stage and get you nothing. Nothing but a single feature in a tiny roundup on the internet nobody pays attention to, and when questioned the publicist would shrug, claim she has no control over who takes up her press release emails, and say that's the business of publicity.

"They'd stop you at distribution. They'd stop you everywhere.

"Peters's team would literally *take a cut* fiscally in order to keep the Benedicts happy. Call the failure of the book a loss, shrug, and move on to the next.

"Do you hear me, Bryony? Under Amelia they would make it impossible for you to succeed, then they'd all blame your book's failure on you, and then with your sales record you'd never publish anything, with anyone else, ever again."

"Everybody here is horrible," I whisper. "All of this . . . it's just . . . one big, straitjacketed monopoly."

"Not all of it. Florence Peters, though, doesn't have the freedom to take you on. That's why I kept hinting to you that she wasn't a good fit."

"Yeah, because she's a 'morning person' you said, not because, oh, I don't know, *she's part of some underground publishing ring*."

"She's not out to *murder* you," Jack says. "The unfortunate fact is, publishing is a business. It's a business just as much as, if not more than, it is an art—to everyone's disappointment. The Benedict family has *ownership* over Artemis."

"Yes, but this is Media Row."

"Different imprint. Same ownership."

"Then we try Havanna."

"Same ownership."

"Curtis," I say heatedly.

"Same ownership. And they can refuse working with whomever they want."

"Then I'm stuck." I throw my hands out. "Artemis owns everything."

"Not necessarily. It's just tricky. You just happened to enter the innermost circle of one of the most powerful families in the business. And then, unfortunately, you were so good at what you did, you went off and became irreplaceable."

I scoff. "Those are strong words when Amelia likes to say *the absolute opposite* about me. To my face."

Jack frowns at me. "And when did you start the terrible habit of believing her? She's the world's biggest liar."

"No. I think that title belongs to you." I scoff. "Look, Jack, this has been *terrific*, but I have to go. And if I haven't made it clear enough, I want you to leave me alone. Consider this my official termination—"

Jack's face twists. "Bryony, don't be like this. We're just scraping the surface here. This is going to take some time to explain—"

"I don't want explanations, Jack. Really, I don't." I shake my head. He's getting to me.

I can feel it. Feel myself slipping.

Five more minutes of conversation with this man and I'll be back under his wing, inside Amelia's coop.

"If you were honest with me and really had my best interests at heart, you would've shared this—*all* of this—with me a long time ago." I move toward the door, then cringe inwardly, remembering I left my jacket hanging on the seat.

Forget it.

It's a casualty in this battle.

"It's not that simple." Jack picks it up and trails after me. "I didn't *know* most of this until recently."

"You *work* with her. *Her*," I hiss, pushing the door open. "What kind of person are you for working with someone so—so—"

"Deceptive? Color me deceived myself," Jack says. "Again, Bryony, most of this, I didn't *know*. Of course I knew she was a handful. We *all* do. But it wasn't until lately, as I was trying to get you out of this mess—"

"But you knew *some* of it." I wheel around. Look him in the face. "Tell me this, Jack. Did you send out my manuscript this past year? To anyone? At all?"

And at this his face falls.

And I know my answer.

"I have a plan. Just trust me. *Please*."

He holds out the jacket to me.

His eyes are steady, a heavy deep green, as if he has gathered up every conversation we've had in the past two years, every tear dropped, every text sent in the midnight hours, every moment shared that will forever be seared into both our memories and is now relaying all of it in his eyes. Saying with them, *Trust me. You may not like me in this moment, but TRUST ME.*

Well.

That trust is gone now.

And I rip my eyes from his, leaving him standing at the corner, holding the jacket out for me.

"Goodbye, Jack," I call over my shoulder, and I begin to run. Run like my life depends on it. Across the street. Around the corner.

And out of his life forever.

CHAPTER 21

Yun Hee: Teacher sorry to disturb you

Bryony: You have not disturbed me at all. What is up?

Yun Hee: I am gone

Bryony: Gone? Gone . . . how?

Yun Hee: Not there

Bryony: In Florence? Are you . . . wanting to be gone? Want gone?

Yun Hee: No

Bryony: Lost?

Yun Hee: Yes. Or yessssssssssssss

Bryony: One "yes" is perfect. No problem. I can help you. What street are you on?

Yun Hee: No street I am on train in New York City

Bryony: What?! Okay. Which train?

Yun Hee: A rapid-transit system. The MTA New York City Transit

Bryony: Yes. The subway. Do you know the letter of the train you are on?

Yun Hee: 2

Bryony: Letter

Yun Hee: A

Bryony: And do you see a name going across the screen?

Yun Hee: NO SMOKING

Bryony: Name of a street?

Yun Hee: NO WEAPONS ALLOWED

Bryony: Nope. Other long, digital name of next stop?
Look up. Look. Up.
Yun Hee: URINATING IN PUBLIC WILL COST YOU
Bryony: I'm on my way.

• • •

Thankfully, swinging by the thirty-three-mile-long route of the A
Train with clues of "many trees by church" and "man with Snoopy
balloon" was enough for my sleuthing skills, and it only took three
hours to find Yun Hee and make my way to my flat, where I now drop
my purse onto the floor.

I don't know why I ended up back here.

I suppose it has something to do with the fact that Gloria is waiting at her place right now like a sweet puppy. Eager to hear how the
meeting went. And I don't have the heart to tell her.

Right now, I don't have the heart to tell anyone anything.

I am at a new low.

One rung lower than needing to be around my sister to cheer me
up. Now I just want to be alone.

Well, except for the random moments I have to wind my way
through the city to rescue well-meaning students who thought it wise
to "study" the metro system for the test in real life when they've been
in America a total of two weeks.

That's it.

I'll have to start doing field trips to the subway with my classes. I
mean, how many times do I have to go find a student stranded on the
metro before I learn this lesson?

I begin to make a note about adding in a "field trip" when I stop
myself.

But of course.

Never mind.

I order food in, and somewhere in the next six hours, eat it. The hum of a series of baking shows on television adds noise to the emptiness. I'll probably shuffle back over to Gloria's in the morning. It's too depressing here. Who knows? I'll probably take her up on the (continuous) offer to bunk together again. I'm on month-to-month now. About to be out of a job. Two jobs. Might as well.

I don't know what exactly I was hoping to gain by being here, but whatever it was, it never came.

Inspiration?

Hardly.

Just bleak reality.

But then, in the middle of the night, I shoot up in bed.

With a solution.

CHAPTER 22

"What in the—"

Halfway down page 1, I'm a little surprised.

By the end of the chapter, a little disbelieving frown has settled on my face.

And by the second half of the manuscript, my shoulders have landed in a hunched position over my computer. Like a gremlin. One hand taps the down arrow as I continue to rake my eyes over the screen, while the other hand has settled over my lips. Like I'm a shocked witness to a hang-gliding tragedy.

Like a disbelieving athlete to an unbearably bad score at the Olympics.

I *wrote* this?

THIS?

This rubble?

This nonsense?

THIS?

Plot holes *abound*. And I mean ABOUND.

As for characters, *what characters?*

Just a hodgepodge of names going in and out—a stream of what has to be a *hundred* names packed into one book. Do you know how many people I keep to my published books? How many characters my readers can be expected to remember? Eight.

There may be a couple randoms in there—the benevolent mailman, the randomly crabby grocer working the night shift—but I learned with my first book two *years* ago to keep the names and characters to a minimum.

Susanna made sure of it.

She's taught me a lot, actually, more than I ever realized.

I pop off the top of the ChapStick tube I've worked my way through since I started my plan at 2:00 a.m. It's halfway gone now; I can't help the incessant biting-on-my-lower-lip habit when I'm wholly focused. I have to pause once in my reading to look up *Can someone die from eating ChapStick?* and go down that rabbit hole. An hour later I resurface from a dozen articles, two YouTube videos (each fifteen minutes long), and three personal testimonies via social media. Long story short, I bought a spatula in the shape of a dinosaur from an ad I regret already, but I'm going to live with my despicable ChapStick-eating habit.

My plan initially *was* simple.

I had *planned* to do a quick read-through of *Water Under the Bridge*—more like a perusal even. Skim a few pages, make sure it was up to par (as I was so certain it was), then print, bring Jack the book, and offer it up like the sacrifice it is.

But then . . . well, then I read the first line.

And sure enough . . . Florence was right.

Jack was right.

In fact, it was a terrible reality check when I had to admit he was being soft on me all this time. Is that why he didn't send it? Is that part of it? A lot of uncertainties have left me frustratingly dubious, but one thing at least is for sure.

This book is awful.

I hadn't realized how much Susanna had taught me in the editorial process of that first book. So much that is common sense now, second nature even, is missing in *Water Under the Bridge*.

It has potential, yes. Just. Like. Jack. And. Florence. Said.

But without any edits it stops there: potential.

It takes me five days of working nonstop to rewrite.

And I mean a solid don't-sleep-eat-breathe kind of five days.

Gloria checks on me about once a day. Stuffs something food related under my nose. Refills the jug of water beside me. Adds a potted plant beside my desk for a "happiness factor." Leaves.

There have been times in the past two years when I've been in the zone, but they don't compare to anything like this.

It's an emotional roller coaster and a delicate surgical procedure all at once. It's like being a neurosurgeon working on an airplane during war. My stomach plummets as my eyes reach each new scene, and I gather up the information, assess at a rapid-fire pace, and begin carefully going in with the scalpel. Snipping bits here. Attaching new pieces there. Carefully re-puzzling everything together so that one little changed detail doesn't domino-effect destroy all the other pieces. All the while feeling a heavy load, a tumultuous fear that this'll never work out, then breathing a sigh of relief at each scene end. Another page down. Another piece nicely revamped and integrated.

And then one day around noon, I look up.

Ah. The world.

Light is spotlighting a few specks of dust dancing around the window.

A bird—cardinal, sounds like—is singing outside nearby.

A dog barks in the distance.

I'm absolutely surrounded by plants.

I realize the lights are all off. My apartment gloomy and quiet but for the explosion of light here beside my desk window, and in my mind.

I rub my incredibly scratchy eyes and reach for my water bottle. How long has it been since I blinked?

I take a sip.

Stare at the blinking cursor by the title.

Backspace.

Rewrite the title: *Meet Me Under the Bridge.*

A fresh title to symbolize the protagonist's journey—Gran's journey, really—in leaving her world, and hurts, behind to start fresh on new land and, along the way, building The Bridge and finding immense joy. Comedic relief in her friendships. Love (because, of course, rom-coms must have their love). A powerful message wrapped up in a delightful road trip through the heart.

"The best book yet," I murmur to myself, not out of pride but out of certainty.

This will work.

I press the email button.

Type in Jack's email, an email I never wanted to type again.

But for the sake of The Bridge, for the sake of this *almost* impossible dream of saving it . . .

Time to see how 312 pages could change . . . everything.

CHAPTER 23

"—yes, Maria, I know doctors often scribble their signatures like a flat line with a little squiggle. But if you look here, at the bottom of your practice checks, see how I did mine? Just a nice, curvy line, see? Connect the letters. No, we don't use cursive anytime in life, really, but for the test, they'll want to see if you can write your name like this. Like on the board. Now grab your pencils, and start writing out your signatures on the practice checks— *Are you kidding me?*"

Pencils stop as the students all around me look up midscribble.

The class is packed today.

The next round of GED tests is in four weeks, and I've decided during the wait to go as speedily as I can. My goal is to get as many students through the GED tests as possible in the next two and a half months. And while I have so very little I can control, this I can.

I've extended hours in class time and added evening sessions.

Sure enough, Gloria was halfway right, and I've ended up opening my home for group study sessions—particularly for the students who are close to taking their tests.

I went back to work last week. The hour after I shot off that email to Jack.

Realized I couldn't sit on my hands any longer. I had to go.

Had to do.

It's been helpful, this rushing around, teaching the students as quickly and efficiently as I can. Grading tests. Printing off extra practice tests.

Mr. Platt in the level above secretly resents me for this. Five students moved up to his advanced level just yesterday, and the look on his face when I knocked on the door surrounded by them, saying with a cheery, overbright, "Look who passed their level 4 exams!" was priceless.

I don't blame him.

We're all stressed.

But it's not going to stop me from trying to get them moved up and to graduation level before the semester ends.

Now we're in class, and I'm teaching through lesson 22 on writing checks.

And it's been going *great*.

Until I get the email from Jack.

"*Unbelievable*," I hiss, staring at the email.

"Teacher?"

Lakshmi is frowning at me, concern etched across her face. Pencils are drooping in students' hands all around.

"Yes . . . ," I say distractedly, but one hand has found its way to my hip, and I've started breathing like an angry hippo about to charge. "All fine."

"You don't . . . ," Lakshmi says hesitantly, "look fine."

"Not the definition of fine." Fen points at his dictionary, then up at me. "More like—"

"Keep writing."

The sound of thirty-five pieces of lead scribbling on papers fills the room again. And it's like this—this deathly but for the scribbling silence—for another five minutes until . . .

"Murderous expression," Socorro announces loudly.

All eyes turn to him. He props up his dictionary for all to see. There's a zoomed-in picture of a bald male on the page, with a beet-red face and flared nostrils. I think he might be holding a hatchet.

"Teacher, you look like murderous expression," Socorro says with the satisfaction of a job well done.

"Keep. *Writing*," I say again, this time with a definitive snap. Pencils pick up. Heads drop to their papers.

I swivel around to face the blackboard, back to the students, and read the email again while picking up the eraser and beginning to erase the board.

The nerve.

The absolute *nerve.*

Jack is threatening to . . . to *sue* me?

Me.

My ex-boyfriend of a whole seven days is now prepared to sue.

Well, Gloria's had her share of fascinating dinner party stories to share from sore ex-lovers, and now, apparently, it's my turn to pull my weight. Entertain the masses with a tale of unbelievable revenge over cheese sausages on toothpicks.

When I turned in the email with the *Meet Me Under the Bridge* manuscript last week, I was courteous. In fact, I assumed (apparently wrongly) that this would be a dream come true for Brooks Publishing.

A joy. A relief. I was polite. I was professional. I pretended none of the pain he and they had caused me existed.

And with my email I would have proof, in writing, that I was a responsible person. A tactical, logical, reasonable adult. Somebody other publishers would love to have as a writer on their team.

The email had gone like this:

Dear Jack,

In accordance with my contractual duties, I am attaching my next manuscript.

You will note that the title has changed. This is true, and I assume that given there are, according to Amelia's wishes, no references to children or any other discrepancies she wishes to acknowledge, this will not be a problem. Give it a read and I think you will find that I have saved my final, favorite work for last.

I sincerely hope that with *Meet Me Under the Bridge*,

Amelia and the team will receive their greatest wish in securing her as the rom-com writer of her time. After this manuscript, consider my contract completed.

Best regards,
Bryony Page

It took two hours to receive a reply from Jack.
And in it were the simple words:

Dear Bryony,
    Absolutely not.

Which was *maddening*, but no matter.

Fine. He wanted to play the immature, irrational child? I would lean even further into my role as the rational, mature adult.

I simply worked around him and forwarded the manuscript to the rest of the team.

It took approximately thirty minutes to get a series of celebratory messages.

Thank you for your prompt work, Bryony!
Another winner, no doubt. Very much looking forward to diving in.
Received and accepted. Thank you for your submission.

Susanna's came last. Twelve hours after everyone else's emails came in. She had dropped everything. Read the manuscript. And her reply to everyone was soothing to my weary, bandaged soul.

Bryony,
    You have outdone yourself. This is, by far, the best manuscript you have ever brought to my desk. Thank

you for your upstanding work. You should be incredibly proud of yourself. I know I am.
Susanna

And then, just as I was feeling a little happy, just a *glimpse* of it, I got another email privately from Jack, after which an email thread ensued.

> **Jack:** I am not accepting this manuscript.
> **Me:** Well, this is the one I'm giving. And the team has accepted it.
> **Jack:** We need to talk. Face-to-face.
> **Me:** I am completing my contractual duties and giving you my thirty days. I have looked into the contract we signed, and apparently we need notice in writing. Consider this my notice in writing.

I then deleted his next six emails.

It took a massive amount of self-control, but I did it.

Gloria stood behind me as I did so, rubbing my shoulders soothingly and telling me I was doing the right and brave thing, not because she thought so, really, but because I had asked her to. *I* needed confirmation here. *I* didn't want any lingering doubts.

So she trusted my gut instead of hers and gave me what I needed: unconditional support.

And then . . . this email slipped through the cracks while teaching this morning.

I opened and read it, simply because of the dreadful subject line: Notice of Pending Lawsuit: Bryony Page X Sterling Literary Agency

It read:

> Bryony Page,
>   In accordance with the terms of your contract, section 13 subset 3b: Writer will perform Promotional

Services, if any, at the times provided in Part 1 or, subject to Writer's prior professional commitments and reasonable availability, at such other times as Publisher may reasonably request and, if requested, as part of the Promotional Services, will sit for video- and audio-recorded interviews, which Publisher may reproduce, distribute, display, perform and adapt for promotional purposes. All reasonable expenses incurred by Writer in performing Promotional Services will be paid by Publisher.

You were expected to attend and support a book launch tour, running from July 18 to August 1, and any spontaneous events thereafter. You have failed to perform such duties and left without notice. Reasonable efforts of communication on the part of the literary agency were made, and you have failed in this regard as well.

If you do not attend the final event of Amelia Benedict's tour, we regret to inform you that you will be charged with failure to comply and face criminal punishment.

See attachment below for information regarding tour date and time.

We look forward to seeing you in attendance.

Jack Sterling
Senior Acquisitions Agent
Sterling Literary Agency

I'm breathing *fire*.

"Teacher?"

Saliha draws me out of myself, and I look at their faces. Follow the trail of their expressions back to my hand on the board. See why the students are staring at me that way.

The board is covered in practice sentences with action verbs but for the single circle of area directly in front of me, where apparently I had been swirling the eraser over and over until it was one perfectly clear space on a board otherwise covered with words.

Hastily I set the eraser down.

"Teacher," Socorro begins, "are you ok—"

"Unhinged?" Fen puts in, finger on his dictionary.

"Yes, I am *fine*. I got news that is—" I'm trying to find the word, but the pesky ball of flames in my chest is making it difficult.

"Demented?" Socorro interjects, pointing to another word.

"*Unfortunate*," I throw out, before he can start on a round of insults. "I just found out some . . . *unbelievable* news . . . and I'm having a hard time processing it."

"What are you going to do?" Miho says in her polite, careful voice.

"Do?" I suck in a breath. Look down at the email. "I don't know. I suppose . . ."

I can't be sued.

I *really, really* can't be sued.

The words feel like sticky tacky in my mouth. "I suppose I'm going to go to"—I read the attached location—"*The Bright Show*."

My stomach churns.

The biggest, most viewed morning television show in all of history.

CHAPTER 24

The building is huge.

Tunnels and turns that make no logical sense. Signs everywhere. People everywhere.

Throw in my nerves and I'm an absolute wreck.

Gloria has dressed me in the smartest ensemble of my entire life. When she heard what had transpired, it took roughly two minutes of stunned silence before she broke out of her frozen position, grabbed her purse and my elbow, and announced shrilly, "Well, if you're going to go, you'll need a revenge outfit!"

Apparently, the goal was to remind everyone behind the scenes that I was the brains and the power behind this massive machine in motion, and that while they put me under their thumb through this humiliating venture, the reality is that I was taking my "big brain" and "creative genius" (her words, not mine) with me and never stepping in Jack's sights again.

I don't feel like I'm going to get any revenge here, of course not, but at the very least I feel like a professional in what she laid out for me. My pantsuit gives off dignified vibes. The black satin pant legs swish slightly with each footfall, little whispers of encouragement to keep going. I can do this. Nobody looks at me like I'm out of place.

Nobody looks at me here, really, at all.

I'm invisible. Just another somebody employee walking through on her errands. And that's good for me.

I pull a wash of brown curls behind my shoulder.

Pause in the tap-tapping of my low-slung, much-too-expensive-but-will-wear-forever heels at the sign on the wall.

There's a set of big blue doors opposite. The one I was directed to look for in the ensuing emails from last week. I didn't even read them. Gloria took over. Read and communicated the information to me.

And here we are.

Big blue double doors.

People moving in and out with importance.

Penny spots me from some sort of foyer inside and rushes toward me. "Bryony! There you are!" Grinning widely, she takes me up around the shoulders and ushers me inside.

I follow numbly.

The world already is starting to spin a little.

Everything is starting to feel like a dream.

That's because you need to breathe, Bryony. You have literally cut off your oxygen and are about to pass out.

I take in two huge gulps of air.

Continue the simple act of moving forward.

There are no windows. We are in the heart of this massive building, it feels. And behind me, I hear the click of a door shutting.

The walls are bright yellow, forcefully so. Even the batch of sunflowers on the receptionist's desk seems to scream, *"BE HAPPY!! WE'RE ALL SOOOO HAPPY!!"*

Susanna, for her part, is sitting on the edge of a chair in the corner, seeming equally as uncomfortable as me. A receptionist is hidden behind the massive bouquet of flowers. A small cluster of people surround Amelia, and I avert my eyes immediately. I don't want to know who they are. I don't want to see or talk to any of them.

Susanna spots me and her eyes light up. She pops up from her chair quietly and is at my side in a moment.

"Bryony!" she says in a hush and gives my hands a little squeeze.

It seems we are on the same page here.

"Hello." I smile softly.

"This book." Her eyes are wide, trying it seems to express the depth and weight of her words. "Your book," she says more quietly.

"I just wanted to tell you. It's . . . going to make the world a little bit brighter."

I press my lips into a grateful, if bittersweet, smile. Thankful for the reminder in all of this of what I have to hope for.

There *is* hope today.

But then my brows knit together. Susanna's an editor. Not in marketing. Not in publicity. Why is she here?

As if she can read my thoughts, she gives my hands a squeeze and says, "I just wanted to be here to cheer you on."

My eyes glisten momentarily before I push the tears back in. I nod, noting how personal this is. She never showed up voluntarily for any of Amelia's other books. But she's here for mine. She knows: this book, especially, is mine.

Amelia is set to go live at 8:00 a.m. sharp, and while she answers fluffy questions here and there on this fluff show, there is a moment at the end where she announces her next book. Forty emails must've flown through my inbox this week over the announcement. Sales wanting to announce *Meet Me Under the Bridge* at the final moment. Marketing wanting to wait to keep the attention on the current book that has just launched. Editorial even jumping in with their thoughts here and there.

Everybody had an opinion and emotions got involved, but in the end, editorial (of all departments) and Susanna specifically was the one to convince the team that while *The Seven-Year Holiday* is strong, *Meet Me Under the Bridge* is going to be the big hit. The wonderbook. The, in her words, "perfect rom-com to satisfy hearts and minds."

They even got the graphic designers to throw all projects aside to focus solely on creating the perfect cover for the announcement.

When I saw it, I cried.

It's unlike any of Amelia's previous books. More tame in colors. More muted in palette. A watercolor rendering of the building. Still illustrated, as rom-com covers are, but simpler. Two figures beneath the bridge. A cascading stream falling gently on either side of Amelia's name at the bottom.

It's the most beautiful cover I have ever seen.

Perfectly fitting for the story.

Setting the expectations well. People will find love in this story. People will laugh, I can only hope, at the surprising characters who fill up the pages. In time they will fall in love with the characters. But there is also something deeper to be expected in *Meet Me Under the Bridge*. Something to learn about cultures. About growing and widening your world beyond your neighbor's fence line. About forgiveness. And letting go. And healing.

And for all of those things I am grateful. I am grateful that today I will get to see it shared with the world. Even if from behind a wall.

Like a mouse, watching the scene unfold from a quiet corner.

"I don't *like* this shade of yellow. I said *specifically* 'honey-butter yellow.' Not whatever—whatever this is."

Amelia's voice creeps out of the cluster of people in the corner, and in a glimpse I catch her ensemble. To be fair, she does look like one of Barbie's guests invited to a midnight neon roller-skating party. Her highlighter-yellow pencil skirt looks three inches too short and boxy. The tweed yellow blazer over the yellow blouse looks like someone did indeed color it inch-by-inch moments ago. In fact, there almost seem to be strikes of highlighter crisscrossing all over the shirt.

"Oh dear." Penny brushes a hair from her face. She looks rather smart today. And at ease. In fact, I don't think I've ever seen her looking so happy. "I'll just—go see what I can find. Hello, Bryony."

And to my shock, I hear a little *snap* and can swear I see the tip of a highlighter peeking out of her trouser pocket as she slips her hand in. She gives me a crazed smile. Everything about her is off today. She even seems *un*surprised to see me. Like I've been here all along. Which, I don't know . . .

"*Do that*," Amelia spits after her.

You know, I never did understand those people who talk about color complementing. How oranges suit some people's skin color while reds or greens suit others. It all just sounded like the kind of thing bored middle school girls did at a sleepover for fun. Like those personality tests where the answers are all pretty much the same. Just now you're defined by a different color. Or animal. Or tree.

But today? Looking at Amelia?

I get it.

Yellow does *not* suit her.

Her face looks pale and sickly between the bright yellow of her ensemble and the bright yellow of her hair. The pink on her lips looks vibrant—too vibrant. She looks a little like a two-dimensional sketch a child would make. Circle for the head. Choppy yellow hair that curls at the ends in one massive, 1950s flight attendant swoop. Blocky yellow clothes. Sticks for legs.

Huh.

Well, isn't that interesting? Learn something new every day.

A door swings opens and a man strides in, glances up at one of the many clocks on the wall, and claps his hands. He seems like a busy man. The kind of man who loves to glance up at clocks and find he's ten seconds away from being late and destroying his career and everything he's ever held dear. An adrenaline junkie, perfect for a career in television.

"Let's take you back, ladies!" the man says, and before I know it, I'm being pressed from behind toward Amelia and the door off to the side of the receptionist desk.

"Oh dear. Well, I guess we're out of time." Penny wheels around to face the door, completely unsympathetic despite the *tsk-tsk* she's given. In fact, she looks absolutely euphoric.

Poor dear.

She's snapping. Snapping before my very eyes.

Amelia is fuming. People are tugging at her from behind, too, and if her hair wasn't so massive right now, I wouldn't be surprised to find steam shooting from her ears.

At least there's no sign of Jack here.

I'm surprised.

But relieved.

I honestly didn't know how I would be able to face him.

The man swings open another door, and our little troop follows him up one hallway and down the next. Door after door after door opens until at last we are at a humble-looking little brown door and he grasps the knob. He pauses, turns and gives us a "shh" sound with his finger pressed to his lips, and opens the door.

I take in a breath.

The room is massive.

Back door to a shining stage in the distance. People are already seated for the live event. Melinda May is already sitting on a teal couch with somebody, one shiny pointy heel crossed over the other. We wait a few seconds as she speaks some inaudible words, and then a laugh ripples around the room.

He motions for us to walk ahead.

It seems impossible for anyone to hear us, really. Not unless somebody in a moment of leaning into intrusive thoughts let out a scream or something.

People in black T-shirts are hovering at various points in the background, moving spotlights, shifting cameras. Flipping pages. Everybody is concentrated on the conversation occurring between Melinda and her guest. Everyone painfully focused while Melinda herself leans back and takes a sip of coffee. Like none of this is really around her. Like she's actually sitting in a little nook at a breakfast table somewhere fabulous like Cape Cod, having a chat with her little friend.

Wait.

I squint. And correct myself. A little friend named Anna Kendrick.

"You sit here." The man points to Amelia—who looks even more aggravated that he didn't refer to her by name. In fact, he's acting like he doesn't know who she is at all—though to be fair, *Anna Kendrick* is onstage, and from the weekly lineup I read in the receptionist area, Tim Tebow is coming on tomorrow.

Amelia finds her way to the black chair and motions to a woman nearby, who jumps into action beside the man with a string of electronic devices. She's already pushing back Amelia's hair to clip the mic onto her blouse as he says, "She's going to get you set up and tell you everything you need to know. Now you." He points at me now. "You come with me."

"Oh. Okay." I admit I become a little nervous under his direct stare.

Of course I know I have a job to do, but the reality is, there's a 99 percent chance this is a marshmallow interview. It's a casual, fun-loving television program for the population of America just cracking open their eyes and settling down to a show while the eggs simmer. Cute little mugs of coffee are involved. Half the time somebody is called to do the Hokey Pokey blindfolded. Pranks with people popping out of couches. Surprise station-wide gifts of vehicles and hot tubs with two hundred screaming, out-of-control participants.

This isn't an intelligent bookstore interview where a fight breaks out among two teams trying to decide whether the protagonist was "alluding to something deeper with the disposable straw on page 112." This is pure, easy entertainment.

Amelia's specialty.

My work here is just to suffer in silence and avoid ending up in court.

The man flips his hand over and beckons me toward him.

Penny and Susanna start to walk behind me, but he holds up his hand. "Just her."

"O . . . kay," I say feebly. "See you on the other side." I toss a little smile over my shoulder toward Penny and Susanna.

"Have fun!" Penny says, her hands in little excited balls at her sides.

It's an entirely out-of-place comment given the situation, but at least I'm acknowledged here.

"Step lightly," he says as we move around lights and cords snaking along the concrete floor and various shadowy figures all quietly doing their jobs. Everybody is listening intently to the interview. There's a focus here like none other.

Finally we come to a little door. Unpainted. Something someone in passing would easily take for a storage closet full of mops and buckets. But no buckets are inside. Just an empty room. And a single metal folding chair.

Okay. I'm definitely dying here. Amelia has hired a hit man.

"Here you go," he says and I turn to him. He's trying to usher me in with his hand. There's even a little flicker of a friendly smile attached that in this lighting looks very much like a horror movie.

"I'm not . . . sure," I say tentatively.

I don't want to be rude here, even in the face of apparent death, it seems, so I find myself negotiating politely with my kidnapper. "It's just a little . . . lonely looking. What about . . . um . . . one of those other rooms? I'm sure I could sit in the receptionist area where we came in?"

"Mics here." He ignores me and steps inside. "The room is soundproof—"

Not, for the record, something I'd recommend a kidnapper announce in a pro-con list for why his victim should come inside.

"—and you can see the screen live on the wall."

I take a couple of steps inside and look above the door. Sure enough, there's Melinda on her vibrant green couch with her vibrant pink lipstick and her big smile and yellow sunshine mug that says "LET'S MAKE IT A BEAUTIFUL BRIGHT MORNING!"

The man behind me has taken up a remote control and is tapping at the screen. The sound goes up. Melinda's voice surrounds us.

A woman is suddenly at my side delicately clipping a mic on my blouse.

"Here's the remote." The man places it in my hand.

"Well, I—"

"Water bottles are in the corner."

Well. It's not a kidnapping at least. More like prison. But the nice, air-conditioned, and stocked with Scandinavian mountain–sourced water in a mini fridge type.

"Your agent is just getting mic'd up now."

"My . . . agent?" I feel that familiar pinch in my chest. "Why . . . ?"

He shuts the door.

After a little inspection to ensure there's no electricity line running through the chair, I take a seat.

Well well well.

So I'm in the show's "secret room." How many of the celebrities who come on here have their own people for such purposes? Makes sense if you think about it. All those celebrities being unusually hilarious at eight in the morning when put on the spot. Maybe this is where all their improv specialists sit, throwing out lines through mics in their ears.

"All right, I'm ready," Jack says, opening the door and stepping inside. He looks around for a chair and the stage manager takes approximately one millisecond to snap his head back and hiss, "Chair!"

Three humans emerge simultaneously, each carrying a chair.

The manager grabs the one closest and rests it on the floor beside me. He listens to something in his ear for a moment, then nods, takes the remote from my hand, presses Mute, and sets it back in Jack's. "I believe we're ready," he says, and I'm not sure exactly whom he's directing his words to—us or the people in his headset.

Regardless, he grabs the doorknob, says, "Five minutes," and pulls it shut.

Leaving Jack and me together.

In this soundproof room.

Alone.

My brow rises at the sight of a mic line running from the collar of Jack's shirt.

Jack is straight to business. "The job is simple, Bryony. Answer the questions—honestly, to the best of your ability—and this should all be over in thirty-six minutes." He pauses. "I'm sorry it had to come to this."

"It's fine," I reply politely. I'm sitting straight up. As in, rod straight toward the ceiling.

"Do you want to . . . talk . . . for a moment?" he says tentatively.

I shake my head firmly. Decide to stare at the screen. "No. I'd rather not say anything that could get me sued, thank you very much. Once is enough for a lifetime."

Jack rubs his face. Looks at me for several long moments. Then nods at the floor. "Here we go. And, Bryony?"

He leaves my name so maddeningly long in the air I eventually reply with a tart, "What?"

"Just know, I was always and will always root for you."

Something draws his attention in his earpiece, and he nods. "Audio is on," he says to me and unmutes the screen. Why does he get the earpiece? Where is mine?

What is going on?

Melinda's voice comes out loud through the screen. "And here to welcome us on this bright and beautiful Thursday morning. You all know her. You've all heard her name. The queen of fiction herself. Let's all give a warm welcome to Amelia Benedict!"

The camera pans to hundreds of fans standing, cheering, whistling all around. Multiple people are wearing the show's "signature colors." It's a room of bright pink and pearls. I squint. Is that . . . is that Yun Hee?

The camera pans over to Amelia, who is now standing, leaning forward, hugging Melinda like they are dear, dear friends.

"Oh my goodness, how *long* has it been since you've been on?" Melinda says as she squeezes Amelia. "*So* good to have you on again."

"I have thought of *nothing else* all week," Amelia says brightly. It's her classic "welcome on" line. The one I heard repeated a dozen times at every location we went to.

"Come. Come and grab a seat and tell us, how *are* you doing?" Melinda grabs her mug of coffee someone has just repoured and sits down. She crosses one leg over the other. "*The Seven-Year Holiday* has just launched."

"That's right. Three weeks ago." Her face is one massive grin. No one would connect the jab Amelia *just* took, but the reality is, the team had been trying to get her on *The Bright Show* for launch day and was denied (something about Martha Stewart showing people how to pot tomatoes), and Amelia was, in a word, furious.

"It's just such a pity we couldn't have connected on the big day." Amelia flashes a bright smile.

"Isn't it?" Melinda grins back, looking not sorry at all. "Anyway, you are here now." She gives Amelia's knee a big pat. One that starts with a hearty pat and morphs into a stronger body-jiggling shake. "Tell us how it's been. I hear you have a *riveting* story about a rogue"—and she turns to face the cameras with a *get a load of this* look—"*squirrel* that entered a bookstore during an event. Apparently you fed it from *your hand*?"

And for several minutes I sit there in tense silence beside Jack, watching as Amelia talks and laughs about all the various menial aspects of her life that she fluffs up with bogus details to sound interesting. She did not, in fact, save the squirrel's life at the bookstore. The squirrel ran in through the open door before the start of the event, and her response was to scream and throw peanuts at it until it ran away.

Melinda is chuckling like this is the *best*, most *fabulous* story of her life as Amelia finishes. "Well, look at that, folks. Amelia has captured even the hearts of woodland animals with her fabulous books. Now *about* those books, I'm wanting to hear more."

And here's the pivot.

I'm waiting for the elementary-level question. The "Tell us all, what would your characters drink in the morning? Coffee? Or tea?"

Which is why I'm stunned when her voice suddenly changes, and she says very seriously, "How specifically does the incident of 1942 affect the way Rose's grandmother related to her granddaughter during the cup and saucer moment in chapter 12? Would the outcome have been different if her grandmother had not experienced these issues?"

"What?" I bite my lip. This is *absolutely* not what I was expecting and, from the look on Amelia's face, a surprise to her as well. I mean, last time she was on, Melinda had her play the "tube of lipstick game" and pick color ranges that were most suited to her characters (alongside a free lipstick bag for every person in the studio).

"Well," I begin, thinking rapidly. It takes a moment. I have to admit, my brain has been swirling with thoughts of *Meet Me Under the Bridge* the past week; it's hard to think back three books ago. But after a few seconds, it clicks. "I guess I would say," I begin through the mic, assuming I'm speaking directly into Amelia's ear, "Rose's grandmother offered up that specific cup and saucer during that scene because the Patricia saucer related to her time in Japan, when her husband was stationed in the air force during World War II—which is how Rose's mother, Patricia, got her name. It symbolized her reminding her granddaughter how precious her mother was to her and simultaneously symbolized letting go of toxic habits in order to put more attention toward cherishing her granddaughter. Though they had lost their mother and daughter, Patricia was the bond that united them."

Jack has muted the screen while I speak, no doubt so I can focus, and I watch the screen as I speak. There is a screen behind Amelia's head with moving text of what I said. I can only see the bottom half of the screen, but it's obvious someone is typing out what I (through Amelia) say.

Amelia is gesturing widely with her hands, smiling and laughing with the perfect entertainer face as she always does.

"Oh," I add after a few moments, "and yes, that scene would have been entirely different if Rose's grandmother hadn't had those experiences in life. The entire book would be pivoted, in fact."

I watch in silence as Amelia's mouth moves with confidence, her lips and hands moving in rhythm as she gives her answers with grand expressions.

Melinda nods. Nods again.

Jack unmutes as Melinda talks again. He's a bit slow on the clicker, and her words come in after she begins her sentence. "—so interesting, Amelia. Thank you for sharing this with us. And a follow-up question: When Rose is in the bookstore seeking information about the history of the cup, she gets an unexpected answer about her grandmother's tumultuous past. What do you think this says broadly about the creation of storytelling? Do you feel like she should have found the cup?"

I frown. "What cup? I'm sorry, but I think you are mistaken. In *A Room for Rose* there is no scene about discovering a cup."

It's muted again.

And I can see Amelia splaying her hands out, speaking, and Melinda leaning forward. Nodding intently. Oddly, grinning.

I mean, this isn't *that* exciting of an answer.

Jack unmutes again.

"Fascinating," Melinda says. "And do you think Bill's love for Rose is why she holds that cup so dear?"

My brows shoot up. "Who's Bill?"

And I have to be crazy, but it looks like Amelia is nodding with a confident, "Absolutely."

But there are my words on the screen behind her. Right? I can't see the top of the screen, but what *I* am saying is being typed over her head.

"Mm-hmm." Melinda looks enraptured. "And how long did it take Bill to realize he needed to escape back into the city?"

"What city?" I say, my voice rising. "I don't— There's no city involved in this story. Maybe . . ." My wheels are turning, trying to process what's going on here. "Maybe you're thinking of one of my earlier stories? *Sunset over Santorini*?"

But Melinda is nodding and bobbing her heel as she listens while Amelia answers.

"Amazing," Melinda says.

"What's amazing?" I cast a bewildered glance over to Jack for the first time. "This is not what I said," I hiss. "I don't—"

And there Jack is, however, with a curious little smile on his face. The tiniest flicker.

And it hits me.

Hard.

In the chest.

I've seen that expression on his face. The memory of those first days, the first time we ended up peeling off to do something not specifically work related. We were having a business lunch. It was going well. I was sharing my thoughts about a manuscript; he was bouncing back ideas. It was merely two weeks after our first meeting. And then his phone alarm went off. He made a face as if he knew he was caught losing track of time and had just remembered another commitment.

He said, "Care to continue this conversation on the move?"

And before I knew it, my feet were on the fan side of a peewee field, and I was motioning madly with the other moms and dads and aunts and uncles for a little three-and-a-half-year-old boy named Jack—named after his uncle Jack—after he hit the ball with his little bat and started doing front rolls instead of running to first base.

We didn't end up talking more about work that day. But we did talk about what felt like everything else under the sun. And that day, when his nephew slowly front-rolled his way to first base, was when I first saw that look on Jack's face. Pride.

Quiet pride.

And that's exactly how he is looking at *me* now.

"And for all new or soon-to-be fans out there, I think it's time we do a fun little game with your backlist of books. A hot seat, if you will. Shall we, everyone?"

Amelia's smile looks stiff as Melinda glances around the audience, and an eruption of cheers ensues.

"I think we have our answer." Melinda laughs as she shifts her attention back to the camera and audiences everywhere. "Okay, Amelia, the rules are simple. I name a character; you name what book they're in. Ready?"

"Sounds fun." Amelia grins. I can see her mind though. She's just as confused about this as me. There are no fancy lipsticks to draw on dolls blindfolded. There's no dramatic story to unfold here. Just . . . quiz work. Dull at that for the nonreader. And yet the audience is going *wild* for it.

Melinda draws up a finger.

Pauses as we hear a buzzer.

"And here we go. Josie," she says, and all of a sudden, the timer starts.

"*Sunset over Santorini*," I say like rapid fire, spurred on by the sound of the timer ticking loudly over the speaker.

"*A Room for Rose*," I hear Amelia say with a confident smile.

"What?" This time I stand. Point at the TV. "No. *No*."

"Denton?" Melinda says challengingly.

"*A Leap of Faith*," I spout.

"*A Room for Rose* also." Amelia grins even wider.

"Perfect," Melinda says.

"*WHAT*?" I cry out. I look to Jack now accusingly. "What's going on?"

And then a thought comes to mind. A terrible, horrible thought.

First Jack threatens to sue. Now this. Is he somehow trying to *destroy* my life entirely? The vengeful agent who couldn't handle his client leaving him? The angry lover who has now locked me into this safe room and broken my mic system and *nobody* will believe me, that I gave the *right* answers? That I was doing my *absolute best* to do the right thing and get out of here?

I have no evidence.

Nobody will believe me.

It's just Jack and me in here. All alone.

"Haley Frydman?" Melinda says.

"*Smuggler's Paradise.*" I know full well it won't come through, but I have to try anyway.

"The butcher in *The Seven-Year Holiday* who collects cotton candy," Amelia says promptly, then pauses, catching herself.

"Interesting," Melinda says. "Cotton candy, you say?"

"Well . . . ," Amelia says, then coughs, looking a little puzzled at her own response. She recrosses her legs. "Anyway." She gives a little laugh and picks up her coffee mug. "Hot seat, am I right?" She chuckles, blows into her coffee, then takes a sip.

Melinda laughs heartily. A little too heartily. A "ha-ha-ha," and then she crosses her legs again with a more serious expression. "It *is* a funny little game, isn't it?" She gives a pointed look to the audience, and they laugh all the more.

Melinda sits back and shifts gears. You can see it on her face as she uncrosses her legs. "And now, if you haven't been holding on to your seats already, folks, *buckle up* now, because we have an exclusive announcement here at *The Bright Show* this morning." Melinda's teeth seem to glow even whiter as her smile just bursts with anticipation.

She points toward the screen behind her. "Folks, the author of *all of these books* we discussed this morning, right here, right now, the *true* author we have come to love and admire for her stories chock-full of wit *and* substance, *this* author has written what I can only believe to be the most sizzling story of the year next year, actually jumping off from firsthand experience herself—"

Amelia's smile flickers in surprise.

And then it flashes up on-screen.

The cover of *Meet Me Under the Bridge* in all its glory.

"*Meet Me Under the Bridge*," Melinda cries triumphantly. "And isn't it absolutely *stunning*?"

I feel a slight quake, like a group of people have just stopped outside the door.

I reach for the wall beside me, steadying myself.

She's right. The cover is absolutely stunning.

Even though I've looked at it a dozen times, I can't help taking in an admiring breath as I see it announced for the first time to others. I find myself stepping toward the screen, but a foot away, watching people's reactions. Feeling little drops of pleasure as I see their nods of acceptance of this new work. Of admiration. They love it too.

"Can you tell us, Amelia, what this book is going to be about?" Melinda says.

And I'm ready for this.

Of all books, of all the stories I've ever written, this one is dearest to my heart.

But this time as Amelia begins to speak, something horrible happens.

I hear my own voice coming over the speakers, over the . . . over the *television* . . . as well?

"It's about a bridge in Newport," Amelia begins, just as I, holding the wall, say, "It's about a teacher who builds up an ESL program in the small town of Florence—"

"And the . . ."—Amelia's voice slows down as her eyes pop wide—"the bridge . . . breaks and . . ." Her eyes swivel off camera to a giant box that has just arrived onstage on her left—a large nondescript box with a nondescript door that looks *quite a bit* like the one I walked inside just a few minutes ago. "*What the—*"

And then, out of nowhere, there is a slam and a rush of air as all four walls around Jack and me fall to the ground. The wall I was just holding on to has collapsed beneath my fingertips.

And my hand is still raised up, holding nothing but air, as I look out.

I'm standing in the middle of the stage, staring at Amelia and Melinda on one side, and two hundred audience members on the other.

CHAPTER 25

"Oh my word, folks," Melinda is saying above the claps and cries of awe. She practically yells over everyone as she points to the screen over her head. "It looks like we missed a little detail on that cover."

And then to my *shock* Amelia Benedict's name dissolves and my own name—MY OWN NAME—emerges in its place. Big, bright, and bold.

BRYONY PAGE.

And above it, #1 Bestselling Ghostwriter.

My stomach has flown to my throat.

I am about to throw up. I clutch my heart, eyes giant and round.

But then I feel the quiet press of my hand, and I look down to see Jack giving it a light pressure to balance me again.

I take a breath, and when he sees I'm okay, he lets go.

"This is— No, this—" Amelia's quaking words are flying underneath the cheers and chants and claps of everyone around us, and she moves to stand, shifting her attention and increasingly furious expression from Melinda, to Jack, to the traitorous cover, to me.

"It was *you*!" Her finger points in all directions, then it seems to land ultimately on me. "And you!" She points at Jack. "The both of you have worked against me since the beginning. Stealing my books. Making up this—this *ridiculous*—"

"Don't forget me!" Penny steps out from the woodwork backstage. She gives an overbright smile, looking incredibly proud of herself. Waves to the crowd.

And then I see it, the mic on her collar as well.

The Bright Show put me in a soundproof room and wheeled it ever so slowly onstage. And Penny? Was she the one feeding Amelia her lines all this time? No wonder it sounded off. I mean, Haley Frydman, the butcher in *The Seven-Year Holiday* who collects cotton candy?!

Amelia, after some guidance from the stage officers, marches off-stage, headed no doubt for her nearest lawyer. But that will be another matter for my brain to face when my body is *not* currently on live TV in front of *millions of people*.

"So as you can see, folks," Melinda says, holding her cup up as a man comes by and fills it, flashing a smile to the camera, "it looks to me like the wool has been *fascinatingly* pulled over all our eyes the past two years, and right now, for the first time, we are looking at the true author of *Sunset over Santorini*, *Smuggler's Paradise*, *A Room for Rose*, *A Leap of Faith*, *The Seven-Year Holiday*, and who knows?" she says with a shrug and a laugh. "Maybe more. But let's hear from the author herself. Bryony, let's grab you a cup of coffee."

She motions for me with a pat on the couch to sit beside her.

This isn't *bad*.

I'm in shock, but none of this is *bad*.

In fact, it's *good*.

I find myself reminding me of that over and over, forcing myself to settle into this new reality.

On wobbly legs I begin to move forward, and then she adds with a snap and gestures to Jack. "Oh, and I'm given to understand that you are under a contract of confidentiality, and it was imperative that you be completely oblivious to this entire reveal," Melinda says. "So, with respect to that, we're also going to need your agent up here. Jack, get on up here!" she says with a massive wave.

I feel the slightest pressure on my lower back as Jack encourages me forward, and together we go to the couch.

The couch.

On *The Bright Show*.

In the most surreal moment.

Of my entire life.

"So," Melinda says brightly as I numbly hold a coffee mug into which a man is currently pouring coffee, "tell us . . . everything. How long have you been writing Amelia's books?"

"I . . ." I feel a hiccup of pressure on my throat.

"No comment from Bryony Page," Jack interrupts with a smile and a gentle hand over my forearm. "But I'll let you personally know from my own witness, two years."

"That's an incredible amount of writing in a short amount of time. How did you do it?"

"I . . ." It's confusing. She's looking directly at me, prompting *me* with her eyes.

"Bryony Page is incredibly hardworking," Jack jumps in. "Not only has she committed to teaching ESL to adult immigrants and refugees at The Bridge for the past fifteen years, following in the steps of her grandmother, but she continues to work faithfully teaching these students during the day and writing all of the books by night. And weekends." He laughs. "And lunch breaks. And every spare moment she can."

"Wow," Melinda says, and I see a flicker of real-live approval in her eyes. Admiration. And it feels like a balm to my soul after years of being misunderstood. "And can you tell us more about this fascinating place, Bryony? The Bridge? I've been told that this is the real-life setting of *Meet Me Under the Bridge*."

I hesitate.

I'm not sure if I can speak to the story. It was accepted as part of my contract this past week. The book belongs to Amelia now.

And as though Jack knows what I'm thinking, he leans over and whispers quietly to me, "I told you I wasn't going to accept your manuscript. This book is yours."

"Brooks isn't taking it?" I whisper back, all while Melinda smiles as the happy third wheel, looking entirely accustomed to fervent whispers on the couch on live TV between couples. Or former couples. Or just people.

"I didn't say that," he says. "I said *I* didn't accept the manuscript on Amelia's behalf. Every publisher under the sun will want this book when it gets publicity like this. Even those, perhaps, with a list," he says suggestively.

He smiles and nods at Melinda as though to say, "*There's a lot more to this behind the scenes, but this isn't the time for that conversation. This is the time to tell the world about your book. Just trust me.*"

Trust him.

I take a breath.

Feeling the barriers break down.

My chest open up.

"And as for that second book under your contract with Amelia," Jack says louder, "I advise you, as your agent, if you'll have me, to terminate the contract, given that there simply will not be time with your new life. As an author under your own name. With your very busy life teaching students at The Bridge. And who knows?" Jack shrugs. "Maybe you'll find time for hearing out and forgiving a very stupid man who made a stupid mistake in the past too."

A rush of "oooohs" goes round the audience, and Melinda's eyes spark with joy. "And as if today couldn't get any brighter, folks, *here* it looks like"—she throws out a hand at us—"we have *love* in the mix too. Oh, my heart." She claps her palm on her chest, then points brazenly at the two of us. "So what is this between you two?"

My cheeks are hot and must be flaring pink. I open my mouth, but Jack jumps in. "That might be a great question for another day, Melinda. In the meantime, you were asking Bryony Page about *Meet Me Under the Bridge.*"

He looks to me with expectation.

I notice Jack is adding my full name in every sentence he can. It's a plan. A tactic. He's searing my name into people's memories. Reminding them over and over and over again with that cover on-screen: *BRYONY PAGE. BRYONY PAGE. BRYONY PAGE.*

And now—with the romantic intrigue and the hint of a second visit—there's a plan there too. Securing getting me on *The Bright Show* a second time.

The man is an absolute genius.

"Right," I say, after an intake of breath. "The Bridge. Well. The Bridge is a place very special to my heart . . ."

And so I go on, sharing all about The Bridge. The people. The troubles financially and how the threat of having to shut down inspired me to write this story. I delicately step around any implications of writing for Amelia, keep everything aboveboard. And whenever I get close, Jack is there to jump in. Squeeze my hand. Interject a strategic word here and there that keeps me from saying anything that could get me in trouble.

The audience absolutely eats it all up.

Every time he touches my hand.

Every time he compliments me.

They seem to love not just my works but also the way Jack so openly and proudly props me up. Supports me. Cheers me on. Keeps me—legally, that is—from harm.

My thoughts fly to my next book.

Wouldn't it be fun to write about such a charming agent in shining armor?

I feel a zing and the itch to grab my notebook, start plotting out points now.

Huh. I didn't know if I would ever be able to write again after all this.

"Well, this has been positively fascinating," Melinda says, for the fiftieth time this morning. "Bryony—Page," she adds, with a surreptitious look at Jack and a curvy little smile, "I think I can speak on behalf of everyone here today and say we are *in awe* of your dedication to the place behind this incredible story to come." She glances at Jack, who mouths the date, then she says, "March of next year, folks. That's what we're aiming for. *Meet Me Under the Bridge*. And we have heard your struggles. Your triumphs. Your loyalty and sacrifice, and I have *no doubt* that the publication of this book will reap many benefits for this incredible organization that will keep it on its feet. *But*—"

Water forms in my eyes as I comprehend her words.

"—just to be sure," she says, her grin widening, "on behalf of *The Bright Show*, we want to offer a *permanent partnership* and add this wonderful and meaningful organization to our charity list. Starting with this."

And before I know it, two staff members in bright yellow T-shirts come onstage, carrying on their shoulders a massive check, with the number two followed by a *lengthy* line of zeros, and the words *The Bridge* in the recipient line.

I can't even think.

I'm frozen.

Frozen in shock.

I don't think I'll ever be able to move again.

My mouth has dropped open, and an unnerving chill runs through my body.

I've turned to plastic. Right here. On this green couch.

"Very good signature!" somebody calls out in the audience.

Socorro?

Melinda laughs. Points to the audience. "And this might be a nice time to give you one *more* surprise," Melinda says. "Will the students and former students under BRYONY PAGE who have been able to join us today please take a moment to stand?"

And then I see it.

Dozens and dozens of people in bright pink moving to stand. Grins splayed across their faces. Newer faces and those from early days. Serghei. Fen. Miho. Saliha.

And at the front are Gran and Gloria. Gran looking out of place in her bright pink T-shirt instead of silk chiffon. Wiping her eyes with a loose handkerchief as they all clap.

And that's when I can't take it anymore.

And I begin to cry too. Big, fat elephant tears that streak down my cheeks and most definitely ruin my makeup.

As the room begins to heave with cheers and hugs and celebratory words, Melinda takes her mug and moves close to the camera and the front of the stage as she always does at the end of every show.

"Well, folks," Melinda says, smiling at the camera. "It looks like we've had another bright and beautiful morning here on *The Bright Show*. Together, let's go out there and make our day *great*."

CHAPTER 26

"What did you do?" I say under my breath, looking up at Jack as the clapping ensues around us and lights shut off.

Somebody is swiftly removing my mic and Jack's.

People are in a haze around us, movement flying by all around, but we are in the center of the tornado. Eyes locked on each other. The quiet in the storm.

"This has got to be the prank of the year for them. News of this is going to hit every outlet from NYC to Taiwan," I say.

"I never liked conventional marketing and publicity." Jack grins. "Think outside the box, I say."

"You're going to be fired. You're going to be *sued*," I reply.

And at this, that confident little grin lights up his face. "Bryony." He dips his chin down. "I'm a little better at contracts than you think."

"Speaking *of*, how about that threat of suing me?"

"I tried every which way to get you here. And legally to pull this off you needed to be clueless. It was a last resort. Well, aside from cameras in your face at four in the morning and Amelia saying, 'Good morning, BRYONY PAGE!' They did like that idea."

I shudder, imagining it.

"No, but once they heard this plan they were pretty hooked," he continues.

"You're at least going to lose your reputation. You can't just rat out your authors. And *Amelia Benedict* at that."

He shrugs. "I knew the risk." A significant pause follows. The crow's-feet at his temples crinkle as he looks at me with those proud green eyes. "Worst-case scenario, it was still worth it."

And I feel the walls around my heart crack a bit more.

He's risked everything. Who knows what the fallout of betraying Amelia Benedict will be? Who knows how much that will cost him?

"I hear The Bridge could be hiring. I'm very good at English," he says.

And I laugh. It's the first laugh between us since all this happened.

I put my hand on his arm. Laugh some more, picture Jack standing at a board, growing furiously impatient over the explanation of an orange. Shouting eventually, "*Or-ANGE. This is an OR-ANGE!*" I shake my head. "No."

He smiles at my laughter, all the way till my laughter runs out.

"Hey," he says more seriously, jokes aside now.

"Yeah?"

"I'm sorry. I *was* wrong for lying to you about sending the manuscript off. That was on me. And it's not an excuse, but to be clear, after the books under Amelia took off, I was told to keep you at all costs. And at the time, for a long time, I let the excuse of your book needing work and your resistance to work on it lead the manipulation.

"And for some of that time, for a long time, I lied to myself. Telling myself you were in a great place. You had growing success. I upped your margins. You had a steady stream of income. And publishing out there, in the big world, 99 percent of the time would get you nothing. More than likely, you'd be paying in time and energy for the privilege of making a few bucks in an overly saturated market. Particularly with the way *Meet Me Under the Bridge* looked when you first sent it. It had"—he shrugs—"it was just going to be extremely difficult to get it sold in that condition. And I don't blame you, Bryony. People love their first novels, but they also tend to cling too hard to them. They become their untouchable project. Their baby. Especially when there's a deeper purpose behind it.

"To be honest, it wasn't until I met the students themselves that I could understand your attachment to the place, and your mission. And by the time I was completely on board, I realized we had gotten ourselves so deep in a web within the Amelia world that it would be near impossible to get you out—unless I did something drastic.

"I spent the past four months trying to get you out, though The Foundry Literary resisted all my efforts. I was *trying* to convince them still when you found out.

"So. I'm sorry. I'm sorry for everything. And I was wrong to make decisions *for* you instead of *with* you. I was wrong for not being 100 percent honest. I was wrong for choosing to deceive myself for a long time and tell myself this was better for you when it wasn't my choice to make. And I'm not *asking* for anything here, anything bigger." He shrugs again and gives a vulnerable rub of his chin as he works out his next words. "I just . . . hoped . . . you could forgive me. Because I *am* really sorry, Bryony."

I stare at him for a long time, my face frozen. This. *This* is what Jack does. He can convince you of anything.

"Are you crazy?" I say at last.

This takes him by surprise. "What? Well." He's rubbing the back of his neck now. "I just . . . hoped . . ."

"You think I would let you go after you risk your entire career for me? You are *stupid*—"

"Painfully so."

"And it was *very, very, very, VERY wrong* to lie to me—"

"I know, Bryony. I'm so sorry—"

"But the stupidest thing of all here is to risk your job for me. To threaten to *sue* me just so . . . I could be . . . happy. You must think I'm an idiot."

His eyes are clouded, confused. "Well. I—"

"I'm not letting you out of my sight *again*, sir." I close the gap between us so his chin is at my forehead. "This close, see? You're going to be stuck to my side forever. I certainly hope you thought this through, because that's how it's going to be."

He's grinning as the tension releases from his shoulders and I cling fast. "It'll be a little challenging to fly to Italy to sell your book this way."

"We'll buy a double-seater," I say, and kiss him before he can come up with another word.

"Somebody catch this!" Melinda says distantly in the fog.

"This better not be a publicity stunt." I pull back momentarily with a grin.

He chuckles low and whispers in my ear, "I warned you I'm not a conventional agent, Bryony Page."

And he leans down, tucking a lock behind my ear.

His hands thread through my curls, clutching me as his lips meet mine with an unspoken agreement to never be so far away again.

EPILOGUE

"This heartwarming paean to forgiveness and found family wrapped in a delightful romp and romance is, in many ways, the perfect rom-com. *Meet Me Under the Bridge* is a triumph."

—#1 *NYT* bestselling author Anne Sanderworth

"Shall I take your bags, madam?"

"Stop it. You're creeping me out." I blow out a frosty breath as I hold my suitcase while bouncing on my toes.

"Madam would quietly prefer I take the bags." Penny reaches for the handle.

"No. I've got it," I say, holding firm.

"Madam says no, but really she is begging me to relieve her arm of the luggage to protect her delicate writing hands."

Penny is tugging at my bags.

"Jack, stop her. People are going to think I'm a horrible person," I say to him, who watches, bemused, while we stand at the entrance doors to the tour bus, waiting for them to open. People are loitering around, cameras out.

"They already know about the two of you," he says casually, ignoring the flash of cameras all around. "The posts will say 'Bryony Page and Penny Matthews at It Again.'"

The day Penny lost her mind and highlighted all over Amelia's blouse during the outrageous stunt, I hired her. Well, technically Jack did. He said, and I quote, "Penny Matthews is going to be the best PA of your life."

And he was right.

Honestly, half the time I go to autograph books, people want her to sign it too. With a highlighter.

In addition to being the world's best assistant, Penny has become one of my closest friends. And turns out, her calligraphy skills are absolutely to die for.

Honestly, next to my chicken-scratch signature (the same one my students ridicule me about still), her loopy *y*'s and crossed *t*'s are works of art.

She addresses all the invitations to both book events and fundraisers for The Bridge. Of which there are many.

I've dropped down to half time at The Bridge—it was a difficult decision, but in the end, one for which I was immediately grateful once the tour schedule was in place. Tuesday and Thursday mornings to noon at The Bridge, usually followed up with a lunch date with Gran and Gloria. And the rest of the week, I write. And tour. And just, in general, do whatever I want.

Most of the time with Jack.

And I love it.

I love it all.

"So sorry, I got hung up!" Gloria races across the parking lot, one massive suitcase sliding against the pavement in each hand.

I nudge Jack. "C'mon. Go help her, will you?"

But he nods to a space behind her. "Why? She's got *him*."

And sure enough, my face breaks into a wide smile as I glimpse Albrecht closing the trunk of the car, lugging another four various articles in his arms.

Albrecht, my quirky German student, came after all. The two fell for each other several months ago, after Gloria had enough of him trailing after her, stalking her every time she went to her car after bowling, and said, "What is *wrong* with you?" And he announced, "You walk haphazardly and you are like a squirrel. Easily distracted. I must make sure you're safe."

She said, "Do you *hate* me?"

To which he replied, "You talk a lot. Almost too much. We should get you coffee to protect your voice. It is . . . too pretty to lose."

They've been together ever since.

I grin madly, about as madly as I have been ever since my entire life flipped on its head seven months ago. Never in my life did I think I would be going on tour. And yet . . . life has a funny way of surprising you. Sometimes in ways you never dreamed possible.

"Back for round two!" The doors open and Trina is sitting on her seat, grinning down at us.

"Only riding with the best!" I step on board and give her a hug.

It's been only a few weeks since we traveled down the East Coast for *Meet Me Under the Bridge.* Now, according to Mona, it's time to head west. And frankly, I can think of no happier circumstances than road tripping to see the mountains, and a few bookstores, with this crew to share the adventure of it all.

Jack, for his part, has kept most of his clients. He was fired from the agency, of course—with plenty of threats of suing he has masterfully averted like a skilled cat burglar—but almost all of his authors parted to stick with him. Turns out, more people in the publishing industry were impressed by his "ingenious" stunt than anyone could have anticipated. That, plus the fact that I had under-estimated exactly how much dislike everyone unanimously had for Amelia Benedict and all she stood for. It's hard to know, sometimes, exactly how people feel when they're too afraid of the consequences to show it.

So Jack formed his own agency.

Sterling Literary.

And given both his clientele and his fascinating publicity stunt, Sterling Literary has become one of the most exclusive and sought-after agencies for authors of all time.

Just yesterday he hired on two more of my former students to help with translation in foreign rights.

"You ready?" Jack asks. "What?" he says when he sees my face.

"Oh, I was just thinking," I say, shaking my head with a smile. "About . . ."

"About the first time we met. Did you think it would shake out like this?" I ask, not really because I don't know the answer. More like I just want to hear him say it. Again.

And he knows this.

His eyes soften as the busyness around us swirls to slow motion, and with all the intensity and sweetness of his golden green eyes, he steps forward, kissing me softly with one foot on the stairs.

"I wouldn't have been found on West 74th Street in that bowling shop, wandering around for a bowling bag, if I wasn't hoping, desperately, for things to turn out exactly as they have."

We kiss again, at least until Gloria starts to whistle and nudges Jack's back while complaining, "C'mon, you two bowling bag–hauling cuties. It's freezing."

And the rest of the day we laugh and drink our coffee and huddle around our computers and papers and games and interweaving existence—all of us squeezing into the little dinette booth as the bus carries us down the interstate. And cars pull up to our sides and slow down as the people inside press camera phones to the windows. Taking pictures. Photos to share with others.

A great big graphic of the cover of *Meet Me Under the Bridge* spans multiple windows, along with dozens of students and former students smiling with me in front of The Bridge.

And in bold black lettering above it are the words:

BRYONY PAGE'S #1 *NEW YORK TIMES*
BESTSELLING NOVEL,
MEET ME UNDER THE BRIDGE,
NOW AVAILABLE.
EVERYWHERE.

DISCUSSION QUESTIONS

1. Aspiring author Bryony Page attends her first writers conference bursting with optimism, only to find rejection. Have you ever dealt with incredible disappointment in a situation, and were you able to persevere through it or not? What life lessons did you gain from that experience?

2. If Bryony did not have that moment with Jack where he found her answer intriguing and set the course of her life in a new direction, what do you think she should've done? What would have been something wise given her dreams and aspirations?

3. Despite agreeing to sign up as a ghostwriter in exchange for getting her own book published, Bryony deals with great frustration in somebody else taking credit for her hard work. Have you ever experienced this frustration? How should that be handled? Do you think Bryony should have done anything differently or was it just her cross to bear?

4. What is the range of emotions and thoughts you have had when you've had to forgive someone? Have you ever identified with Bryony and her sense of betrayal with Jack, and if so, how?

5. Would you like to be an author on a tour bus traveling the country? Why or why not?

6. Which scene or moment in this book made you chuckle? Why?

7. Do you think you would enjoy Jack or Bryony's career more? Why?

8. Jack was humbled and learned in his story how his own motivations changed the way he saw things. Have you ever justified or rationalized your wrong actions until they seemed "right"? Have

you ever witnessed someone else do this? How have people done this throughout history?

9. What would you do if you suddenly had the chance to destroy your real-life enemy? Would you act on it or not?

10. Which character's weakness do you identify with most? Why?

11. The ESL students are an interesting group who are all under one school roof with one common goal: to learn English. As a former ESL teacher to adult immigrants myself, I know only too well how fun and challenging it can be to have so many different worldviews represented. What are some problems that could come up in conversations in the classroom (speaking from experience, they certainly happen), but also, what are some beautiful moments that you think could happen (those certainly happen, as well!). When in your life have you learned from another person's culture and life experience?

12. Which character's strength do you identify with most? Why?

13. Who is your favorite character and why?

14. Bryony kept her ghostwriting a secret from nearly everyone around her for years. Do you think you could hold in a secret from everyone for a long time? Do you think it's healthy to?

15. What is your favorite scene and/or quote and why? *(Side note: I'd love to hear your answer to this! Please don't hesitate to message me on Instagram or tag me with your answer at @ourfriendlyfarmhouse. —Melissa)*

LOOKING FOR MORE
GREAT READS?
LOOK NO FURTHER!

Visit us online to learn more:
tnzfiction.com

Or scan the below code and sign up to receive email updates
on new releases, giveaways, book deals, and more:

@tnzfiction

ABOUT THE AUTHOR

Taylor Meo Photography

MELISSA FERGUSON is the bestselling author of titles including *How to Plot a Payback*, *Meet Me in the Margins*, and *Famous for a Living*. She lives in Tennessee with her husband and children in their growing farmhouse lifestyle and writes heartwarming romantic comedies that have been featured in such places as *The Hollywood Reporter*, *Travel + Leisure*, and *The New York Post*. Follow Melissa with over 800,000 other subscribers on Instagram and TikTok at @ourfriendlyfarmhouse or her newsletter: melissaferguson.com.